THE NORMA GENE

by M. E. Roufa

Published by Bitingduck Press
ISBN 978-1-938463-41-9
For information contact
Bitingduck Press, LLC
Montreal • Altadena
notifications@bitingduckpress.com
http://www.bitingduckpress.com
Cover art © 2015 by Melanie Forster
Icons designed by Freepik (www.flaticon.com)

Publisher's Cataloging-in-Publication
Roufa, Michelle [1969 -   ]

The Norma Gene/by Michelle Roufa –1st ed.—
Altadena, CA: Bitingduck Press, 2015
p. cm.

ISBN 978-1-938463-41-9

[1. Science fiction, American 2. Cloning—fiction
3. Motion picture actors and actresses, movie stars—Marilyn Monroe—fiction 4. United
States—Presidents—Abraham Lincoln—fiction
5. Walt Disney World (Fla.) —fiction] I. Title

LCCN 2014920795

For my parents

Who always knew I had it in me
and possibly put it there.

Even the most perfect reproduction of a work of art is lacking in one element: its presence in time and space, its unique existence at the place where it happens to be. This unique existence of the work of art determined the history to which it was subject throughout the time of its existence.
—*Walter Benjamin. "The Work of Art In The Age Of Mechanical Reproduction"*

How many legs does a dog have if you call the tail a leg? Four. Calling the tail a leg doesn't make it a leg.
—*Abraham Lincoln*

Prologue

ABRAHAM LINCOLN FINKELSTEIN CAME into the world much in the same way as all other clones: a wet and screaming combination of science and love and especially money, millions of research dollars made flesh. His parents, Marvin and Miriam Finkelstein, spared no expense to ensure for him what all loving parents hoped for their children: health and intelligence and the right number of fingers and toes, plus the genetic capacity to someday completely right the balance of the world. No one bothered to consult Abraham Lincoln, who may have had his own opinion on the subject of his twenty-first century regeneration. He was, after all, long dead.

Little Abe's birth was attended with very little fanfare. No reporters, no lurking paparazzi lining the halls of the maternity ward, no historical ethicists picketing outside. This was remarkable. In vitro cloning of human beings, living and post-living, had been common for over thirty years, but the Finkelstein baby still managed to be a first. There were no Abraham Lincolns before him (not counting, of course, the 19th-century Alpha), and were not likely to be any after. After the furor over Baby Hitler, the cloning of dictators, presidents and other "crucial" historical figures was prohibited, punishable by incarceration of both host parents after the fact—and if caught in time, enforced abortion.[1] Which made Abe an illegal, a genetic fugitive. Fortunately, his parents had the necessary money and pull to falsify a "natural" birth certificate. But they couldn't resist giving him his own name. It would be hard to blame them; they were patriotic, they loved him, they did pay for him. And by the time he reached maturity, he wouldn't be able to hide in a Presidents' Day used-car sale anyway.

So mommy, daddy, and baby went home just like any other family, and baby was tucked into his (tastefully subtle) red, white, and blue bassinet. And as he settled down to sleep, little Abe's mother softly whispered to him—just like every other new mother does—"You are going to change the world."

---

1 In the United Kingdom, these crimes were taken even less lightly than that. While no one actually believed in the divine right of kings anymore, the Labour party refused to take any chances. The possibility of a Tudor or Plantagenet clone someday challenging the throne led to the passage of the Windsor Act, charging anyone caught "birthing, fertilizing, or collecting genetic material" from any member of any royal family with high treason... a capital offense. This despite the fact that the Hitler clone not only failed to live up to his "potential," his sense of inferiority and petty vindictiveness kept him from rising past assistant manager at McDonald's.

1

THERE ARE SOME FACTS everyone seems to know about Abraham Lincoln; "everyone" meaning all those people who live in America who have ever learned anything about American history—a number that manages to shrink every year, despite the success of the "Full Contact American History" video game franchise. Everyone knows that he grew up in a log cabin. That he was our 16th President. That he was assassinated at Ford's Theater by John Wlikes Booth.

There are other facts about Abraham Lincoln that are less well known, but still readily available to the interested scholar. That he was six feet four inches tall. That he was the first President to have a beard while in office. That he had a wart on his right cheek.

Then there are some facts about Abraham Lincoln that were known to only one man, and the handful of people that man entrusted them to. His favorite food was mashed potatoes. He couldn't carry a tune to save his life. He was allergic to kiwi fruit, or would have been if he had ever had the opportunity to try one. And there wasn't much he loved more than the smell of laundry fresh out of the dryer. The man in question wasn't sure whether it was the heat of the dryer, or the chemicals in the fabric softener sheet, or even just the memories of growing up and smelling his mother's old Kenmore spinning as he came home from school. But after a long day, when nothing seemed to go right, opening the dryer after a fresh load was done and getting that first smell of freshly washed cotton was like coming home.

Of course, whether the real, bona fide, 1800s Abraham Lincoln had the same Proustian connection when he removed his own softly-scented unmentionables from the dryer will never be known, electric clothes dryers not having been invented for another century. It's not even known whether he ever buried his face into a freshly starched shirt hanging on a clothesline. But shirt-face-burying was exactly what the only other Abe Lincoln in American history was doing without regard to any recorded precedents, and it was making him very happy.

Abe transferred all of the clothes into the basket and made his way into his bedroom for a folding session. He wasn't the neatest person on earth, but he liked doing things in order, and since he first learned to fold laundry on his bed, his bed was where he planned to fold laundry forever, until the day the nice folks at the nursing home did it for him. Or till the mean folks at the nursing home made him wear the same dirty smock every day, and folding locations became irrelevant. Whatever he could afford. He was only 36; there was plenty of time to worry about that sort of thing later. Years later. Even though the original Abraham Lincoln had only made it to 56 years old, Abe had no reason to believe he wouldn't make it to a ripe old age. There was no evidence at all connecting clones to any sort of automatic repetitions of the lives of their historical predecessors. For one thing, there was no evidence at all connecting clones to any sort of automatic repetitions of the lives of their historical predecessors. For another thing, he hated the theater.

First the shirts went into one pile, the underwear into another, the socks into a third, all other items into a fourth, to be dealt with last. He lowered himself carefully onto the edge of the bed, pulled the pyramid of socks toward him, and started pairing them off and balling them together. It was steady, rhythmic work, practically robotic. He didn't even look at the pile, only at the cotton toes to make sure they lined up. Abe bought his clothes in multiples. It wasn't an act of obsessive-compulsion so much as ease, but there was something satisfying in knowing, as he balled his socks together, that he never had to line them up next to each other to make sure they would match. A sock that matched another sock that matched every other sock only presented a problem when one came up missing. Which happened rarely enough, but each time it did was vaguely unsettling. Had it been the left or the right? The first one he took off, or the second? If it turned up in the next load, would he even know it? Or would an even number of socks in the next load only mean that yet another unmatched sock had somehow disappeared? In other words, the greatest strength of having an infinity of perfectly identical socks was also its largest drawback—without variations, there was no way to keep track of any individual one. Not that there was any need, of course. A sock was a sock was a sock. And a white sock even more so. But when you were a clone, the question of differentiating and individuality became a bit more far-reaching.

Abe reached for another sock. He noticed it had a slightly thinner texture than the one he picked up previously. Was it older? More worn? He momentarily debated unballing all of his socks and starting over, pairing them up by thickness. Then he realized that this was crazy. But it was a thought.

He moved on and started folding his pile of identical white undershorts. They didn't give him the same problems the socks did. Good thing, too. Obsessing about socks was reasonably normal. Obsessing about your underwear was crazy.

You didn't have to be Abraham Lincoln to know that much.

Placing the last balled sock snugly into place within the top dresser drawer, Abe hummed contentedly. His life might not be historically important or even politically relevant, but it was his life, and it was satisfying.

It was also about to change.

2

THE BELL RANG AND Abe got up from his casual perch on top of the battered regulation-issue desk, trying to look friendly and understanding. The students slumped out, making as much noise and exhibiting as much nonchalant disdain as their five-and-a-half- to six-foot frames could sustain without appearing forced. "See you tomorrow!" he called out, as he gathered up the pile of essays the kids had left for him—all 13-point type and wide margins, the modern equivalent of extra-wide penmanship to stretch three-quarters of a page of ideas into two pages. Doomed to repeat history again, he mumbled to himself. Bring on the farce. It wasn't a good joke, or even an original one, but it was sarcastic and also true, and helped him face yet another room full of the Ungrateful. At least this was his Advanced Placement class. They may not have been significantly smarter or more interested than their lower-level counterparts, but at least they were academically obligated to give the appearance of making an effort. In return, it was his job to reward their quest for information with the promise of entertainment. So there you had it. Today's reward was 1865: a nice lengthy screening, in installments, of *Gone With The Wind*.

Abe had fallen into teaching American History by default. His parents had had loftier goals for him; law school, obviously, then politics. Or at least a career in letters. Miriam Finkelstein had put all the silent pressure on him that she was capable of mustering, but they both knew she had already played her role. She would no more have forced him to become a future president than she would have revealed his heredity to the press. It was their private secret. Every mother wanted to do the best for their children. She had given him the best start she was capable of achieving. The rest was—had to be—up to him. She believed his genetic destiny would be enough to make him great. Abe, on the other hand, could only see it as a stumbling block. It was like growing up in the wake of an overachieving older sibling, but on such an overwhelmingly larger scale it was almost paralyzing. He may have had Abraham Lincoln's body and even his mind, but his crushing sense of inferiority was all his own. So: school valedictorian, that much he gave her, and at Yale his unmistakable intelligence and natural debating talents insisted on setting him apart, but that was as far as he was willing to concede to his mother's happiness. To be honest, he had always secretly hoped to be a basketball star. But apparently for all his height, old Abe Lincoln couldn't hit a bank shot if his life depended on it. Which, funnily enough, it never did.

American History was at least respectable in his mother's eyes; it didn't preclude Abe's eventually going to law school or into politics, and it did have a certain resonance to his legacy. She would have preferred a professorship, or at least his going back to grad school and getting a Master's, but when he graduated from Yale with an American History degree, without even honors, teaching seemed like a natural fit. It was a private preparatory school, the salary was reasonably good, and it allowed him to help people, even to shape the future, albeit on a much smaller scale. Deep down, he knew, he liked underachieving. It kept him from having to fail.

Actually it hadn't been such a bad class today, Abe reflected as he headed back to his car at the end of the long day (staff meeting, Debate team meeting, "voluntary" attendance at Parent-Teacher exploratory meeting). The discussion had gone from slave narratives to slave memoirs to the politics of memory. How tenuous the hold of personal recollections could be, in the face of a communal search for identity. Whether it was appropriate to pad the truth, to invent memories, if doing so could help elucidate the greater truth of historical experience. And can memory ever document truth at all? If your quest were to find the unadulterated truth about any given historical experience, would you go back if it were possible? Sometimes his kids amazed him with the connections they were able to make, the conclusions they reached. Other days they just amazed him with how many places they could abandon their gum. He infinitely preferred the former.

His good mood made it almost to the door of his car. As he clicked off his security alarm, he couldn't help but notice the caricature staring back at him from the hood of his car—a stick figure Abe Lincoln carefully delineated in shaving cream (he hoped), showing off a profoundly enhanced penis. Underneath was scrawled "FOUR SCORE AND 7 INCHES." You had to give them points for historical contiguity, Abe allowed. He knew the student artist (or artists) responsible for defiling his Ford had no idea of the true connection between himself and Lincoln. His family had never told anyone for fear of possible prosecution, and he had spent too much of his life both scared and embarrassed by the affiliation to ever lay claim to it now. Still, from the time he hit his growth spurt after puberty, he had never been able to escape the comparison. Now in his early thirties, the resemblance was unmistakable. That his name was Abraham only compounded the problem. At least this prank was actually funny.

Abe wiped the shaving cream off as best he could with the sleeve of his jacket. It had been due at the dry cleaners for a few wearings now anyway. He tried wiping the excess off his sleeve with his hand, then without thinking wiped the hand off onto his perfectly clean pants. Great. The very indignity of it all made him smile. That, along with the other fact that he alone knew intimately—as it turned out, Abraham Lincoln had been a particularly well-endowed man.

3

NORMA OOMPHED HER BODY out of bed and wiggled the sleep from her eyes on her usual route to the mirror. Lids half-closed, lips puffy, she caught herself catching herself, wondering for the zillionth time whether today would be the day she snapped, the day she Marilynated. How did it happen? She wondered. What was the trigger? Was there a warning sign, an audible click in your head that snapped you into a budding Stepford mistress? Or did it tiptoe in slowly on crows' feet, quietly kicking you into submission? Whispering, *you can be perfect, you can have men at your feet...* You can be fat and ridiculous and a dime a dozen, she told herself firmly, and headed for the shower.

There were the meetings, of course. It was Wednesday; there would be one tomorrow night. She could pop in just to see what it was like, join the half-dozen or so other women in town searching for meaning in their lives, striving to avoid preordained destinies—and in the process, usually goading each other right into the familiar patterns. *Once a Norma Jeane, always a Marilyn* went the joke, but the nature vs. nurture jury on that one was still out. Was it worth the risk? Norma sighed, sliding the soap over her thigh. She was about to turn thirty, could feel it even though it still didn't show on the outside (two years till decrepitude, she thought grimly, then suppressed it), and she wasn't particularly happy as she was. What did she have to lose?

She would go to work; she would think it over. She had to run some errands on the way back home anyhow. Maybe she would take a quick look in, if the place was on her way. Maybe.

One thing clonologists guessed from the start was the inherent mental need for clones to compare themselves to their genetic predecessors: mentally, physically, even spiritually. And no one felt the brunt of that psychic confusion more than the Marilyns. Bearing the name without the glory, frizzy-haired, tending toward chubbiness and easily addicted to almost anything, there was no way for a Marilyn to avoid the glaring differences between themselves and their alpha. The lure of post-op glamor was fierce. The Normalyn movement, archetype for all clone support groups, was inevitable.

Originally Marilyns Anonymous, until it became evident that anonymity for a Marilyn (even without the plastic surgery) was pretty much impossible, Normalyn served as a gathering house for Marilyns—and the Norma Jeanes who were desperate not to become them. You are okay just the way you are, the club literature stressed. But if you want to change yourself completely, that's okay too. Here are some beauty tips.

In the first years of the cloning boom, before regulation became legally and eugenically necessary, a glut of new old babies was gleefully dumped upon the American genetic scene without any attention to possible social consequences. InstaClone™, Celebra-Clone, and other recklessly enterprising fertility startups took the public's money and gave them exactly what they wanted—the public wanting, in remarkable but not surprising percentages, Kim Kardashians, Michael Jordans, and Marilyn Monroes. There were approximately 1300 Marilyns floating around in the world, nearly all in the United States, 80% of them between the ages of 25-35. So even the plasticked platinumed perfect copies weren't exceptional in any real sense. Try living up to that.

Pulling into the parking lot of the Lord and Taylor's quadrant of the mall, Norma was surprised to find it nearly empty. She checked her dashboard clock and then her watch, ready to kick herself for possibly undersleeping. But no, it was just before 9, she was right on time. She steered her berry-red convertible (Obvious? Probably. It was her one concession to Marilynhood) into one of the nearest of the farthest-away spaces. Employees were Not Encouraged to occupy the prime mall parking slots; those were for the Express Privilege of Customers, store bulletins repeatedly asserted, and even on an empty lot day Norma wasn't going to risk being caught and lectured.

As she maneuvered the convertible roof up, Norma heard rather than saw the Land Cruiser approaching. Her car, standing out like a flamingo in the arctic in the near-empty parking lot, probably made her a target to begin with. But as the giant roaring luxury truck bore down on her, Norma couldn't pretend it wasn't personal.

The coal-colored SUV coasted into the slot directly behind hers in the sea of empty spaces, the sound of its door opening only just preceding the hush of its engine shutting down. There was no mistaking—or escaping—the classic opening move in the mating dance of twenty-first century suburbia. Norma gathered her jacket and purse and slowly got out of her car, the door locking behind her automatically with an irritatingly perky chirp. She walked quickly, but the light clicks of her sabrina heels were no match for the decidedly unladylike clomping of the boots behind her. Eyes focused straight ahead of her at the gleaming chrome and glass doors of her destination, Norma steeled herself against the inevitable *Hey lady.*

"Hey, lady!" The voice was deep, amiable, a bit butch. Shosha closed in on her, nudging her hip gently, then slid a bitch-black manicured hand (Chanel, of course) around Norma's shoulder. Norma smiled diplomatically. Shosha ran the cosmetics floor at Lord's, and as a lowly perfume artist, Norma was required to look up to her. Which, at 5 foot 5 to Shosha's 5 foot 1 in boots, was rather difficult.

Norma's relationship with her boss was reasonable, if occasionally more uncomfortable than she wanted to admit. But after almost two years in the department, Norma had yet to find they had anything in common. Dressed in an ever-changing succession of expensive bondage wear in black leather and platinum, even despite her lack of height Shosha would have been an incredibly menacing figure if she were even the least bit unself-conscious. Standing still behind a counter or posed against a wall, not speaking, Shosha was regal, poised, hard. She had the look down. But statuesque silence wasn't Shosha's strong suit, and the second she opened her mouth, or moved her body more than an inch or two, the whole femme fatale façade fell apart. There was something like a puppy about Shosha. Too eager to please, too unsure of her body, too prone to overexcitement. There was no escaping it: underneath the almost perfect hardass bitch-goddess exterior, Shosha was a nerd. Clothing that looked fresh off a Milan runway on a store mannequin would magically transform on her body into something from the latest Klingon convention. She also seemed to have an acute crush on Norma.

"Hey, lady," Shosha repeated, now so on top of Norma that some sort acknowledgement could no longer be avoided. "Hey, Shosh," Norma responded, their eyes presumably meeting through each other's UV-protected lenses (Norma's, vintage cats-eyes with rhinestones; Shosha's, severe black rectangles with the exact width of side supports required by fashion that particular season). "Place is a wasteland today."

"Yeah," Shosha nodded, practically bouncing with joy at the interchange. "Yeah, I think it's because of the cold snap. Only supposed to be 65 today. I bet Maxine will be selling a lot of cashmere, don't you think?"

Norma shrugged politely. The funny thing was, Shosha was probably right. No matter how long she lived in Florida, Norma would never get used to her neighbors' tendency to label two days in a row cooler than 75 degrees a "cold snap."

Seeing that talking about the weather hadn't turned into the conversational springboard she'd hoped, Shosha pushed on. "Say, Norma, I really like your dress. You look seriously fine, girlfriend. Where'd you get it?" Norma cringed at Shosha's foray into slang, then at the question, finding herself suddenly in a real dilemma. The dress had been her mother's. Admitting this meant a guaranteed lengthy conversation, but lying could just as easily lead to the same result—and might require serious brainwork on top of the ordinary discomfort. Thinking fast, Norma gave the best answer she could come up with, one that she knew had only the tiniest chance of success: "Oh my God—What's that over there?"

"What?" Shosha swirled around, following Norma's gaze. There was nothing actually over there. But amazingly enough, the ruse worked. While Shosha paused to scan the empty horizon for signs of whatever it was she was supposed to be shocked and/or awed by, Norma quickly made her escape through the shining store doors. That Bugs Bunny was a genius.

4

STEPPING INTO THE EMPTY store first thing in the morning was always the best part of the day for Norma. The small amount of warm sunlight that was allowed through the glass doors and past security made the chrome and glass counters sparkle like freshly cut diamonds. It was no wonder the store layout required customers to pass through Jewelry before any other department. But first thing in the morning, before anyone arrived, every countertop and display case had that irresistible polished gleam.

It was those initial moments that were always the most dangerous for Norma. Everything shining, everything desirable, and no one around to see. Just to slip something, anything into her purse. A compact, a scarf, a pair of earrings—even just one earring—and she would be steady to face the day. As always, she suppressed the urge. Everything was electronically tagged, traceable not just through the security gates but all the way to your home should you get that far, and no earring in the world was worth that disgrace and humiliation. Though once there was that pair of snakeskin Louboutin slingbacks...

Norma wasn't a smoker, had never been into drugs, and didn't even drink all that much except at parties where, let's face it, social lubrication was practically the law. But the itch to take things was constantly present. Working as a sales clerk in a department store had to be the absolutely worst occupation for a kleptomaniac, second only to (possibly) pearl diving. But despite all the temptations, so far she had mostly been good. If only because she knew that once she allowed herself to take even the smallest thing, she wouldn't be able to quit. Ever. And the image of a future of being beaten up in a prison cell for surreptitiously pocketing another prisoner's shiny lucky shiv was just too horrifying to fathom.

Fortunately, Norma's job didn't require her to spend any time being tempted behind the vitrines. All she had to do was stand in front of the perfume counters, smile invitingly, and spray the living daylights out of anyone who dared to pause nearby. On busy days, it was a lot of fun. When things were slower, and people lingered longer over things they had no intention of buying, it became much harder not to misbehave. And when things were really really slow, she secretly used the mannequins for target practice.

"Would you like to try *Illusions*?" Norma cooed, for what had to be the millionth time. Brandishing the perfume bottle as if it were a work of art, as if it were a diamond tiara, as if it were a staplegun. All depending on her mood, and on the facial expressions of the passing customers. But always with the same seductive smile. To spritz or not to spritz. So much for her Liberal Arts degree. Still, it was steady work, not too demanding, and it paid well enough to satisfy her food and footwear needs. My God, she shuddered in response to the thought. Steady work? Not demanding? Paid reasonably well? The self-justifying clichés had slid through her mind so easily. Ah, the rallying cry of the horizontally mobile. File clerks and desk clerks and shop clerks, unite! We have nothing to lose but our ambition! Could it possibly be that bad? Yes. Yes, it was that bad. It wasn't that she lacked ambition. She owned the same dog-eared copy of *What Color is Your Parachute?* as the next twentysomething occupational drifter. But while she was very good at choosing colors, picking which way to leap proved too daunting. She was good with people and she liked to shop. What had begun as a stopgap job while she tried to find herself had become a reasonably lucrative location where she could be found. At least it wasn't show business.

"Would you like to try *Illusions?*" When she had first started, she thought the fragrance was lovely. Now it was the noxious aroma of hell. Toilet Water had become more than a product category; it was a reasonable description. Every day she would subconsciously hope that the scent would change into something more bearable. Gasoline. Sauerkraut. Fresh dog vomit. Anything but this cloying sweetness. And its mitigating factors were minor. At least the bottle was beautiful and fit sensuously into her hand. And the name could be said many ways, in various inflections, depending on her mood. She pitied the poor souls promoting *Penetration.*

At least Shosha had (so far) defended her from the parent company's latest promotional proposal. What better way to sell *Illusions* than to have the sales representatives look like the famous icons of the past? All the one-name glamour girls had been listed, with costume and make-up suggestions, to fool the customer into believing they had stepped into a world of illusions themselves: Garbo, Dietrich, Hepburn (both Kate and Audrey varieties), and of course, the magnificent Ms. Monroe. Norma knew it was only a matter of time before the marketing goons laid down the law. Maybe if worst came to worst they'd let her pose as Cher. But she doubted it. There was only one name likely to show up on their very short list when they looked at her employee photo. And no matter how many stars she wished on, that name wouldn't be Beyonce's.

Would you like to try *Delusion*?

5

A BE SLID BEHIND THE wheel and started the engine. His car was practically ancient at this point, without fingerprint ignition or computerized autopilot, let alone a reasonably uniform paint job, making it an easy target for parking lot pranksters. He had found it toilet-papered, wallpapered, and vanished altogether—having been pushed by the more industrious students to the farthest-away student lot, to a nearby street's fire hydrant (125 dollar ticket, thank you very much), and on one particularly memorable occasion to the 30-yard line of the football field. At least the shaving cream caricature rubbed off without a trace. From the car, anyhow.

It was a beautiful, sunny, cliché-worthy Florida day. The sun beat down charmingly on the giant gym shoe poised precariously over the Largest Foot Locker In The World, casting its strikingly athletic shadow over the neighboring fast food restaurants and tourist-friendly mini-malls. A pair of impossibly long laces hovered unenthusiastically in the heat, as if knowing they were fighting a losing battle. Though Abe had driven past it for most of his life, it still gave him an unsettled feeling. Why a giant sneaker? Or at least, why a giant sneaker so high up in the air that people couldn't be photographed next to it? It was the only tourist attraction in town that he could think of that wasn't there to be posed in front of, next to, or inside. As if no one had ever told the owner that if an object—however extraordinary—couldn't be captured by visitors to prove its existence back wherever they came from, it might as well not have existed at all. Unlike almost any other city in America, Orlando only truly existed in photographs and shared videos. A place that could only be experienced from someplace else.

That was the problem with teaching history in this town. As far as his students saw it, there was no history. And technically, they were sort of right. Orlando simply had no past. No historical one, at any rate. Built whole out of unlivable swampland, everything from the faux-plantations and colonial-style developments down to the very grass and trees was transplanted or man-made. Even the bodies of water that dotted the scenery had been carefully fabricated, painstakingly recreated to mimic what developers considered to be the ideal Southern scenery. Or the depths of the Pacific Ocean. Or the veldt. There was even an Eiffel tower. Other than the handfuls of people who actually lived there, only the crocodiles and flying insects (the mosquito had long been considered the state bird) truly belonged. There were some actual birds that were indigenous to the area, herons and cranes and wild turkeys, but they were so fantastical in shape and behavior as to seem animatronic themselves.

So how do you teach about the founding fathers when there is a Hall of Presidents right around the corner with every last one of them sitting in historically correct robotic poses? Where westward expansion and the Gold Rush are not only locally evident phenomena but outright encouraged activities on an ongoing everyday basis? How can you treat history as a living document when everything around you is fake? Sometimes it felt like the only lesson his students wanted to learn about history was how profitably they could be doomed to repeat it.

And frankly, thanks to the marvels of the exact same worship of physical replication, when it came right down to it he himself was as fake as they came. His factual history negated his biological history negated his personal history negated any possible sense of self. There was nothing he could do that can't be done. Nothing he could say that can't be sung. All the rest is commentary.

Still, today hadn't been that bad. He'd ended the discussion by mentioning the upcoming traveling Smithsonian exhibit, which would bring the original draft of the Emancipation Proclamation to town, among other important historical documents and artifacts. It took a long time to convince the students that there was anything to be gained by—as they put it—looking at a dirty piece of paper in a glass box. Even though Abe was sure that box would somehow manage to be surrounded by dancing robots in powdered wigs and bass-heavy electronic music. But by the end of the discussion he felt like one or two might find their way over to the Mouse Museum after all. If there was nothing on Netflix. Okay, so it was a long shot. But a real piece of history didn't make its way to Orlando every day, and he believed it was his task as a History teacher to try to persuade them. He would go to the opening ceremony tonight, he would come back with some heartrending or stimulating stories about his own impressions, and maybe someone would get excited enough to show up. That is, if he could come up with a heartrending or stimulating impression from a dirty piece of paper in a glass box (which would in all likelihood actually be acrylic). Or at least from one of the peruked robots.

Following the curve of the road into the sunlight, Abe spotted a billboard for the upcoming exhibition. He made a mental note of the sign's location to tell his students tomorrow. Once an event could claim a billboard, it graduated from being a mere happening to an Attraction, and became noteworthy, promising fun and excitement. While the enlarged copy of the Proclamation itself seemed every bit as un-attractiony as he could possibly dare to hope, it had been jazzed up with a burst of fireworks behind it, and what looked like a waterslide-shaped American flag. Abe prayed it wasn't there because of any actual American flag-shaped waterslide. Every time you thought this town had reached its maximum capacity for silliness, Abe thought, you found your concept of "maximum" was impossibly shortsighted. As he drove past another billboard, this one for the Cured Meat Dancing Troupe (with Upside-Down Coasters! Brought to you by Hormel!), a stream of sunlight passed through two of the painted Meat Dancers and hit Abe squarely in the face with such unexpected brightness it caused his eyes to water. Without thinking, Abe wiped his eyes with his sleeve and immediately felt a blinding pain as residual globs of shaving cream oozed into his eyes. The slimy sting was excruciating, thousands of white-hot slugs crawling over his corneas. Instinctively, he reached up to wipe the pain away with his other sleeve, only to be hit with the same pain again, made worse by the humiliating sense of his own stupidity. He flailed his arms wildly, completely losing control of the wheel and any remaining common sense. At the last possible moment he remembered the brakes. As his foot hit the floor, he heard the two sounds you never want to hear in conjunction: a blaring car horn followed by squealing tires and the crunch of metal.

The first thing he saw when he was able to force his still-tearing eyelids open was a red strapless evening gown pressed against his windshield. This was odd. Odder still, though comforting, was the fact that the dress was empty. Abe panicked. He had hit the Invisible Woman.

6

NORMA PEELED OUT OF the dry cleaners with a complaining squeal of tires. She was going to be late. Again. Her ten-minute break had stretched to twenty already, and she was still miles away from the mall. Late meant another dressing-down by Shosha, which meant another guilty half-apology from Shosha for being "Too hard on her," which meant fending off Shosha's inevitable invitation to an expiatory round of drinks "someplace quiet." But at least she had the dress back. Or rather, the Dress. A long straight column of silk, bias cut and dangerously naked of details, it was in that shade of red for which lipstick manufacturers are still flagellating themselves trying to come up with the right name. To say Norma looked amazing in the Dress would be like saying people need oxygen to live. To say she really could not afford the Dress would be like saying people need to not be trampled by wildebeests to live. Some facts are more relevant than others.

The dress was a designer piece, one of a kind, as close to haute couture as Norma would ever see in her life. It had been sent to the store with a shipment of ready-to-wear as a retail experiment, or perhaps by mistake. It cost $18,000, more than half a year's pay for Norma. When the word spread throughout the store of its arrival, Norma was one of the many breathless store clerks who sneaked it off the rack to try it on, pretending to act like it wasn't such a big deal, while secretly practicing lines like "I'd like to thank the Academy, my publicist, and of course God..." As soon as the silk insinuated itself around the curves of Norma's body, she knew she belonged to it. And she knew what she had to do. She stuffed it in her bag and made a run for it.

Later that night, after the Dress forced her to drink a bottle of chardonnay and pose in front of the mirror in every conceivable position short of Downward Facing Dog, Norma suddenly remembered the word Stealing. Also the word Wrong, and the word Prison. When the next mental leap brought her to the words Jumpsuit and Orange, the Dress suddenly weakened its silken grip. It had suddenly become permanently overaccessorized with visions of shiny silver handcuffs and fat home-monitoring anklets. She had to take it back. And would have had it back on its rack just seconds after the store reopened if it weren't for the tiny snag of fabric staring at her from the neckline. Somehow that malicious dress had mutilated itself just to prove its domination over her life. She couldn't return it that way. She would be caught; she would be fired; she would be Sent Down. An appropriate term, exactly how her throat felt at the thought of it: sent down to the bottom of her stomach. Just as her dinner was suddenly motivated to feel Sent Up. "This is all your fault!" she yelled at the Dress. "I am yelling at a dress!" she yelled back at herself. "I am going to bed!" She would sort it out in the morning. She knew there was a good tailor at her dry cleaners, who did rush work for only a tiny extra charge; she would take it there.

Now, coming from the cleaners with the Dress seamlessly (literally) mended, Norma was on a tear (please God not literally) to get back to the store. So far, the rumors on the floor had gotten as far as the word "missing," without yet having reached the damning word "stolen." Because the dress was so expensive, no one would dream of triggering the GPS tracer before its automatic activation kicked in. Activating the satellite tracker automatically notified store headquarters in New York, and in the kind of backwards logic that could only make sense in retail, she knew that the more valuable the item was, the more incentive there would be to pretend it wasn't missing at all. A false alarm would cost just as many jobs as a real one; it paid for them to wait. Too many giggling clerks had had the dress through their hands and on their bodies for there to be more than a general alarm. It was misplaced; it would turn up. And if not, if it really were stolen (which it is NOT, Norma thought), the electronic tracer would automatically check to make sure it was still in the store on its regular sweep after 24 hours. No harm, no foul. All Norma had to do is slip it into any dressing room in the store and it would probably be accepted without much question. She decided to focus her efforts on Designer Menswear. There were three women clerks in the department, all of them tall and good-looking enough to pin blame on, while still being tall and good-looking enough to probably avoid real harassment. A dumpy girl being caught with stolen couture would be a capital crime. A lovely one could giggle and say "Wasn't me" in just the right way, and most of the store cops would fall all over themselves making excuses for her. Still, Norma didn't want to take any chances. Only half watching for cops as she sped through yellow lights, cutting it closer to Dress-red at each intersection, she finally concocted a plan. She would go up to Menswear, she would latch onto the first businessman who looked like he was about to try something on, would take him to the dressing room—how she would do this, she wasn't—maybe if—

The next thing Norma knew, her car was stopped halfway over a curb, intersected with another car. The other driver was flailing his arms like someone with a nerve disease, or as if his airbag had been filled with gnats. She was breathing fast, but otherwise okay. Her car seemed okay. His car seemed—fuck. He had hit the Dress.

7

ABE WAS OUT OF the car first. He was incredibly relieved to see that it wasn't a headless woman, but some sort of evening gown. However, if that gown could be a woman, he had no doubt it would look exactly like the woman rushing toward him from the other car. Beautiful. Curvaceous. And the most beautiful skin he had ever seen on a human being. He wanted to touch it, just to see what it felt like. How could she be possible? She was just feet away now. He was dazed by her. It was a crucial moment for him. Poised on the tip of his tongue were a number of the most sensationally stupid attempts at conversation that ever plagued the human male.

Fortunately, she spoke first. "Oh my God—is it okay?"

"I'm fine," he started to answer, touched by this dazzling confirmation of her inner loveliness, her beautiful show of concern. Then he realized the pronoun wasn't quite right. It. Thing. Car! He checked the front corner of his car where they had connected, and it looked okay. It took a lot to dent a car these days, the panels had done their job and bounced back into shape after impact, but still, if she was that worried for his sake, then he owed it to her to take the worry seriously. "Not a scratch. It's fine, really. Is yours all right?" He looked up to where he thought her eyes would be, only to find she wasn't there after all. She had bypassed him altogether in favor of the windshield, and was going over the bagged dress as if it were covered in Braille. She hadn't heard a word he'd said.

A bit peevishly, he raised his voice. "It's okay—I'm fine."

"What?" The dress seemed okay. A couple of smudges, but the dry cleaner's bag seemed to have protected it from the worst damage. It could be worse. Only then did Norma remember that there was another person on the scene. She tucked the precious dress over her arm, then strode toward him, smiling her *Illusions* smile.

"I'm sorry. It was my fault."

"No, it was my fault," he answered, gallantly.

"No, no, really, it was my fault."

There was a pause.

There was another, longer pause. She faltered. "Um, this is the part where you're supposed to insist it was your fault."

Abe looked startled. Even if he hadn't made an oath that he wouldn't apologize unnecessarily, and hadn't just broken it (but that didn't count; it was what you were supposed to say), he would never have taken responsibility for something that so clearly wasn't his fault as this. "But it was your fault."

Norma was shocked. Had she lost her touch? "Are you *sure* it wasn't your fault?" She leaned in breathily.

Abe swallowed. Was she attempting to seduce him? He had seen that sort of thing in movies. Would she offer to go out with him if he changed his story? Would she try to kiss him to change his mind if he held out a bit longer? He'd seen movies where that happened—overly broad comedies at any rate. So that put it in the realm of possible, however hugely unlikely. He might never see another woman this beautiful again, and certainly not in such weighted circumstances. He decided to take the chance. "I think so," he responded slowly, in a tone he hoped was seductively unsure but merely sounded learning-disabled. "You turned right in front of me. You ran the stop sign and turned right into my lane, right in front of me. I would have had to swerve into traffic to get away from you. See—your car hit mine." He swallowed again, trying not to look too deeply into her eyes. He held eye contact, mentally signaling that a change of mind—of heart—might just be possible. Would she take the bait?

Norma eyed the positions of the two cars, noted the fact that her car didn't seem to be damaged in any way, remembered the orange jumpsuit and switched personalities. No more Illusions.

"Then I'm really sorry. Look, I have to run. Here's my information." She scribbled her phone number and address on a perfume-sample card and tucked it into his shirt pocket. "Sorry—bye!" She jumped into the convertible, this time safely fastening the passenger side seatbelt over the dress with a motherly caress, then sped off. She had only a few precious minutes left to get to the Designer Men's Department to do the real damage control.

Abe watched her car disappear down the road without moving. She hadn't kissed him. She hadn't touched him even, unless he counted the brief moments her hand had come in contact with his pocket. He didn't even know her name. So why did he feel like he had already slept with her, sometime years ago? He pulled her card out of his pocket. Norma. He was momentarily taken aback. Such an uninspiring name for such a gorgeous woman. The card smelled amazing. He would have to do something about this.

In one fluid motion, Abe picked up a rock on the side of the road and smashed it again and again into the side reflector of his car, until he managed to crack it. There. Turns out she had damaged his car in the accident after all. Now he HAD to call her. She owed him. It was the best Abe had felt all day.

It wasn't until three miles down the road later that Abe realized he had smashed up the car on the wrong side.

8

PULLING BACK INTO THE parking lot at Lord's, Norma kept trying to clear her head. Something was bothering her. She couldn't figure out what it was, but she knew it had something to do with the accident. She pulled up the parking brake and scrutinized the dress again, but it seemed to be fine. That was the most important thing. And she was fine. She stretched, feeling the curve of her spine and the way her neck moved when she turned her head sinuously around in all directions, then followed suit with her shoulders. Knees, ankles also fine. So it wasn't her. The car had seemed all right, and the guy was right, the accident had been her fault, so even if there was a problem with the car, she could deal with it later. But she didn't think it was the car. Which left the other car, the other driver...

Something clicked. She suddenly remembered the other driver, and the way he had looked at her, the way he looked himself. Like he knew her. No, it wasn't that. Like she knew him. The more she thought back, the more certain she was that she had seen him someplace before, maybe even that they had met. Which was really strange, now that she thought of it, because he hadn't mentioned it. And people who had met Norma before always mentioned it. Heck, people who had never come in contact with Norma before frequently insisted that they had met, either because they thought they had (thanks to the Marilyn Monroe thing), or just to get in her pants. And here this guy, who she was growing more and more sure she knew from someplace, if she could just put her finger on where, who even seemed (now that she thought about it) like he was hoping to get into her pants too at some point during the proceedings, hadn't recognized her at all. Strange. Who was he?

She hadn't slept with him. Had she?

She did a quick rundown in her head of all the possibilities of times when she might, maybe, possibly, have maybe been in a situation where that might remotely have happened and she wouldn't have remembered, and decided no. She was never that bad. And even if she had been, if he didn't remember her after *that*, she might as well throw herself off a cliff then and there. He was cute, though. Why is it that when you finally meet a cute, decent guy, she thought, the first thing you do is smash into his car?

She shook her head. Whoever he was, this was the absolute last thing she needed to be worrying about right now. The absolute first thing she needed to be worrying about was how to get the dress back into the store without anyone catching on that she was the one who had taken it out in the first place. She looked over at the red shapely form strapped securely beside her in the passenger seat. The theme to *Mission Impossible* began to play in her head. She was ready.

Getting into the store was the hardest part. First the dress had to be removed from the dry cleaning bag (dead giveaway) and restored to its store hanger from under the seat. Then it had to be inspected again for any tears or stains or fingerprints (how did you check a dress for fingerprints? I don't know! Just check it!) Suddenly Norma was panicking and probably leaving thousands of panic-stained fingerprints all over the dress, but fortunately—as she reassured herself, talking herself down from the panic—they didn't show. Not without a microscope anyhow. And anyone who would think to take a microscope to a dress like that wouldn't be in Couture in the first place. Well, not without a warrant. She panicked again. She talked herself down again. If she could have slapped herself, she would have. *Mission Impossible. Mission Impossible.* She calmed down. Next it had to be slipped into a shopping bag large enough to keep it relatively hidden and unwrinkled, but not so large to arouse curiosity. Especially not Shosha's curiosity. One of the better—and worse—things about a life in retail is the shared obsession with shopping. "Omigodwhatdidyouget?" being the breathless password to a sorority of bargain hunters and designer-hounds and shoe fetishists, each with her (and occasionally his) own rating system against which every new purchase had to be immediately evaluated. Whatever you bought, from the smallest tin of lip gloss to the largest full-length coat, had to be taken out, shown off, given a price point with specific reference to how much you had saved—or alternately, how exorbitantly you had splurged. Next came the Pause, during which the assessment took place, followed by the delighted approval of everyone, which was either wholehearted or entirely fake, and clearly telegraphed as such. No one would ever say, "That's the ugliest thing I've ever seen," or "My God, whatever made you think you could pull that color off?" or "You were robbed." That went against the code. But they made sure you could tell they thought so. Similarly, when they thought you made an amazing score, and wanted you dead, the best you would get would be the same applauding round of blank delight. On the surface, all shoppers were equals and there was no jealousy. Otherwise, no one would share where they found their treasures. But deep down, inside every true shopper's heart was another true shopper's sharpened stiletto.

And Shosha was no exception.

So after much deliberation, Norma decided it had to be a beat up, older shopping bag, telegraphing that this wasn't a new purchase. Even though putting such a lovely dress into a battered bag seemed somehow sacrilegious. So nothing too old. Finally she settled on a reasonably middle-aged, medium-sized bag from the anchor store across the mall. It was familiar enough that it wouldn't invite any comment, and more importantly, she could throw it in the trash without any regrets once it had served its purpose. Norma hoarded old shopping bags the way some people saved their used gift-wrap or collected souvenir spoons. She kept them neatly folded under her bed and in the trunk of her car, never knowing when one might come in handy for just such an occasion as this. She ranked them according to quality (the nicest shops tended to have the nicest bags, with real cloth straps and bags that were of such a strong fibrous paper that they seemed like cloth themselves) and design (her absolute favorites came from a Chinese department store, she only had two but they screamed with color and bright graphics and blazing pictograms that looked incredibly stylish, even though for all she knew could actually have read "Guess who just paid 3000 times more than these cost to make!" or "Help! I am 4 years old and am being forced to work in a shopping bag factory for two cents an hour!") Occasionally she actually would reuse them, and it was always a matter of much consideration which one was worth putting into service, knowing that paper bags are flimsy things, and each journey could be their last.

It wasn't so much a matter of the bag itself, she reasoned, but what the bag *stood for.* Each bag was more than a bag, it was a brand. The ones worth saving, that is. Carrying it made the user a person who shopped at that store, and because people assume that no one carries a shopping bag unless they shopped at that store recently, it made them someone who shopped there on a regular basis. Just as much as the Fendi baguette she dreamed of someday carrying, Norma felt that a Fendi shopping bag said things about her, things that she liked to have said. Not that she had one of those bags yet, either, but if she did... Showing up at work with her lunch in a little bag from the high-end lingerie shop on a regular basis said that she had an exciting sex life. No one had to know that it was the same bag, or that the purchase was made several months ago. The same was true for a bag from an exclusive shoe shop that she carefully employed to carry an extra sweater or some other trifle once a season. And she treasured her little robin's-egg bag from a trip to Tiffany's a handful of years ago on a tourist trip to New York. Not just any Tiffany's either—*The* Tiffany and Company, the Fifth Avenue flagship, the Audrey Hepburn original, though the bag itself didn't show it, unfortunately. So what if she only bought a mini bottle of perfume? She had a Tiffany shopping bag, just the size a jewelry box would fit into, and someday she would use it to carry her lunch, or her makeup pouch, or some other *je ne sais quoi*, and Norma felt confident that the effect—on whomever she needed to be devastated—would be devastating. Maybe that was why Norma was one of the highest-ranking salesgirls of the *Illusions* perfume line in the state, year after year. While she never saw artifice as anything but superficial, she never saw that superficiality as a weakness. She couldn't remember a time when she didn't fully comprehend the power of illusions. She may have been born into the job.

Mission Impossible... The dress was in the bag, she was out of the car, she was walking across the parking lot. Walking casually, a just-coming-back-from-lunch walk. Pausing at the electric doors just before they opened, so as to make sure the coast seemed clear. A quick scan in both directions didn't turn up anything out of the ordinary. Norma glided in, her gait a combination of "I work here" authority and "I'm still on my lunch break" insouciance. The former to keep salespeople who didn't know her from asking if she wanted anything, the latter to keep the ones who did from wanting things from her. It was a trick to pull off, but you didn't spend years spritzing people with perfume who only wanted to be left alone without acquiring certain skills. Ensnaring those people with the perfect walk was one of her favorite challenges. So naturally she knew a range of perfect walks by heart.

The clicks of her heels on the polished floors echoed her heartbeats like castanets as she passed through Costume and Fine Jewelry, past the scarves and fancy hats that no one ever bought and finally onto the carpeted floors that signaled the beginning of the clothing departments. From there her pathway through the labyrinth of racks to get to Menswear resembled a drunken line dance—forward a few steps, then a few to the right, then around, then forward again, occasionally turning as if to take a second look at an item the way a casual shopper might. Just as she suspected, the Men's Suits department was completely deserted. No one wore business suits in Florida, and the few who might would be too busy actually working at whatever suit-wearing job they did to even think about stopping into the mall on their lunch hour to pick out a new one. The *Mission Impossible* theme just getting to the good bit in her head, Norma dashed into the dressing room and pulled back the curtains of the attendant's cubicle, flinging the dress out of her bag and carefully burying it among the rack of discarded suits waiting to be pressed and replaced on the sales floor, intertwining it as much as possible with another garment so it looked like the two had been tried on together. Now to get back to her station. *Mission* accomplished. Bit of an anticlimax, really. Almost disappointed, she dumped her shopping bag and headed out of the dressing room. Only then did she realize that she was not alone.

A very small man with very suspicious eyes was staring at her.

"Hey!" He said. "You're not supposed to be in here."

If it was possible for a human being to look like a frog, this man was him. Short in stature, with large bulging eyes and curiously elongated arms and legs on a scrawny body, there was something well, *oozy* about him. He also was not wearing pants. The suit trousers he was changing into, or out of, were still at half mast. Norma shuddered. She debated whether or not to admit that she worked there. Had he seen her hiding the dress or hadn't he? She decided to play it safe. There was one advantage to a man so uniformly unattractive: with so little likelihood of a Mrs. Frog in his life, he would probably take the fall for her if she needed him to. She'd sweet-talked worse.

In one graceful gesture, Norma grabbed a suit off the rack—carefully sizing it up to be certain it was absolutely wrong in as many ways as possible—and tried to look as casual as she could under the circumstances.

"Excuse me," she said to him, breathily, gazing into his eyes with her most liquid stare. "Could you possibly help me?"

Norma held the suit up, her eye contact never wavering. The man gulped, but said nothing. He stared at her, his eyes bulging ever so slightly more. Norma was half afraid that his tongue would shoot out and check her nose for bugs. Then the man spoke. Even his voice was fairly froglike. "Me?"

Norma broke eye contact to look around. There was no one around. No one. Yes, you. Either you or the manne-quin over there. Without a head. And I'm not looking at the mannequin. She raised her eyebrows slightly. Clearly she'd found a winner. But it was too late to turn and run, and for all she knew she was running out of time. *Mission Impossible.* The misguided sequel, starring the Muppets. She had to get away from the dress, though, and she couldn't afford an eyewitness, and it while she completely trusted Mr. Headless over there, leaving Kermit to his own devices was too much of a gamble. She returned her eyes to his, and resumed her sultry request.

"Uh huh... I was just wondering if you could do me a favor. I was trying to decide if this suit would be right for my boyfriend, and, well..." she paused, and looked down at her feet shyly, giving the impression that she was blush-ing—damn she could act!—"I was just wondering, since you're kind of the same size as him, whether you might try it on, so I could see how it looks?" She raised her eyes back up to his, and bit her lip ever so slightly. She was a pro at this. The effect of her white teeth against her red lip, her big trusting eyes looking into his, her chest rising slightly as she breathed in... the kind of look that's specially calibrated to make a hardened master criminal drop his gun and raise his other gun... boop boop a doo, baby...

The frogman swallowed, his fly apparently unmoved in any way. In fact, he was quickly taking the time to pull up his pants and fasten them as tightly as possible. "Let me guess—you think if you butter me up, I'll buy you that dress, huh?" Shit. He'd seen it then. "Look, I don't have that kind of money. Or that kind of time."

Norma was flabbergasted. Far in the distance she saw another clerk approaching. She knew she'd be asked what she was doing in his department, and her lunch break was definitely over. She needed to change tactics. "I'll give you fifty bucks."

"To try on a suit?"

"To shut up about the dress."

For the first time, his eyes lit up, with a quick oleaginous gleam. "Oh I see...your boyfriend won't buy you the dress, so you try to lure some sucker in here to buy it for you—but you don't want him to know so now you're trying to buy me off... Yeah, I'd like to 'try on the suit...'" Now it was his turn to look suggestively, which was nowhere near such a pretty sight.

"Oh my God! Eww!" It was all Norma could do not to lose her breakfast, right there in the cubicle. There were bad pickup lines, and bad pickup moments, but she'd never been accused of prostitution before—welcome to a new low, baby. And at the same time, a teeny tiny part of her fashion-loving brain was processing how, if he hadn't already mentioned that he couldn't afford the dress, and if he was even a little bit cuter... *ew! ew! ew! ew! ew!!!* Norma made a mental note to find a brain surgeon to have whatever piece had formed that thought removed.

Somehow she kept her head. Vomiting on his shoes wouldn't be a good idea. She just had to make a graceful exit somehow. And soon, because the Menswear clerk was now just yards away.

"I mean, no. You've got it all wrong."

The frogman saw her increasing panic, saw the

approaching store clerk, and made a quick mental calculation. "Well, it's going to take a lot more than fifty dollars."

"How much?" Norma didn't have much more than the fifty she had offered, but what was she going to do? With relief she noticed that the clerk had turned off to the side and was straightening the nearby tie display—that bought her another minute or two at least. Why hadn't she thought of rummaging messily through all the ties on every table as a first line of defense? And the money! Why had she offered him a bribe in the first place, when for all he knew she was just misplacing a dress? She couldn't even really afford the fifty—what was she thinking?—and now his assumption that she was at his mercy effectively put her there.

"Go out with me."

Norma tried going back to her original story. "I can't. I have a boyfriend. He's very jealous."

"Then I'll tell him you're giving happy endings in the men's dressing room at Lord and Taylor's for cocktail dresses."

"You're bluffing."

"So are you."

For the first time, Norma smiled. At least he was smart. She hadn't had a date in a long time, so even if it was as awful as she was sure it would be, at least it would be someone else paying for dinner and treating her like she mattered. It was hard to say no to that. Deep down it was always hard to say no to being wanted. She gave him her number, then started to walk away.

"Hang on." He grabbed her arm, and started dialing the number she gave him. Deep within her handbag, her cell phone started to ring. He grinned. "Just checking."

Norma started to leave again, then stopped. Somehow

she still felt she needed to explain herself. "It wasn't a cocktail dress. It was couture."

Their eyes met. The frogman spoke first. "Then I wouldn't have just told the boyfriend."

9

WELL, IT WASN'T THE turnout he had hoped, but it could have been worse. After two weeks of plugging, reminding, and offering extra credit, Abe had finally been able to convince a grand total of nine students to agree to come to the Emancipation Proclamation exhibit's opening party. Given the peripatetic nature of high school students in general, and of a couple of the students on the list in particular, he genuinely only expected to see about half of that number. But still, the exhibit would be in town for several weeks, and if even one of those students could be sufficiently jazzed up by anything he or she saw tonight, maybe it would be enough to excite a dozen more. It was a long shot, but it was a party, which meant there would hopefully be something exciting going on above and beyond the actual excitement of the rare historical documents that were the raison d'être of the show. And if all else failed, alcohol would in all likelihood be served, and Abe had already decided to turn a blind eye to any underage maneuverings in that department. After all, he reasoned, there was no legal drinking age in the 19th century. That was a living history lesson right there. He had no doubt that the kids were going to pretend they didn't know him. It wouldn't cost him anything to return the favor.

He scanned the crowd hopefully, but he had arrived early and there was no sign of anyone he knew. He had to hand it to the theme park "imagini-storians" who put the exhibit together: there was a real nod toward verisimilitude everywhere he looked. The hall itself was set up with life-sized moving dioramas of the torments of slavery, of the underground railroad, and several scenes of Abraham Lincoln's own life and Presidency, all with information-rich signs and interactive screens that visitors could use to seek more information or to park their used cups. There was a scale model of Lincoln's boyhood Kentucky log cabin, about the size of a New York studio apartment, for visitors to explore, and a display of clothing the former president had worn, including his distinctive stovepipe hat (far furrier than Abe would have expected). Abe stopped to take in one of his animatronic doppelgangers, this one delivering the Gettysburg address. No matter how many times he came upon an image of Lincoln, in whatever form, it never failed to arrest him. From the worst caricature at the cheesiest used car dealership sale, to the commanding statue in the Memorial in Washington D.C., all of them seemed to speak to Abe.

And he always wanted to ask them the same question: *Who am I?* As if all of them—from the portraits painted by men who had actually known the man, to the creepy men wearing fake beards—would somehow, somewhere, have the answer. He knew that what he was feeling was just garden-variety existential angst, and that he was lucky enough to have the other Abes there to stand in for the answer if he wanted them to—whereas years earlier Sartre asked the same question and, having no one specific to ask, got the answer *Well, I guess I'm nobody then.* But still. Looking into those plastic eyes, his own eyes, his own features but not, Abe still felt an odd connection. He decided he wanted a drink. He hadn't seen a bar anywhere, which was a relief considering that the only flat surfaces in the room were the cases at the far end that were set up displaying the Proclamation and a selection of other significant documents. But shouldn't there be waiters bringing around trays of champagne or something? Had he come too early?

He felt a tap on his shoulder. "What are you doing out here? You're late!" Abe turned to face a man he'd never seen before, who looked just the tiniest bit too irritated to be angry, or possibly the other way around. "Didn't the service tell you to use the staff entrance?" Abe gaped at him, his face as almost as empty of intelligence as the robot behind him. Abe pointed to himself, wordlessly, making the comparison to the animatronic model even more vivid. The man stared back, as if startled by Abe's clear show of stupidity, then just gave Abe a shove toward a door marked Staff. "Just go. Get in your costume, and start bringing around trays of champagne... people are waiting!"

His head spinning a bit even without the benefit of the champagne that he was now apparently supposed to be on the giving end of, instead of the receiving, Abe backed through the door into what turned out to be a staging area with a small galley kitchen. Once again, people seemed to be expecting him and pissed at him at the same time. He was told he was late and a bundle of black and white clothes was pressed into his hands.

"Where..." he started, but before he could finish, he was pointed to the door marked *Men's.*

"Oh, you've got to be kidding me." Abe looked down at his reflection in the mirror and almost literally felt his stomach sink. The clothes fit, which was impressive, considering no one there knew him. When first faced with the decision of whether to put the costume on or not, he had he had chosen the lesser evil, assuming that once he tried squeezing his lanky six-foot-four inch frame into whatever size garment they handed him, he had an easy way out to explain that they had the wrong man. He didn't expect that the pants would fit, let alone the shirt. Certainly not the jacket. But of all the things he didn't expect, of all the nightmares on top of nightmares he didn't expect when he made the first mistake of not explaining the mix-up immediately, he truly didn't expect what he beheld now, looking at himself in the dirty mirror bolted to the wall of the staff bathroom of the exhibit hall. Even before tying on the bow tie, it was painful to see.

They had dressed him as Abraham Lincoln.

10

A BE WALKED OUT OF the bathroom still in his socks, not
even waiting to change back into his street clothes. He
needed to find the manager and explain. He couldn't do this.
He wouldn't even play Lincoln back in elementary school
plays; he certainly wasn't going to start now by starring in
Abe Lincoln: the Cocktail Waitress Years. But what he saw
when he exited the bathroom brought him to a standstill.
The staging area was filled with Lincolns, all dressed exactly
like he was. A few wore the traditional beard, a couple were
women, but all of them bore more than passing resem-
blances to the 16th president, all wore the costume, and the
only major difference between them and him, other than
genetically, was that he didn't have a tray of champagne.
Or shoes. A point that was quickly screamed at him by the
same man who had accosted him earlier.

"I'm not..." Abe tried to explain, as the manager bore down
on him, his face getting redder. Their eyes met and Abe
gathered his courage together—no matter how angry this
man was, Abe had the facts on his side. "I'm not a waiter!"

"Of course you're not—you're an impersonator! They're
not expecting perfection—just competence. Shoes! Tray!"

The other Lincolns had started to exit the kitchen in
pairs, and Abe could hear the muffled sounds of applause
and appreciative laughter as they made their way into the

hall. Clearly this was supposed to be a grand entrance, and his delay—or rather, the delay of whoever they thought he was—had spoiled the overall effect. Instead of ten pairs of Lincolns together in double file, only nine pairs of Lincolns exited in formation, with a solitary solo Lincoln trailing behind. Thanks to him, it wasn't quite a score. Abe wondered if he should apologize for that too, then decided the man probably wouldn't appreciate the humor.

As Abe was lacing up his shoes, the back door opened and a tall gangly boy of about 19 came rushing in from the parking lot, looking very flustered. He threw his jacket off onto a nearby chair and looked beseechingly at the man, who Abe had by now concluded must be running the event.

"I am so sorry I'm late. My car got a flat and I didn't have the number here to call... it's okay if you don't pay me the whole amount, but I can get suited up real fast if you still need me...?" The kid looked at the man and then at Abe, just as the man was looking at Abe and then at him. Only Abe wasn't looking from anyone to anyone, because for the first time, he was the only one in the room who knew exactly what was going on.

The kid stared at Abe incredulously. "They sent a replacement already? I didn't tell them I wasn't coming in. I didn't even tell them I was running late. Dude—that is so uncool." The kid actually looked like he was about to cry. From the looks of his clothes, his beaten-up shirt and frayed khakis, and the worn-down look of his shoes, it was clear that he wasn't doing these jobs just for the fun of them.

Abe got up from his chair, his unlaced shoe already off, the stockinged foot clawing at the laced one. "Oh no," he said reassuringly... "I'm just —" he groped for a word, "—freelance. I was here to see the exhibit, and um..." He looked at the manager, but he was offering no help, "...this guy grabbed me to fill in. But you can see I wasn't any good. I'll just change out of this so you can take over... come on..."

Abe headed to the bathroom to change back into his own clothing as quickly as possible, which wasn't quick enough. Handing over the costume, he smiled at the kid. "How'd you get started being Lincoln?"

"Oh, I dunno," he answered. "Pays better than being Howard Stern."

So there you had it.

With a sense of relief, Abe exited the bathroom into an empty kitchen. He thought about helping himself to an entire bottle of champagne as hazard pay, but didn't want to risk another run-in with the source of the hazard. So instead he decided to rejoin the party he had come to attend in the first place.

Since he had last been in the hall, it had undergone a subtle yet unnerving transformation. The addition of a hundred more people, now holding drinks and hors d'oeuvres—not to mention the 19 people dressed as Abraham Lincoln serving them—made all of the historical exhibits seem a lot less educational and a lot more like really bad conceptual art. Then again, as far as he could tell no one was actually looking at the exhibits. Of course, Abe realized with another mental thud, this party was yet one more place for people to be seen and to tell people they had gone to; another theme event. No different from any other party opening an art exhibit or theatrical performance, or honestly, if they had parties for that sort of thing, new rides at the theme park just outside the building's back gates. With a fresh burst of cynicism, Abe wondered how many of the people gathered there actually knew what the Emancipation Proclamation was, or even in which of the clearly marked handful of cases it was located. Whether, when asked tomorrow what event they had attended, they would mention having seen the document—the original preliminary manuscript, written in Lincoln's own handwriting with comments added by his Secretary of State, valuable beyond comparison—or whether they would just say they were at "that Lincoln thing" and leave it at that. Then again, most of his own students were only deigning to show up for extra credit—if they even bothered to come—and was that really any better? Was the purpose of preserving these artifacts, this proof of history, merely in order for people to appreciate them with constant reverence? Or was it enough that people simply continued to gather in their presence for any reason, however trivial, just to continue to bear witness that they still existed? Questions like that had made Abe decide to become an American History teacher in the first place. Even though he knew that the answers to those questions was simply that most Americans didn't care about either appreciating historical artifacts, or appearing in their presence, without alcohol or people in costumes or talking animals or other spectacles. Which, ironically, was probably what was bringing an awful lot of people there that night. Also there would be fireworks.

Abe flagged down a nearby Lincoln and helped himself to some wine. He hoped it would be the kid, but it was no one he recognized, so to speak. But as impersonators went, this one had the look down. The right basic height, the right hollow cheeks, and the right hair, which went a long way. Even knowing he looked nothing like him, really, as always it still sent a bizarre chill through Abe, like looking through a funhouse mirror. Or a regular mirror after waking up with a particularly bad hangover. He reached for a glass, but the waiter pulled the tray away.

"Aren't you supposed to be serving?" he asked suspiciously.

"No," Abe answered, exasperated. "I'm not an impersonator."

"You should be," the waiter responded. "You're a little too bony, but in the right clothes you would look just like him. Did anyone ever tell you that?"

"You're the first." Abe answered, taking a glass off the tray. What did he mean, too bony? He tried to check out his reflection in the reflective surfaces protecting the nearest dioramas, but they kept being blocked by prettier people doing the same thing, only with much pouffier hair and clothing. He knew he wasn't bonier than Lincoln; that was impossible, but he still wanted to feel at least partially attractive in his own right... and each outside opinion negating that was worth at least a few minutes in front of a mirror obsessing.

He wondered if any of his own students had bothered to show up, but in the crush of people he couldn't spot anyone. He wondered idly how many of the kids would be counting on that to insist that they had been there when in fact they were currently at the movies or slouched in front of the television at home. And if he took their word for it— which he pretty much had to do, let's face it—how many kids who hadn't signed up or expressed an interest would suddenly show up at his desk tomorrow afternoon to insist that they were here too—"You know, toward the back, near the, um—important stuff. I came late." Abe was a patsy, he was too honest, he was constantly being taken advantage of. He might never be fully respected by his students, but they genuinely liked him. He was just fine with them liking him for the wrong reasons. It kept them paying attention in class, or at least pretending to pay attention (even if it came with the price of never-ending abuse of his car). And Abe really loved the idea that once in a while, because they were paying attention, some of the lessons he was teaching were breaking through, just as right now he really loved the idea that maybe somewhere in that room, one, two, even all nine of those students were mingling and possibly even looking at the displays (the ones you could see through all the partygoers), or reading the information cards (the ones you could read through the mood lighting), or gazing in wonder at the Proclamation itself (instead of throwing up in the parking lot after sucking down one too many pilfered glasses of wine).

He decided to wander over to the lighted cases himself, to drink in the reason he was there. It was fairly easy; as he suspected, no one was paying them the slightest bit of attention. There were several small cases, built of glass and hewn wood to better mesh with their Civil War Era surroundings, arranged in a loose triangular formation so there could be little doubt which was the main attraction. And yet all of them were small treasures, next to which everything in the room—from the ridiculous multi-thousand dollar dioramas to the cheapest-looking but still priceless slave underclothing—was mere kitsch. They ranged from signed letters documenting Lincoln's thoughts on slavery and emancipation, a copy of The District of Columbia Emancipation Act, which set all slaves in Washington D.C. free in 1862 and led to the larger Proclamation itself nine years later, one of the few existing sets of photographs of the final draft of the Emancipation Proclamation, written in Lincoln's handwriting, tragically destroyed in the Great Chicago Fire in 1871. And in the largest case, spread out under softly-glowing spotlights, was the preliminary draft of the Proclamation, beginning with the words "I, Abraham Lincoln, President of the United States of America" in Lincoln's scratchy yet compellingly beautiful handwriting, the capital A's somewhat darker than the other letters, rising from the page, befitting the man and the country. This was only the first draft of the manuscript; the official document was in the National Archives with other historical Acts and Proclamations, but it was written in an anonymous clerk's fine calligraphy and had long been considered of lesser historical interest. So much so that it hadn't even made the tour, poor thing. This was the real deal.

It was only a rough draft, but judging from the tiny amount of emendations, the ideas had flowed from Lincoln's pen onto the paper wholly formed. Perhaps there had been a first first draft prior to this one, with more corrections. Perhaps there had been twenty abandoned first sentences. But somehow Abe didn't think so. It read like the work of a brilliant mind committed to a point, one more concerned with stating what was right than with political expediency. Nothing like the final draft, the one destroyed by fire in Chicago, also on display in the form of a series of large blown-up photographs. Here you could see the messy form of how a political speech was built by committee. Words were added, scratched out, occasionally invaded the margins. Comments were appended by William Seward, Lincoln's Secretary of State. And in the most charming touch, whole paragraphs of text were cut and pasted—actually cut and pasted, out of a book or a leaflet or some other printed source—right into the middle of the manuscript. Abe couldn't help but grin at the thought of his forebear reaching that part of his writing, stopping, taking the Act of Congress he wanted to quote, dipping his pen into the inkwell and realizing that there was no way he wanted to write down all those words if he didn't darn well have to... then grabbing a pair of scissors and a pot of glue and saying to hell with it. The pages, faded with age, stained and worn, were haunting in their untidiness.

But on this draft, the real one—Lincoln's own draft in Abe's opinion—the ideas still seemed alive, fresh from the pen. If the penmanship hadn't been so old-fashioned, it might have been written within the last week, the ink still seemed so strong. Abe couldn't look away. He longed to break the glass, to run his fingers over the lines, to retrace the letters. What made him choose the words he picked? And why the ones he corrected? They belonged to him, somehow. In some distant part of his mind he almost felt like he *remembered* these pages, but of course that was impossible. It could only have been that he had seen their images in a book somewhere, or on the Web. He never came across anything related to Lincoln that he didn't stop and inhale, so it could easily have been buried in his memory banks from a single glance ages ago. The thought passed. All he knew is that he was communing with this writing, these pages, because they were so unique, so rough. It had nothing to do with slavery, or the Civil War, or even history, or any of the reasons he thought he was there for. Instead, he found himself looking at a piece of someone's mind at work, evidence of his hands on the paper in the patchwork of text, of his association with his colleague Seward... he was eavesdropping on a complete moment in a man's life. Of his own life, sort of, he couldn't help but feel. As if he had been there.

A tap on his elbow broke him out of his reverie and brought him back to the present and his own skin. It was the angry man from earlier in the evening, the man from the kitchen. Abe flinched, half expecting to be thrown back into the staff bathroom and forced into new indignities, possibly involving a stovepipe hat. But the man didn't seem at all angry now. If anything, he had a slightly bemused expression on his face, though that disappeared as Abe looked back at him, fading into a politely blank smile. Abe stepped aside, making room for him at the display. He hoped he was merely in the way. But the stranger kept looking at him, as if their former connection meant a conversation was in order. Abe had the vaguely uneasy sense that he was supposed to apologize. Then again, in most awkward social situations he had the feeling that he was supposed to apologize. But years of then being asked "What are you apologizing for?" followed by his saying he was sorry for apologizing had finally cured him of the habit. Not of the impulse though.

The man kept looking at him, almost sizing him up. Abe tried to walk away, but he was hedged in between the display case and the man's body—there was no way for him to get past him without saying something, even if that something was just "excuse me," and it was starting to dawn on him that he was hoping to catch Abe into a conversation if he made the mistake of speaking first. The ritual dance of the uncomfortable male partygoer, small talk division.

Finally he spoke. "So what does it mean to be a freelance Lincoln?"

"Excuse me?" Abe had no idea what he was talking about.

"You said you were a freelance Lincoln impersonator. Back in the Green Room."

The green room? Did he mean the kitchen? Abe shook his head, confused. He vaguely remembered the comment, but there was so much going on at the time that it was hard to believe anyone else had picked up on it. And with all the other assumptions about who he wasn't, and all the humiliating dressing up and dressing down it had led to, the fact that this was what this man had come to talk to him about was pretty disconcerting.

"No, actually," he confessed, "I'm a history teacher. I just said that to the kid to make him feel better."

"Why would it make him feel better?"

"Well, he seemed pretty upset to think his job was taken out from under him. It seemed like adding insult to injury for him to think he could be replaced by somebody right off the street. Plus he really seemed to need the work."

"Nah, it would have been good for him. He's always late—would have served him right to lose a gig, especially to someone pulled off the street. He's too cocky because he's top of the list."

"Top of the list?"

"When people want a Lincoln and they look through the photo book, they usually pull him. He's not the best look-alike, but he's got the right height and the right bones, and because he's young and has that soulful puppydog-eyes look he's got some sex appeal thing—you know, sexy Illinois-Junior-Senator-Lincoln. Good for bachelorette parties and bat mitzvahs and stuff. You know what I'm talking about."

Abe couldn't think of a single scenario in which a bat mitzvah or bachelorette party would go hand in hand with anything resembling an Abraham Lincoln impersonator, let alone a sexy Abraham Lincoln impersonator, but he de-cided to keep that to himself. He nodded, uncomfortably, and made a move toward the rest of the room. The man held out his hand, blocking him.

"Harold Harmon."

"Abe Finkelstein," Abe responded automatically, wishing immediately that he'd made something up.

"Abe, huh? You don't say."

"I don't say what?"

"Well, you can't tell me I'm the first person to notice the coincidence that your name is Abraham, and you look so much like Abraham Lincoln?"

Abe tried to smile casually. He hated when this happened. "Why, no. You're the first."

Harold took it in stride. "Me and about a million other people, huh. I get it."

"The other coincidence, which is really freaky, is that my last name is Finkelstein." Abe said

"Yeah? Why's that?" Harold leaned in, interested.

"Well, considering how much I look like Marvin Finkelstein."

"Marvin?"

"My dad. Excuse me." Abe sidled past him and hightailed his way through the crowd to his car.

11

L'OISEAU UNIQUE WAS ONE of the nicest restaurants in that section of town, if you liked dodo. Holding true to the unwritten Orlando law that no business can be successful without being themed, L'Oiseau Unique billed itself as "a fine French bistro devoted to America's oldest, newest and most exciting land fowl." Whether the dodo was, or was not, actually America's most exciting bird, was of course open to debate, but that L'Oiseau Unique was devoted to it was absolutely without question. Diners could choose from "recently-sequenced" or "farm-raised" varieties of the bird, shipped from the handful of nations that had managed to perfect the cloning process. The differences were negligible, and were most likely highlighted in order to produce a sense of connoisseurship in snobbish diners. The birds had been brought back from extinction to be enjoyed cold or hot, prepared countless ways. This being Orlando, of course, diners could also have chicken or steak.

The prices were a little higher than the norm, the napkins were of actual linen and the glasses were of fine enough crystal that a few tended to escape from the restaurant in customers' purses on the occasional evening despite the higher class of diner—again, this being Orlando, home of the obligatory souvenir. Norma could feel her kitten heels sinking into the carpet slightly as she followed the hostess to their table. She had never been here before and she was glad she had dressed up for the occasion. Not *dressed up*-dressed up, she hadn't wanted to send any signals. She certainly didn't want her date to think she liked him enough to get dolled up just for him. But she liked to fit with her surroundings, or even better to rise above them so they set her off like a jewel in a ring, and she was certainly ready to shine here. And while no venue in this town was ever likely to be a place to run into locals, a place that attracted a wealthier crowd was never a bad thing. If she met someone new while she was here, and if that someone new asked for her number...? Well, anything could happen.

And if not, at any rate she had read that dodo was full of anti-oxidants and Omega-3 fatty acids, which were very good for the brain.

As they got to their table, her escort pulled her chair out for her before sitting down himself. He was incredibly solicitous. Norma couldn't help but feel like this was the kind of date she had wanted to be taken on for quite some time. If only the company were better. She didn't want to be the kind of person who judged people based on their looks, but she just couldn't get past his. Something about the way his Adam's apple kept bobbing up and down, like a gumball trying to parallel park. Or the way his lips curled just slightly over his teeth. And it didn't help that he was so much shorter than she was. She watched him as he read over the wine list, his slightly bulging eyes scanning up and down and up and down, and was again reminded of a frog. It would never work. Plus, how could you ever fall for someone you were only dating out of blackmail?

"Nice place, right?" he said.

"It's beautiful," she replied, and meant it. She followed his eyes, taking in the candles on the table, the flower arrangements, the view out the windows of the fake pond with a little bridge spanning it, filled with water lilies and even... some... lily pads.

Oh dear.

No, it would never work.

"I take all my dates here. There's just something about this place." He was saying. "I don't know what it is... I guess it's that thing the French call the *je ne sais quoi.* Anyhow, I hope you like dodo. Though they also have chicken and steak."

"I love dodo." Norma smiled. She had only tried it once, as a child with her parents, and found it tough and stringy. America's oldest, newest and most exciting land fowl had this effect on a lot of people, but a lot of people also found Picasso's art to be boxy and unflattering and Shostakovich's music to sound like cats set loose in a piano factory. It was rare and expensive and got great reviews from people who also got great reviews, therefore officially she loved it, and that was that. "Especially with chardonnay," she added. There was no way she was going to do this—the meal or the date—without a bottle along. His eyes, which had been hopping up and down the narrow menu, came in for a landing in relief at her suggestion.

"Chardonnay," he told the hovering waiter.

"Very good," the waiter said.

"Very good," he echoed to Norma, his eyebrows lifted in happy expectation.

"Good," she said back to him. It was about as enthusiastic as she was willing to get.

"So tell me about yourself." She leaned in, tugging a hole in the silence. It was about as good a start as any. If he was any kind of a talker, that should last her at least through the appetizers, and possibly halfway through the entrée.

As it turned out, he was a particularly longwinded kind of talker. His name was Stuart. He worked for the Mouse.

12

THE FOOD WAS, AS expected, delicious. It was also, as expected, dodo. But this was not actually a bad thing. A distant (not to mention larger and stupider) relative of the pigeon, the dodo could be taught to eat almost anything. As a result, it could also be made to taste like almost anything—nutty, fruity, like meat or like seafood—anything except, oddly enough, chicken. For a good chef who could work past the naturally tough and stringy nature of their flesh, the possibilities were endless.

After the complimentary spicy dodo bruschetta, Norma had a lovely smoked dodo salad on wild greens, followed by roasted dodo tips on toast which were genuinely delicious (though what they were the "tips" of was never properly explained, possibly for good reason). Stuart was a bit less ambitious, moving from a simple dodo-egg omelet to a simpler grilled dodo steak with rice. They decided to pass on dessert. No matter how lovely the calligraphy on the menu cards, there was no way to make "dodo tiramisu" sound tempting. But otherwise, the restaurant was a success. The waiters were certainly attentive. And other than holding a forkful of his omelet out and insisting she try a taste, from his fork, while he was holding it across the table, Stuart's dating comportment was reasonably good. From a distance—albeit a far distance, possibly involving a satellite—Norma believed she appeared to be having a very good time. If she were myopic and deaf, she probably would have been having an excellent evening. If only her escort weren't the man sitting across the table. Or if he were, well, if only he were better looking. Or at least if he would just. Shut. Up.

By the time the appetizers were cleared away, and the arrival of small crystal dishes of pink dodo sherbet to cleanse the palate (nothing like dodo to prepare you for the taste of more dodo), Norma realized her conversational opener was also going to be its closing statement. Nearly half an hour had gone by, and Stuart was still talking about himself and his job, without having stopped for even a moment to ask anything about Norma at all. Though to be honest, aside from the ego pinch of being ignored at close range, this suited Norma just fine. He already knew where she worked, and where she worked pretty much encompassed what she did. She didn't want him to know anything about her personal life, and this was the best possible way not to divulge any of it. Plus, people who never stopped talking about themselves were generally easy to stop dating, because all you had to do is stop feigning interest. Once they realized their favorite subject didn't fascinate you, they were very good at arriving at the conclusion that you had "too little in common" all on their own.

Norma didn't know much about the people who earned a living working for the theme parks, but there were enough of them to constitute a small city, and the Mouse ran the biggest ones of all. Everyone she knew seemed to have a story about a friend of a friend who had been there, who had seen the secret underground tunnels that stretched for miles underneath the parks, or heard rumors about the hidden trash tubes that shot garbage straight from the can to the dump ten miles away at speeds of up to a hundred miles an hour. That all the workers were called "cast members" and were sworn to secrecy in a closed society that was almost as tight as Yale's Skull and Bones, but with far sillier outfits. Or so she suspected, never having been to Yale. No one knew what was true and what was false.

And now she was on a date with one of them. And he wasn't just any cast member—he didn't sell any of the millions of hats with ears or stand behind a counter hawking lemonades in novelty cups or work with the seemingly hundreds of thousands of other employees whose only job was to walk through the park with dustpans and brooms making sure not a single gum wrapper ever touched the ground for more than three seconds. He was a featured performer. His only job was to smile and sign autographs and be seen. He was, in fact, a prince.

"It's a pretty good gig, especially since I don't have to wear a head. You really feel bad for the guys who have to wear the heads, especially when the heat gets up in the high nineties. You know, they put fans in the things, and some of the big heads have ice packs—the bears with the hats you know, but still... they fine you if you pass out."

"Really?" Norma tried to look fascinated, but she was mostly appalled. She concentrated on her spoon. It was a very nice spoon.

"Yeah, and twice as much if you pass out in front of the kids. Especially the little ones, because they think they killed you. Traumatizes them for life. It's like going to war every time you go out there wearing one of those big heads. You get hazard pay if it goes over 100 and you only have to work half-hour shifts. But you pass out once in front of the wrong toddler? Oh, it's over. You'll be lucky if they let you push the vomit mop under the coasters they run in the dark…"

"The only guys who get to have no heads are the princes, so I'm kind of lucky. It's great because of the no-head thing, like I said, plus I get a sword, which doesn't mean anything from a combat point of view, but it's a nice touch if any of the kids get too close. Some of them don't always wash their hands, and forget about remembering to wipe their noses—you got to learn how to distance yourself or you're totally gonna get drenched in it, know what I mean?" He grimaced and took a large bite of sherbet. As she watched the pink ice half melting on his lips, Norma thought she could still hear the viscous lump as it made a wet, smacking sound against the back of his throat. Norma, about to take a bite of hers, changed her mind entirely and replaced her spoon on the plate next to its dish. So much for that.

"I don't like the tights, though," he continued. "The big shoulder pads I can live with, but I hate the tights. All the princes have to be *broad of shoulder and slender of leg.*' Some sort of medieval thing I guess. Makes us more phallic, I think. Separates the Princes from the boys, if you know what I mean." He took a giant bite of his breadstick, leering-ly. Norma choked on her glass of wine. She wasn't sure what to make of Stuart at all, she absolutely didn't want to be out with him, especially not where anyone could see them together, but she couldn't say he was boring. "But the tights chafe like a bear. A couple of the guys get a codpiece, but I just have a long doublet and have to deal with it. And I'm lucky because if I walk a bit bow-legged people think I'm in character. But man it can aggravate you when you get a pair where the seams don't line up right on your thighs and it's one of those really hot days when you start to sweat.

And they fine you if they catch you scratching. Especially in front of the kids. Still beats a head, though."

Stuart paused in his monologue to take a gulp of his chardonnay. His vaguely amphibian lips wrapped greedily around the lip of the glass and his eyes half closed as he sipped it down. She could tell that he was enjoying himself, that the restaurant, and the wine, and the way he was dressed and her presence all added to a sense of suave sophistication for him, which he was clearly trying to play up. As he took another sip of wine, his eyes met hers, and his lips made small bubbles on the surface of the wine, with a tiny slurping sound. He cocked an eyebrow as he lowered his glass. He really thought he had every move in the book. But clearly he was not on the same page. Something just didn't add up.

"So... you're a Prince?"

"Yup."

"Like Prince Charming?"

"Nope."

"What do you mean, nope?"

"Guess again."

"I'm supposed to guess?"

"There aren't that many princes. Most women figure it out eventually." He grinned.

"Okay," Norma gave it some thought. "Are you Cinderella's prince?"

"He's Prince Charming, too."

"That's what I thought. Aren't they all Prince Charming?"

"Pretty much, yeah. Though they have names—Prince Phillip, Prince Eric...The Snow White one is just called 'The Prince,' though. Man, he's got an ego. Most people can only tell them apart because they have different-colored hair. But I'm a whole different kind of prince."

"What does that mean?"

"It means you're barking up the wrong princesses. Think of the guys who get their own storyline." Upon saying this, he speared a tomato on his fork with such force that the pulp and a few seeds splattered over his plate like bloody entrails. He clearly loved his work. Norma scoured her brain for all the princes from every fairy tale she could remember from her youth, but the only one that kept coming back to her was the one she would not, could not say to him. Still, he kept looking at her, wanting her to try. "The Prince and the Pauper?"

"Nope,"

"Prince John?"

"He was a lion! And he wears a head!" Now he seemed almost scornful.

Norma decided not to go with "The Prince of Tides" as her next guess. He might not have the sense of humor she thought he did after all. And then she did have that one other thought, the obvious one, but she just didn't dare.

"I'll give you a hint."

"Okay."

"Ribbit."

Oh no he didn't. "What?!"

"You heard me."

"I think you said 'ribbit.'"

"That I did."

Oh yes he did.

And then he did something even more unbelievable. He bugged his eyes out even farther. And then in a move that she really really wished she hadn't seen, he closed his mouth, sucked in a mouthful of air through his nostrils, and expanded his throat into the most froglike display she had ever seen in her life, outside of an actual nature documentary starring the real thing. And then he said "ribbit" again—only still in his same quiet, slightly nasal tenor voice.

Norma couldn't help it—she burst out laughing, loudly enough to get some aggravated glances from the diners at the next tables. It was all she could do to keep the wine still left in her mouth to continue on its route down her throat and not forge a new path upwards through her nasal passages. Somehow, insanely, she had become the social disturbance, and not him. She didn't want to admit to knowing the answer, even now that he had made it obvious, didn't want to say it out loud, even though it was now an established fact. It just seemed too cruel. And also too good to be true. "You're the Frog Prince!"

"At your service, milady. Certainly took you long enough." He stuck his tongue out at her, which fortunately did seem to be a normal length, though he did so in a seamlessly amphibious flicking motion.

"I thought the Frog Prince would wear a head. A big frog head." She had to say it. It was the only polite thing to say.

"He used to. Till I came along. I'm that good." And again he made the frighteningly froglike smile that Norma had noticed when they first met. "Now if I could figure out a way to convince them I don't need the tights, I'd be set for life. Those things chafe like a bear."

13

THE NIGHT WAS BALMY, with the mingled noises of lazy nocturnal insects and frenzied highway traffic. Somewhere a radio was playing a song about love, or maybe about dancing, or maybe about drugs. The singer was roughly 14, already plastic-surgeried to look twice that (or what twice that used to look like, 28 year old women now being required by the dictates of fashion magazines to look 19). So the lyric come-ons were coy nothings, ensuring that her audience knew precisely what she meant, and no one else did. On every lawn, a sprinkler was making a symmetrical arc, spitting a curve of warm slightly sulfurous water just shy of ankle-height, carving out the grassy territory into wedges that stretched beyond onto the pavement, which after much trial and error Norma had learned exactly how to circumnavigate to protect her shoes. Stuart paid no attention to the passing jets, the cuffs of his khakis slowly becoming speckled in moist patterns as he walked Norma to her door.

He wasn't supposed to be there. They had come in separate cars, of course, her first rule of first dates. And she had already told him she had a lovely time, had already shaken his hand and done the lean-in that made the handshake seem just intimate enough not to feel insulting, without allowing for any further contact (a clever trick she had picked up from a fellow perfume spritzer with even more bad-date experience). She had already said goodnight. She hadn't suggested he come over. She certainly hadn't told him where she lived. The date was over. And yet, the whole way back from the restaurant, she could not avoid the sight of his headlights in her rear-view mirror. At first she thought nothing of it. After all, everyone had to take I-Drive at some point or another. Then she assumed it was a coincidence. Then it just started to get creepy. She briefly considered stopping for gas, or taking a roundabout route specifically in order to lose him, but she knew that if she did so, and he did follow her, she wouldn't be able to handle it at all. With every turn bringing her closer to home, she sent out a silent prayer, hoping he would turn off in another direction. But every time she looked back, his car was always there. She was going to have to confront him.

Fortunately, there was only one space in front of her building, her space, reserved for her, and she slid her convertible into it, turned off the ignition and quickly headed for the front door. He would have to find a spot farther away; hopefully it would buy her enough time to get away without having to say anything. If she closed the door before he got to it, he would get the message that the evening was over, and she wouldn't have to be rude to him. Well, not actively, verbally rude anyhow. That was the best solution. That was her plan.

And yet as she headed up the path, there he was a half step behind her, half-hopping to keep up with her as she walked purposefully up to the door of her apartment. There was no way around it. She was going to have to face him.

"Stuart," She said, in the most businesslike voice she could manage. "I don't know—"

"Whoa, slow down," Stuart said, panting slightly. He was out of breath from his sprint after her through the parking lot, and his body language was far from amorous; in fact, he seemed a bit annoyed. "You know, you're really fast on your feet—I guess you didn't see me. Anyhow."

"Stuart," she tried again, but was again interrupted.

"Yeah, yeah. I know. Don't worry, I'm not here to try and get into your bedroom or whatever. I'm not the guy who follows girls home or stalks women, or hides in the bushes and watches them when they're getting undressed later that night—that your window?" He pointed to a nearby window, which as it turned out, was hers.

"No!"

"I'm kidding! Come on... I'm a Prince! Valiant of conduct and true of heart? Okay, okay, really, I just wasn't sure if you were going to want to see me again, you know, I hope you will, I had a really nice time, but that's not the point. The point is, I didn't want you to worry. You dropped your earring back in the parking lot. At the restaurant. I figured you'd want it back."

He held out his hand to her and she reached out and took the long piece of silver. It fell into her palm and glittered softly. "Thank you," she said. "I can't believe you came all this way just for that."

"Well, you know," he said, giving a courtly half bow with a froglike bend to his knees. "Prince." He straightened up and turned away—he didn't even reach to shake her hand again. "Goodnight."

"Goodnight, Stuart."

She smiled as he headed back down the walkway to his car. She also watched till his car drove away, and continued watching until she was sure the car wasn't coming back.

Joke or not, that comment about hiding in the bushes was probably going to linger for a week.

Still smiling, she turned and let herself into her home. Other than the stalker thing, it had been a really lovely evening. Weird, but lovely. She kicked her shoes off and instinctively reached up to remove her earrings, taking off first one, then the other, and laying them next to her keys by the door. Then she realized what she had done and looked down at her hand. Too late, she realized that the long strip of silver wasn't her earring after all. Looking at it more closely, she wasn't entirely sure it was an earring at all. It had no hook or post attached, though it did have a hole at the top... maybe a pendant? It was beautiful, anyhow. A thin strip of silver with a small rounded red disk set into the tip, almost like a garnet. Well, maybe it was a ruse Stuart came up with to get girls—part of the whole gallant, chivalry thing. If so, you had to hand it to him. It certainly was an ambitious approach. And he had excellent taste.

She supposed she would go to the restaurant tomorrow and turn it in to their lost and found. Or at least call them and see whether anyone had reported it missing. First thing in the morning, she would definitely call them. Or at least see if she had a chain that matched.

14

HEY, LADY."

Norma felt her hip get bumped and instinctively swung her hand around and upwards to slap, only to find her hand several inches too high. She recognized the deep contralto just as she stopped her palm from making contact with Shosha's forehead and hair. Smacking your boss was never a good route to career advancement, no matter how satisfying it might feel at the time.

Shosha just chuckled. "Hey—hey! It's just me... don't be so touchy!" she protested, holding her hands up in mock surrender. She really had a way with words.

Norma pointed her bottle of *Illusions* at her with both hands, like a revolver, gamely playing along. Don't be so touchy yourself. But instead she only asked, "You always hip-check your top sales professionals in the line of duty?" Trying to achieve a good balance of professionalism and play—saying "don't touch me" as clearly as she could, while still saying "don't fire me."

"Nah, just you," Shosha said, and winked. Actually winked. "I really like your pendant. Where'd you get it?"

Norma looked down, noticing again Stuart's gift as if for the first time. She stroked it protectively, loving how strangely warm the silver (or white gold? platinum?) felt against her skin. After much (well, okay, a very small amount of) (well okay, next to no) soul searching, she'd left a message at the restaurant saying she'd found a piece of jewelry and if anyone had lost something they could call her and describe it and she'd gladly return it. She had deliberately kept her description very, very vague so her chance of making it hers would be as large as possible. And then left the wrong phone number, so if anyone did call, they would get a local pizza place. So that was taken care of. But one thing continued to puzzle her about it: if Stuart really did get it for her as a ruse to see her again and track her down to where she lived, then why did he tell her she had dropped an earring? Why would he buy her just one earring? Did he have a whole drawer full of single earrings? Or pendants he called earrings? She knew she was overthinking, but it was so strange. And he really acted as if he thought she had dropped it. Could she have accidentally picked it up in the restaurant without realizing it? Had her kleptomania actually progressed to stealing items without her own knowledge? The whole thing was just too strange. She shrugged it off. What was important was that it was hers now. And it was beautiful. And it was getting compliments.

"Thank you." She smiled coyly and decided not to answer where it came from. It was far easier than making something up.

"No really, where'd you get it?" What was it about Shosha, that she never gave anything up? Norma was again reminded of a terrier, all bounce and single-minded determination, and completely unable to read signs. If you could find a terrier who could wear Dolce and Gabbana without drooling on it. "Do we have them here? I think I've seen them here... Would you mind if I got one like it? We could work out a schedule, so we didn't wear them on the same day... I could base it on your shift schedule."

"I didn't get it here." Norma said, as sweetly as possible. "It was a gift. Did you want me for something?" Sometimes when you tossed a ball to a terrier, you could get it to change directions. Or was that only retrievers?

"Hm. I could have sworn we had them here. Oh well. Yeah, actually. I did need to talk to you." She saw the ball! Atta-Shosha! "Can I pull you aside here?"

Shosha led Norma away from the glassiest most mirrored part of the store, to a more secluded section, closer to sunscreens and fake tanners. This was the section people only came to when they knew what they wanted and didn't feel the need to linger. It was a place favored among management for raises and reprimands—more often the latter. Norma's heart sank. "I think I did see them selling the pendants here..." she tried changing the subject back, but the old ball had lost its bounce. Shosha put a protective arm around Norma's shoulder. That meant the news was going to be really bad. "Okay. It's about *Illusions*. You've been doing great numbers. Every time you're out there, trial goes up. But the last month hasn't been great."

Norma protested, "No one's been doing great this month, Shosha. The weather's been cold, I dunno, the economy's down—it's not just me. I know I'm doing better than the girls over selling *Libido*, and they're brand new!"

"Norm." Norma squirmed, rankling under being called "Norm" even more than under the subject of conversation. "I'm not criticizing you. You're doing great. You're the best. But you know how it is, when the numbers go down, we have to do something, and with *Illusions*, well—you know, there's a little something corporate would love to have us doing to push the needle."

"I'm not wearing a costume," Norma said flatly.

"Don't think of it as a costume," Shosha protested. "You're not a clown going to a Halloween party. It's an Illusion. You'd be a part of a bigger Illusion." Shosha was doing her best to sound enticing. Norma could almost hear her capitalizing the word *Illusions* each time she said it, her fingers spreading slightly in subconscious Balanchine jazz hands, willing the marketing gimmick to be more magical than it was.

"It's a costume, Shosha. Don't fall for the hype just because they're spending a little more money on the brochure."

"Oh, I know. But they're spending a lot more money on the outfits too. I've seen a couple of them up at Saks and it's real quality. You'd be surprised. Anyhow, it's out of my hands. Pick who you want to be out of the book, and we'll order you the Illusion. Okay? Or you could let me pick?" Shosha bit her lip hopefully. Norma didn't want to know what Shosha had in mind. But the request startled her. "Wait a second... I get to pick?"

"Of course. It's still fragrance, not fascism."

"You mean I don't have to be Marilyn Monroe?"

"Marilyn Monroe?" Shosha looked her up and down. "You? You'd need some wig—I dunno, I don't see it, but if you want to..." She walked off shaking her head.

Norma was floored. She could be anyone she wanted to be! All of a sudden she couldn't wait to get her hands on the *Illusions* wardrobe catalog—even the idea of being forced to wear a costume suddenly didn't seem so bad. To be anyone at all, even if it was another celebrity; to be told "you don't look anything like fill-in-the-blank celebrity" and to be able to answer, "I know!" and have no rancor about it... just the idea alone was amazing.

She heard the clomp of a platform boot before she saw Shosha back at her elbow. There was the *Illusions* catalog, held open by Shosha's perfectly manicured finger to a familiar figure in a familiar sequined gown, with a very familiar platinum blonde wig and a too, too familiar beauty mark. "Marilyn Monroe!" Shosha said, triumphantly "Wow—I can't believe I never thought about it, but wow, I bet you could pull that off with all the great makeup people here... I'd kill to see that! Oh wow wow wow! What a fantastic idea!"

Damn, Norma thought. Damn damn damn.

15

ABE STEPPED OUT INTO the Florida sunlight, temporarily blinded. It was the man from the party at the exhibit opening. Harold.

"Do you have any idea how hard you are to track down?" Harold asked.

"Not really," Abe responded. "I can pretty much find me whenever I want me."

"You're funny." Harold answered. "Abe was always funny."

"Do you always talk to people in the third person?"

"I was actually talking about Abraham Lincoln. You, know, the president."

"I've heard of him."

Harold pointed at him. "Funny again." Abe didn't know people really did that, point at someone to indicate him or her while still talking to them, but Harold did. It was talking in the third person while still using the second person. As if there was an unseen audience somewhere, and Harold was letting them know exactly to whom he was referring. This is the funny one, right here. Abe felt like he should take a bow. Or bite the outstretched finger. Or point back and say "Observant," or "Annoying." He did none of these things. As in their last encounter, he merely said nothing and hoped the pest would go away.

Then again, the fact that this man had taken however much time to track Abe down meant that he would probably not be shaken off so easily. Abe's first thought was to walk to his car, pleading lateness to some appointment. Then he decided he didn't want this stranger to know what he drove, or his license number, so he stayed put.

"How did you um, track me down?"

"Actually, I ended up taking the last thing you said—Abe Finkelstein son of Marvin. Had a bit of trouble with the whole Steen/Stein thing. But eventually searching through enough public records got me to the DMV and your license plate numbers, and voilà! There I was—and here we are!"

"Here we are."

There was a pause.

No. Something still didn't make sense. "How did you find out where I worked?"

"Well your number's listed, Abe. And you said you were a history teacher. There aren't that many schools around here. Telephone is an amazing thing. You know, Abraham Lincoln invented it."

"No he didn't."

"See? History teacher. That's called heading you off at the pass. In case your next question was going to be 'how do I know you're you?'"

Abe tried to mentally deny that his next question was going to be 'How do you know I'm me?' but it was, so he dropped it. He tried to think of a different question his next question would have been to insist on, then realized how stupid a thing it was to defend. Not as stupid as insisting that Abraham Lincoln invented the telephone, of course. Or that saying that his knowing he didn't was proof that he was a history teacher. But still idiotic. Though maybe not so idiotic as Harold's next question.

"You don't know anyone who looks like Alexander Graham Bell, do you?"

"What?

"Alexander Graham Bell? Inventor of the telephone? Don't play dumb with me. I know you're a history teacher, Abe Finkelstein the history teacher, so you won't get away with it. I don't really need a Graham Bell just now, but it couldn't hurt to have one. Just in case."

Things were starting to make sense to Abe, all of a sudden. "For bat mitzvahs?" he asked, trying not to roll his eyes.

Harold grinned. "I was thinking more along the lines of graduation parties. But you're good! Bat mitzvahs could work!" He pointed at Abe again. "Or sweet sixteens! Because girls are always on the phone! I gotta write this down...! Of course, it doesn't really work without an Alexander Graham Bell." He looked visibly deflated. "But just in case." There was another pause.

"Do you even know what he looked like?"

"No," Abe lied.

"How about Watson?"

"You mean like Sherlock Holmes's Watson?"

"You know a Sherlock Holmes's Watson?" Again, Harold got excited, then caught the look in Abe's eyes. He pointed again, this time with both hands. "Funny! Anyway," he added, putting an arm around Abe as best he could despite their nearly twelve-inch size difference, "I represent celebrity impersonators."

"Really?" said Abe. "I never would have guessed."

Harold pointed. Abe stopped his finger with his hand. "Let me guess. I'm funny."

Harold stopped. "I wasn't going to say that."

"Yes you were."

"I was going to say clever."

No he wasn't. He wasn't. Abe knew it. He wasn't he wasn't he wasn't. He wanted to jump up and down and point his finger at him and poke him. Instead he said what he always said. "I'm sorry." Abe felt like an ass for apologizing again. When was he going to stop apologizing for things? He was going to take a stand. No more apologizing for things that weren't his fault. And certainly no more apologizing for things that weren't even things. No more. Enough.

"Thank you. Apology accepted." Abe wanted to poke Harold in the eye. Repeatedly. Or better yet, himself. With a sharp stick. Yes. Right into his stupid apologizing brain. "Ladies and gentlemen, that squishy popping sound you hear is a sigh of relief from a far too apologetic man. We're sorry for the disturbance." Oh, for fuck's sake, I did it again. Right through the brain itself. With a harpoon.

Meanwhile Harold was apparently still talking. "...about five years now, but when I saw you at the party last week, I saw something I hadn't seen in years. A real magical connection. You really are Abraham Lincoln."

"I'm not interested."

"Let me finish. Look, when I picked you out of the party, you looked like him. Okay, fine. But then, when I saw you in the outfit, you really looked like him. Bonanza. Gold rush. You work for me and if you're any good at acting, you can put your teacher's salary behind you—I promise you. I mean far, far behind you. I can get you TV gigs and maybe into the movies. There's always a need for Lincolns. He's the top President we ever had, except maybe Chris Rock. And in another ten years his popularity will probably pass, and you're what, 30? 35? So if you don't mind dyeing your hair, you'll probably have a really long career. Just think of the money!"

"And you get a cut?"

"Well, of course. I'd be representing you. I'm not stupid."

"I'm really not interested. I love my job. I love teaching. And I hate being Lincoln."

"You hate being Lincoln?"

"More than you'll ever know."

"So you have impersonated Lincoln before."

Abe frowned, caught. "Well, yeah, people have said I looked like him. So for Halloween. Or at school. Only when I was drafted. I hate it. It's not me. Look, I'm late for a... thing. It was really good meeting you. I'll let you know if I see any Alexander Graham Bells. Belli." He smiled.

Abe started to leave, only to be stopped again by Harold's pointing finger. Only this time it wasn't accompanied by the word "Funny." This time it was an arresting point, holding him in place. "Wait. Don't go yet, Abe. There's something I haven't told you. I was hoping you'd want to sign on for your own sake, but that's okay. I know you probably think I'm a big joke, and I guess maybe I am, a little—I mean I'm not, but my job sort of is. But there's big money in celebrity impersonators, and I'm the best spotter there is. People want them for parties, or events, or to sell stuff; I find them. Client wants someone famous like Elvis, I can get them fifty. But I can round them up someone like Marie Curie too. Nine out of ten people at these things have no idea what these people look like, sometimes ten out of ten, but I'll make it my business to know, and I'm gonna provide a decent match. So if there's a portrait, or a video, they'll be able to say 'yeah, that's pretty good.' Maybe even 'wow.' Okay. You think I'm rambling. I'll get to the point; there's a reason I'm so good at representing impersonators. It's not the repping. Almost any talent agent can put their photo book in front of people and almost any actor can buy a wig and look like someone if they're even halfway decent at impressions. It's the spotting. I was a history major in college too, Abe. Double major. History and biology. Did my Ph.D. in Genetic Biology.

"But the thing is, for about three years before I changed over to booking impersonators, I was a clonologist."

16

THE HISTORY OF CLONING was remarkably short and uncomplicated, considering its moral and ethical considerations. Miles and miles of pages were written about "Should We Do It," "Is It Wrong To Do It," "Why God Doesn't Want Us To Do It," "Which Circle Of Hell Are We Going To Be In If We Do It," "Will Our Families Ever Forgive Us If We Do It Or Will We End Up Sleeping On The Futon In The Guest Room For The Rest Of Our Lives," plus multiple variations on the subject of whether it would even be possible. And meanwhile a couple of guys in a lab who never bothered reading that sort of thing just up and cloned somebody.

It all started with the sheep, of course. Everyone remembers Dolly. Named after Dolly Parton, who probably would have been the first human clone herself had the technology been available sooner (scientists being what they are), but when resources are scarce and you're in Scotland... a sheep would have to do. Dolly was a bit of a disaster: very cute and got great press, but she died young from all sorts of medical problems and because of her huge public debut many laws were immediately passed worldwide to try to keep anyone from making any sort of further cloning attempts. Celebrity cloning executives said she was actually a victim of poor representation; that if she had only had a better agent she could have been licensed into immortality via plush toys and bed sheets, and there would be millions of children counting Dollys off to sleep today. Dying young is a windfall when it comes to fame, as anyone can tell you, and that Dolly's developers didn't exploit her celebrity when they had the chance was seen as one of the greater tragedies in children's marketing history.

So the sheep led to cats, which led to other mammals, and the next thing you know (well, not the next thing but in a logical enough progression that all the doomsayers were able to pat themselves on the back gleefully for their foresight) there was a bouncing human baby clone. Her genetic material came from a rich woman who had lost a beloved daughter; her surrogate womb was, easily enough, the same woman's. It made a lot of ethical questions easier, tied the inevitable upcoming nature-vs.-nurture arguments into a neat little mobius strip, and made for an incredibly easy workload for the lab's legal department. Not to mention that it brought the lab a very cozy sum of money. Best of all, because of the risky nature involved, and the woman's extremely personal reasons for wanting the experiment to succeed, she stipulated that there be no publicity for the girl's first few years of life. Losing her child a second time would be heartbreaking enough, she reasoned; losing her in the glare of the media would be devastating. Only a tightly knit international group of scientists knew of her existence, and miraculously, knowing of her was enough for them to wait quietly. If she died, or worse, suffered horribly, they would all have lost together. So they hunkered down and made more mice and cats and horses (or rather one mouse or cat or horse, but a lot of them), and waited to see how little Miranda Grace developed.

And little Miranda Grace developed colic, and croup, and a perpetually runny nose, and dirty fingernails and a smartass tone and the ability to slam doors and scream "I HATE YOU!" at a moment's notice, and was in every other way a perfectly obnoxious, perfectly normal child. And her mother loved her to pieces. And so eventually the press was alerted to the existence of Child X (no name, no city, just the fact of her), and human cloning was officially on.

After Miranda, genetic laboratories that had up till then been so patient and understanding and nicey-nicey with one another suddenly entered a state of warfare. Science for science's sake was all very well and good while the kid might have died, but now there was money to be made. Finding the best way to exploit the blossoming field and corner the market was the new noble calling. So while a couple of altruistic research facilities really did devote their efforts to pursue partial stem-cell cloning for its lifesaving transplant potential, yadda yadda yadda, most of the big players threw their funding into focus groups: what did people want in cloning? Particularly the rich people, those with lots of expendable income? Well, they wanted their old pets back again, they had known that for years—why take a chance on a new kitten when Mr. Tiddlesworth was so good with the yarn thing and looked so cute on the Christmas cards?

And now they had proven that the same sentiment could be exploited in relatives. They also wanted celebrities, though that was soon taken over by professional licensing firms and movie studios until even the best-connected laboratories couldn't get a taste of that action. People also wanted copies of themselves. Children so often didn't get their father's smarts, or looked like the ugly aunt on their mother's side, or just plain let everyone down—why take the chance on ordinary genetics when you could have a carbon copy of what you already knew and eliminate all the unknowns? It was astonishing how literally selfish some people were when they decided to breed. In their minds, having a clone of themselves for a baby took away all the guesswork about what their child would be like—and while a more ethically sensitive scientist would have taken some time to explain to these potential parents that having the same DNA would by no means make the child an identical person, these first pioneers were, as before stated, only in it for the cash. The burgeoning fields of clone counselors and precloning ethicists and the entire clone family-therapy industry (and related self-self-help books) arose as a direct result of this initial oversight. They didn't do all that much good, because the sort of parents who would be grounded enough to realize in time that they were damaging their child with their impossible expectations were far too smart to do anything so narrow-minded as to clone a baby in the first place.

At the overlapping point between hard science and psychology, the field of Clonology came into being. Clonologists were scientists who could understand the genetic nature of a clone's physiology, analyze his or her psyche, and who could also master the life history of the alpha parent so as to best understand the conflicts a cloned individual was facing at every turn. Clonologists were like dramaturges in the theatrical world. They were uniquely capable of understanding how clones thought, and drawing conclusions about why the ones who turned out most like their genetic parents were able to do so, and why so many others were so self-destructive. From a pure research perspective, clonology provided fascinating insights but little information that could be empirically proven—clones, after all, were people, and people refused to behave like lab rats, no matter how frequently you offered them cheese.

But even beyond most parents' refusal to allow their children to be handed over to Science for study from infancy, there was another obstacle. Like most branches of highly advanced science that required multiple degrees, clonology had a fatal flaw: pure research was profoundly expensive, and there was no money in it. On the other hand, if you were a clone, having a clonologist was like having your own personal Sherpa. An ordinary therapist could only guess that you made certain mistakes because of lingering pain from how your mother raised you. But if you had a clonologist, you could know for a fact that one of your chromosomes made you do it. In other words, a clonologist with very little shame who could put enough conviction in his voice could make a lot of money indeed.

Harold had been a very good clonologist.

17

ABE SHIFTED HIS WEIGHT uncomfortably from foot to foot. He didn't like where this conversation was heading. At all. And he couldn't figure out any way to steer free of the deadly iceberg he saw fast approaching. He was already feeling the chill spreading below the surface, tightening in his groin. He did his best to turn back. "That's a pretty big career change. What made you switch?"

Harold smiled. He didn't even seem to notice the conversational focus had changed at all. If anything, from the way he seemed to take the question in stride, Abe got the impression that he was hoping he would be asked that exact question.

As a matter of fact, he was. "Well, I was hoping you would ask that, Abe," Harold said, leaning against the wall comfortably and inviting Abe to do the same. Abe realized with dread that instead of steering into safer waters he had made a mistake of titanic proportions. Whatever Harold wanted from him, he was going to be dragged under whether he liked it or not.

"The fact is, I was never in it to make a buck. You probably can't tell by looking at me, but I was a nerd back in school, really into science, and kind of a history buff, and I thought clonology was the best way to put all that together—I mean, I'm a people person too, you can tell that I'm sure, but the history and the science thing, that was the real pull. But when it came time to go out and work for a living, and start sitting down and doing the research on primary sources— well, you know, real people—they're *boring*. You know what I mean? I would be doing chronological write-ups on these truly *ordinary* ordinary people. I mean, who wants to read the month-by-month biography of the guy who patented a new kind of corrugated box cardboard? But that's what got him rich, and that's what made him feel important, and that's why he wanted a Corrugated Box Junior, so there I was, finding out that he was sad on rainy days in March, and had a weird aversion to wicker, or whatever."

"Wicker?"

"Wicker. Made his skin crawl. Couldn't be in the same room with it."

"You're making this up."

"Why would I make it up? Anyway, who else would come up with a new way to corrugate than a guy who couldn't sleep at night because he kept seeing all these woven raffia laundry hampers coming to attack him? Or is it rattan? Whatever wicker's made of. Whatever. Guy was a nutcase. But that's the thing. It was the only interesting thing about him."

"Sounds pretty interesting to me."

"Okay. Maybe he was a bad example. You're missing my point. Most people who I had to work with didn't even have that. You go to school, you get test cases. They're not Joe Wicker."

"His name was Joe Wicker?" This may have been the greatest thing Abe had heard, ever.

"No, his name wasn't Joe Wicker!" Then, realizing there was possibly a joke lurking behind the misunderstanding,

Harold again grinned and pointed at Abe. Oh no, Abe thought. This again. Sure enough, it came.

"You're very funny." But a lot of the earlier jocularity seemed to have gone out of it. Harold continued, "I was just calling him that, as an example. You've never done that?" He was getting frustrated, and starting to look again like he had at the opening, on the night they had met. The conversation kept getting away with him, and this was obviously much further than he wanted it to go. "My point is, in when you're first going in for your Master's in Clonology, they don't teach you that people are boring. They don't get you started on ordinary case histories of ordinary people who only want to pass along their own ordinary DNA. It's too uninspiring. Just like they don't train doctors with sore throats and broken pinkie fingers.

"They start you on the histories of people whose histories are fun to read. Sports stars. Society leaders. Rock legends. That's how people first get into the discipline. They have you do your workups on *famous* clones. First you study the historical figure, then you study the reason they decided to be cloned, or the reason the person who bought the DNA decided to have them cloned, get the psych workup there, then meet the people or read the transcripts depending on if you're first in line on that particular clone. Then by the time you meet the actual cloned person, you're ready for whatever they throw at you. With a famous person, it's fun. You actually care how the kid's going to turn out, whether he'll be like the alpha or not. You root for them. It's just not the same with real people."

Abe was dumbfounded. He couldn't believe what he just heard. *"Not the same as with real people?"* He knew that Harold didn't mean "real" in the same way that it actually meant in English, as if he were made of wax or a wind-up toy or an animal of some sort—but still. He had never heard anyone refer to clones as not being real people before. He didn't know what to say. He had always prided himself on being against racism, against sexism, against all -isms, really. Well, against all the bad -isms, anyhow, not the good -isms like feminism and socialism and Buddhism. Judaism he was still on the fence about, but then so were most Jews. And like most Jews, he always assumed that when faced with an overt statement against a group of people, he would immediately and unequivocally stand up and not let the racist/sexist/anti-Semitic/homophobic/intolerant statement go by unchallenged. And yet here was a blatantly xenophobic statement, not just aimed at a group of people, but at *his* group of people, and he was going to say nothing? But how could he say something without exposing himself? Even though he was completely aware of the hypocrisy within his silence, and even though he was crushed under the weight of history, of centuries of knowing that the fear of exposure itself was what ought to compel him to say something, that oppression began when ordinary people were afraid to speak out—he couldn't bring himself to speak. He was not an ordinary person. And what would he be speaking up for, or against, anyhow? The criticisms leveled at him were hard to differentiate. Ordinary people were boring. Given the choice of being a real person, or someone unique (even if only unique by way of being the precise opposite of unique), which would you choose?

And Harold wasn't even done talking. He had settled in, his back against the warm brick of the school building, the sun beating against his balding forehead, but he wasn't even breaking a sweat. It looked like an extremely uncomfortable position, but somehow he didn't look at all ill at ease. However much more there was to this story, Harold would take that much time. When Abe fidgeted, Harold ignored it. When he interrupted, Harold bulldozed over him as if he hadn't spoken. Abe realized that he was being wound up, that all this was leading to a sales pitch that Harold may have made dozens of times before. Or that he had planned out well in advance. He wasn't sure whether the realization made things easier, or worse.

"So I graduated, and I got into the real world, and I found that I had to choose my job market. If I wanted to stick to the kind of clones I liked—celebrities, famous people, the really juicy guys—it basically meant staying in academia. Because let's face it, you have to have inside connections if you're ever going to make it at that and meet anyone first-hand. It's all about who you know. I mean literally. That or go for where the money is and deal with the real people. So I did the regular people first for a few years, because six years of post-grad isn't cheap and you have to pay off the rent somehow, plus justify the time and expense and all that, but my heart wasn't in it. You know, I was a great clonologist. Really. I was solid. You should have seen my billings. But I was a star-fucker at heart, and all I was get-ting was nobodies. I can spot a celebrity clone a mile away. But what am I gonna do, chase them down and offer them therapy? Most of them already had someone anyway. Or they couldn't afford it. But, as it turned out, they didn't have agents." He snapped his fingers on both hands and brought them together in a syncopated clapping movement with a smile. "So I threw in the towel and now I do a little bit of therapy, and a lot of impersonator-repping. It's a pretty good living. Kind of my own little niche. Thanks to all my training, you understand, I've got a very good eye."

At that, Harold straightened up. He brushed some dirt from the back of his trousers with his hand, and leaned backwards a bit to look Abe in the eye. Even knowing what was coming next, though, Abe couldn't help but be surprised.

"You can fool some of the people all of the time, and all of the people some of the time, but you can't fool all of the people all of the time." Harold said. "And you can't fool me."

18

WHAT DO YOU WANT from me?" Abe asked. It was a few days later, at a nearby chain restaurant. Once it had become clear that Harold wasn't going away, and that the conversation wasn't going to be any easier or more pleasant, Abe had only manage to stall for time by agreeing to meet again. This place, a "casual dining" establishment whose menu was virtually indistinguishable from any other in the same category, and completely indistinguishable from any in its franchise, was as good a choice as any. The walls were an explosion of "wackiness," with fake taxidermied elephant heads competing with fake traffic signs and possibly fake / possibly real musical instruments on the walls. The impression it gave was that of a madcap decorator gone wild, but Abe was certain that if you went into any other restaurant in the same chain, you would see the exact same saxophone turned at the exact same 37-degree angle and spaced exactly the same distance from the same rabbit in a goalie's mask. Or possibly they had five or six different Corporate-approved designs to "mix it up." But the menu never varied, whether you were in a "zany" place like this one or a "down home" place like the one at the other side of the strip mall, or the middle of the road no-nonsense place across the street. Americans wanted their restaurants themed differently, but they needed the comfort of sameness when it came to food. One nation, under grilled chicken, indivisible. With a side of fries.

Abe ordered a southwestern chicken sandwich with a side of fries. Harold ordered a Cajun chicken sandwich with curly fries. Neither one was fooled by the sauce that they were getting anything different from the other. But both felt satisfied with their individual choices.

"Well," Harold answered, sizing Abe up with a look that was more honest in its intentions than any Abe had seen in his face before. "To be honest, I don't know. At first, I just wanted to tell you that you really should reconsider doing the impersonator work. You could make more than whatever it is you're getting teaching. And full-disclosure, from an agent's-commission standpoint, I don't want to let go of that. You're doing yourself a disservice. It's not rocket science, sure. It's not even real acting, not Shakespeare, anyhow, obviously. But it's easy money and all you have to do is show up. And then you're left with tons of free time to go and devote yourself to higher calling stuff, whatever that is for you. I don't care. So long as I get my cut. So at first I just wanted to track you down out of greed."

"No, thank you," Abe said.

"Yeah, yeah, I know. You're too honest for that. Honest Abe. But that's the thing. The more I thought about it, the more I thought about you... Abe, who are you?"

"What do you mean?"

"Come on. You're not supposed to be here. There are no Abraham Lincoln clones. You don't exist. You're not supposed to, anyhow. I mean, I would have *majored* in you. I was a history major in college, I did my Master's focus on historical clones—if your case study was out there, I would have seen it. You weren't there. Does anyone know about you?"

Abe sighed. "Not till now. And if you don't mind, I'm trying to keep it that way. It's not really who I am." He looked down at his sandwich, half embarrassed, half annoyed. He had always suspected that a conversation like this was probably coming, he feared that it would be inevitable, but no matter how many times he had thought it through, he never bothered to work out a road map of what he would say should the eventuality arise. Still avoiding Harold's eyes, he took a french fry and toyed with it on his plate, lining it up side by side next to another until the two shoestrings matched perfectly. Then he added another. He could feel Harold looking at him, either weighing what to say, or waiting for him to continue talking. Or waiting for him to look up. He tried to find a fourth fry to match the others, but it was getting harder to find another that was the same exact length to be in full harmony with the other three. Finally he found one, placed it in line, then found it tapered to about a quarter of an inch too short. He could feel Harold watching him. Trying to look nonchalant, he ate the fry. Then he scooped up the other three and ate them too. He wouldn't let Harold think they had any significance. They had no significance. But everything he did in front of Harold seemed fraught with meaning, whereas just a few days before, everything was normal. He looked at Harold, hoping to find him looking at anything except for him. But no, sure enough, Harold was watching.

"Fries," Abe said. He gestured toward the fries, trying to seem casual. He ate a few more, as if to prove a point.

"Mnn," Harold grunted.

There was an awkward pause as each man considered how best to change or return to the subject. For all his bravado and salesmanship, Harold was unsure how to deal with Abe now that he had him pinned. His glow of triumph was replaced with the sullen dissatisfaction of a child who finally managed to break his unbreakable toy truck. He had found the single greatest, possibly the single most important person in current American cultural history, and that person was abjectly refusing to have any part in his own importance. He had never met anyone before who didn't want recognition, let alone fame. Harold was stymied.

The truth was, no matter how many times Abe pictured how he might be discovered, the scenario had never quite played out like this. He knew that it probably couldn't be a secret forever; that if he ever got married he would have to tell his wife, for example. And possibly his doctor in a decade or so, since he knew there were bound to be some health problems down the line, which he was going to need help to fight off. He might not have Marfan's Syndrome to worry about (genetic testing had ruled that one out, not that he'd be letting historians know), but untimely death by assassination made it difficult to know what medical challenges a Lincoln who avoided bullets might have encountered in old age. There had been a couple of girlfriends he had thought about telling, and one who he was pretty sure had guessed, but to his relief it had never come to a moment of revelation. Always at the last moment, or when it seemed like a last moment was nearing, he would manage to turn things, or change the subject, or get there first with a well-practiced, "People are always telling me I look like a clone of..." and laughing it off. And the idea was so preposterous, so impossible, so literally and even legally not-possible, that the people would always laugh it off with him. When he was young he had been tormented with fears of being "found out," "caught," unmasked like a superhero in a comic book, his powers taken away and maybe even being forced to leave his family for being abnormal. But as he got older, the fears diminished into simple fears of embarrassment, not wanting to be seen as different or to stand out in any way. Just wanting to blend in. And now as an adult, the fear had mellowed into mild twinges of paranoia whenever anyone looked at him a second too long, or said his full name, or paused and gave him a look when they read it.

And here he was, completely and totally discovered, and he didn't have a clue what to say. After all the years of dreading this day, he would have thought he would have had some battle plan drawn up, some speech prepared, some *something* to say. Never in a million years would he have believed that his response to being outed as Abraham Lincoln's first and only clone would be "Fries."

And he certainly didn't figure on being brought to light in a place like this, of all places, surrounded by ersatz memorabilia and stuffed walruses and waiters with "old-timey" suspenders while suburban stay-at-home moms coaxed their screaming children to eat just one bite, just *one* bite of their chicken fingers and then they could get dessert. He wasn't expecting any fanfare, but he would have liked a bit more gravitas. A realization that floored him, because he had always prided himself on not wanting to be discovered. He had wanted to stay undetected so long that it had become a virtue in his mind, like humility to the Puritans. And now he realized that what he was feeling wasn't simply annoyance at being found out—it was also something else. After spending his entire life in hiding, to be revealed not with a crash of cymbals but with the buzz of a kazoo... he had to admit he was disappointed.

"You can't just stay under a rock like this, you know," Harold said, gesturing with a fry, as if the restaurant were the rock in question. "The world deserves to know about you. You owe it to them."

"Who's them? What do you mean I owe it?" Abe was immediately put off again. The moment of wanting to be appreciated passed as quickly as it had come. It was one thing to want to be recognized, just once, by someone who understood. But it was another thing entirely for that recognition to come with any sort of responsibilities, let alone obligations. "I'm an anomaly, but I'm hardly important. Clones aren't news anymore."

"Yeah but you would be—you would be HUGE! Abraham Lincoln! You were one of our most popular presidents! You wrote the Gettysburg Address! You freed the slaves! Honest Abe—I cannot tell a lie!"

"That was Washington."

"What?"

"'I cannot tell a lie.' That wasn't Lincoln, it was Washington. And he never said it either. It's a myth. Plus I didn't do any of that. President Lincoln did. Well over a century and a half ago. Look at me. Do I look like I freed any slaves?"

"No, of course not."

"That's because I didn't. I just share some DNA. It's no big deal. Except for that, I'm nothing like Abraham Lincoln."

"Right, of course not. I hear you."

Abe returned to his sandwich. It was getting more rubbery each time he put it down, but he was determined to finish it. But he could feel the texture of the chicken resisting his teeth with every bite. Swallowing was going to be a chore. He longed for this lunch to be over.

"You could wear a hat." Harold pounded the table jubilantly.

"Excuse me?" Abe swallowed the piece of chicken much faster than he would have thought possible. He wheezed with the effort of reclaiming his tongue from his throat, still dry from the whiplash. The crazy man banging the table across from him was once again making no sense.

"A stovepipe hat. Nothing says Lincoln faster than a stovepipe hat. Trust me on this, Abe. When I have to send boys out for headshots on short notice, sometimes that's all they need. White shirt, dark jacket, Stove. Pipe. Hat. " He pointed his finger back at Abe. The finger point again. "I've got a great supplier over in Kissimmee. I can get you one by Friday, maybe Thursday if we're lucky."

"Harold," Abe said. "I'm not going to start wearing a top hat just so people will think I look like Abraham Lincoln. I already look way too much like Abraham Lincoln. That's my problem."

"Not a top hat. A stovepipe hat. A top hat won't do you any good at all. You'd look like an idiot."

"I'm pretty sure I'd look like an idiot in either of them. Harold, I appreciate your interest in me. But I don't want anyone to know. I don't know why my parents chose to have me the way they did, but I know they didn't do it for the general public's sake, or I would be out there already. But thank God they didn't, and I got to grow up like every other normal kid and have a real life. Not screwed up and robbing convenience stores or appearing on reality shows or in and out of rehab like all those other firsts. Maybe if I wanted to come out on my own a decade ago it would have been interesting to a few people, but now I'd just be a novelty act. I agreed to meet with you again, and I met with you again. I'm not interested. But thanks for lunch."

Abe got up and started to leave. Harold got up too, and half-touched, half grabbed his arm. "Any time, Abe. My pleasure. But I really think you should think about this. I'll be in touch, okay?"

"That's all right," Abe said as he left, meaning no.

"All right then!" Harold called after him, meaning he wouldn't take no for an answer.

19

"**H**EY, LADY, I GOT something for ya." The voice, as always, grated like a rusty hinge in a Buddhist temple. Two years of working with Shosha, and Norma still hadn't reached the point where she could hear her jovial bray without cringing slightly. But this time, along with the just-too-loud tone and the ever-present clomp of those polished meta-army boots (metal-studded today), was the additional thump of something large and cardboard, almost but not quite making contact with Norma's rear end. Norma whirled around, shocked, but still keeping her "I know you're my boss" smile not far from lips' reach.

"Open it, open it!" Shosha practically jumped up and down, making it almost impossible to continue mentally filing for sexual harassment. She had placed a large wrapped box on the counter in front of Norma. Bigger than a breadbox, too large for even their most expansive gift collection, the box was just the wrong size to be anything that could remotely considered casual or nonthreatening when given by a coworker, let alone a superior who thinks she's your best friend. If it weren't for the fact that the wrapping paper had the word "*Illusions*" repeated in tasteful matte platinum on shiny black moiré paper, with only a small metallic cord in place of a ribbon (who stoops to decorate with elastic cord outside the retail industry?), Norma would have been truly concerned. But since whatever it was must have come from their parent division in some way, whether as part of a special promotion or some sort of outright freebie swag, then whatever it was, if Shosha wanted to unload it on her and call it a gift, she wouldn't go looking it in the mouth.

On a scale of one to ten, with ten being the best gift she had ever received, and one being a regifted pair of mismatched men's socks, the items contained within the box were a solid 5. In their workmanship and beauty, they could qualify for a good 10, though with 2 points lost for their complete lack of originality, leaving them at a solid 8. But in terms of being the sort of present Norma would have desired to receive, they might as well have been made out of three-day-old cat poop. While she feared this day would probably come eventually, she still was living under the impression that Shosha was giving her a choice. Not to mention that the choice would be a long time in coming— certainly not within a week, forced upon her, gift-wrapped no less.

Inside the box was a pile of platinum blonde waves, dancing on top of a rhinestone-covered evening gown the color of her naked flesh. It was indecent what they were trying to do to her. Even without trying the gown on, she felt completely exposed. There before her, snuggled into the box like a glowing jewel, was Marilyn Monroe's birthday suit.

"So, you gonna try it on?" Shosha insisted.

"Now?" Norma hedged. "It's a lousy time. You know you really need me on the floor."

"What, now?" Shosha countered, her voice practically echoing off the decidedly empty floor. "It's deader than dead. C'mon—try it on."

Norma tried again, "I don't think it's going to fit..." She was clawing at excuses desperately, like a kitten fighting to stay out of the bathtub, dreading the almost inevitable drowning.

Shosha's eyes locked with hers. "It's going to fit. I made sure of it." For an instant Norma was almost sure there was something deeper than banter contained in the comment, but then it passed. Sighing, she gathered the box in her arms and headed to the dressing room.

From the day when Eve first discovered the meaning of the word "naked" and simultaneously discovered the perfect fig-leaf ensemble, there have been times in every woman's life when she tries on a piece of clothing that she simply has to have. Sometimes it comes from necessity; Eve's case, for example, and the first woman astronaut's, not to mention ordinary snow- and rain-gear. But even when it comes to fashion-for-fashion's sake, sometimes clothes demand to be owned. When Norma had tried on the Dress, she had existed within one such moment. Now, just a handful of hours later, that coveted red gown—for all its trouble—had become just a wadded up ball in the back of her memory closet.

The Jean Louis dress Marilyn Monroe wore on the occasion of John F. Kennedy's forty-fifth birthday salute at Madison Square Garden was literally breathtaking. As in, breathe in and hold it for the rest of the evening, lady, because there's not enough room in it for both you and your lungs. So form-fitting that Marilyn had had to be sewn into it—and cut out of it—the flesh-colored floor-length gown was a liquid chiffon embrace that somehow managed to convey both sexiness and class. Not Grace Kelly class, admittedly, but the kind of class of that could grant a woman who everyone suspected had slept with the President of the

United States an enhanced status rather than one which diminished them both. It was the color of unashamed nudity, freckled with 6000 hand-sewn beads that sparkled in the spotlights in a rosette pattern, which no one even noticed, they were so busy looking up. The Grucci Brothers couldn't have designed it better. When it was put on the auction block thirty-seven years later, it sold for 1.2 million dollars. And the buyers thought they got a bargain.

While the duplication carefully unfurled in Norma's arms couldn't possibly be as exquisite (or as expensive) as the original, in some ways she suspected it might have surpassed it. For one thing, the advent of stretch fabrics now made it possible to make a dress that could be every bit as closely attached to the body without any surgery. For another, the far less elaborate beadwork weighed much less than the original must have, allowing for even more sinuous movement. This wasn't a chintzy reproduction, either—knowing that their sales force would be wearing the gowns for days at a time, and would be selling an image of glamour to women who would be leaning in within a hairsbreadth of them in order to capture their scent, the billion-dollar fragrance industry refused to take half measures. It was entirely possible that the other *Illusions* saleswomen were being forced to surrender a percentage of their commissions for the privilege of owning their attire, and only her obvious resistance to the entire idea had kept her paycheck intact—Shosha had probably picked up the tab herself. Were it not immediately recognizable to any student of pop culture history, no one would ever know this dress was a costume at all.

Faced with the fact of it, even alone in the dressing room, Norma was almost terrified to try it on. She could find a way to keep from leaving the cubicle somehow, she could figure out a way around Shosha and the whole *Illusions* business strategy in general; those fears were suddenly inconsequential next to the reality of what she found herself about to do. Standing half naked in front of the mirror, holding the dress that—even if it hadn't been a part of her ancestral history—would have still drawn her in by its own magic, Norma was hesitating because she already knew what she would see. It was one thing to not want to parade her secret in front of others. That had always been her personal phobia. But she had also never faced up to her hidden dread—and longing—to reveal her secret to herself. Never played dress-up. Never did the voice. Never even lightened her hair—almost a class 2 misdemeanor in Florida, alongside minor parking violations and wearing sandals with socks under the age of 60. And now here she was, with one of Marilyn's most famous dresses draped sensuously in her arms. And more suggestively, a platinum blonde wig waiting patiently on the dressing room bench to complete the transformation. Like Marilyn herself, the costume wanted nothing less than total commitment. And like Marilyn herself, Norma wasn't sure if she wanted to commit and was sure she really really wanted a drink.

Carefully, even reverently, she started to slide the gown over her head and raised arms, then stopped. If she was going to do this, she was going to do it all the way. Marilyn's dress was sewn onto her for a reason—there wasn't any room inside for anything else but Marilyn. So Norma removed her undergarments and slid the dress on the way Marilyn wore hers—with nothing on underneath but what God gave her. Just as she suspected (or just as the marketing genius behind the promotion had made certain), the dress fit her like a coat of paint. Without even glancing in the mirror, not yet, she turned and picked up the wig. Figuring out the back from the front took a little work before she realized there was a small tag inside, and then it took a little longer to tuck all of her own auburn hair underneath. But finally the transformation was complete. Norma took a step backwards and finally looked at herself in the full-length mirror to see what she had done.

Standing in the tall glass rectangle in front of her was Marilyn Monroe. Norma covered her face with her hands and sobbed.

20

I T HAD STARTED, AS lousy decisions always do, after a bad day at work.

A new standardized test had been implemented, and Abe was mandated to spend the week's class hours teaching his incredibly gifted students the right way to color in preprinted ovals. His bid to coach the debate team had been rejected yet again in favor of the faculty advisor to the student newspaper, a narrow-waisted, narrow-minded woman whose English courses were consistently ranked on students' webpages at the very bottom. Below even the mind-numbingly useless class his school syllabus called Safe Social Networking, but students called Nudes for Prudes. Abe wasn't particularly worked up over missing the opportunity to drill this year's crop of future personal injury lawyers and advertising copywriters in the finer points of avoiding equivocation and shifting the burden of proof. But he could have used the extra cash. Fixing his car's busted headlamp had proved to be more expensive than he reckoned, and he still hadn't lined up a summer job.

Then there was the Lincoln Incident. Caricatures of Abe as Abraham Lincoln had begun cropping up in more and more places. What started as a mildly amusing prank had snowballed into a hallway and internet meme, occasionally amusing, but most often simply profane. It had finally reached the point where school administrators could no longer ignore the postings, and Abe was called in to the Dean's office.

"You need to stop these," he told Abe, waving a particularly egregious poster showing Abe Lincoln (the Lincoln Memorial version) with a caption inviting the cheerleading squad to "sit on my lap and play with my Lincoln Log."

Abe nodded, solemnly. "I'm not really sure how," he responded. "If I show I'm annoyed, they'll just get worse. You know that."

"I know," the Dean agreed. "And if we catch the people responsible, we'll discipline them. But it's your headache, not ours. If you can't keep the students' respect, I'm not sure we can keep you on staff."

Abe promised to do what he could, but what would that be? If there were only a couple of perpetrators, he might stand a chance. But judging from the number and range of originality of the various insults, it seemed far more likely to be a class-wide if not a school-wide endeavor. He'd almost have an easier time figuring out which students were *not* responsible.

Abe hoped the threat to his job stability wasn't serious, but the Dean had a point. If the students disrespected him to such a degree that he had become a laughingstock, what good would his job be? It seemed as though it would only be a matter of weeks, not even months, before someone attempted a similar joke inside his classroom, during his teaching hours. Abe had seen what happened when a teacher couldn't control his class. It never ended well.

Abe headed home in a deep funk, trying to weigh his options but having an increasingly hard time focusing on how to hoist them onto his invisible scale, considering he had no clue what those options were. He could quit, he supposed, but it was the wrong time in the school year to look for another job. He could feel his back up against the wall when Harold called.

Harold had an idea. It was guaranteed to make them rich.

Rich was a word Abe could understand, even if he had no personal frame of reference in which to fit it. Rich could be a very nice thing. In light of his present non-rich circumstances, saying yes to Harold's idiotic scheme suddenly seemed a lot less crazy.

The next morning, Abe woke in a panic, common sense and regret mingling in his mind to form only one word: No. He called Harold immediately and repeatedly, but the call kept going straight to voicemail. Abe sent message after message, all with the same communication: He had changed his mind. He wasn't interested. He was backing out.

Harold never checked his messages. He found long ago that the best way to create the reality you want is to ignore all other potential realities that might intervene. Abe had said yes, and it was on. Abe would be famous. He would be rich.

Interlude

I N THE LATTER END of the last century, a Brahman bull named Chance became an unlikely celebrity. Milky white and big as a meat freezer, with a massive span of curved horns and a cheery glint in his eye, Chance would have been worth a special trip even if he had the personality of a cow. But where a normal bull would gore a nearby stranger faster than you could say "you idiot, get away from that fence," Chance was all heart. Docile and sweet-natured, Chance would allow children to ride on his back and political candidates to pose alongside him and boost their virile American male bona-fides. From Ronald Reagan to Mother Teresa, any celebrity passing through the rolling hills of Swiss Alp, Texas was treated to a photo op with the congenial bull. A celebrity in his own right, Chance starred in movies and on late-night TV. So when, at the ripe old age of 21, Chance started showing his age, it seemed a natural solution for his owners to have him cloned.

It took 189 attempts, but eventually the cloning procedure was successful, and Second Chance was born. A beautiful calf who seemed to instinctively recognize his owners and who immediately claimed his predecessor's favorite shady resting spot under a tree behind the ranch house. Second Chance ate his feed in the same slowly contemplative manner, and showed the same cheery glint when you caught his eye. In fact, Second Chance was identical to Chance in every way. Well, nearly every way. There was the tiny matter of his personality. The first time he threw his owner, dislocating his shoulder and nearly goring him through, it barely gave him pause. Just some youthful spirits, no doubt, he would be sweet as a lamb once he matured. The next time Second Chance sent him to the hospital, this time goring him several times and nearly detaching his scrotum, he was equally sanguine. After all, the ranch had only acquired Chance when he was 7 years old, so clearly anything Second Chance did before reaching that age didn't count.

So they totally didn't expect it when Second Chance died of a stomach ailment not long after reaching his eighth birthday. He had never been ridden, never dandled a toddler between his horns, never posed with any famous nuns. He couldn't be trusted. His owners insisted to the end that they had their bull back, that had he lived longer he would have shown his true personality. Or at least stopped maiming people. But it was not to be.

This may have been the most dramatic proof that cloning a living thing was not the same as duplicating it outright. From C.C., the first cloned kitten, to little baby Miranda, clones were born and loved from their infancy with a passion that began diminishing with every passing year as the object necessarily bent under the weight of their parents' unmet expectations. Where had their lost loved ones gone? Religious leaders saw this as irrefutable evidence of the human soul—the intangible part of a person that separated him or her from the lower beings. If the seat of the soul could not be found, they argued, then it was more evidence that humans were imbued with something intangible directly bestowed by God (conveniently turning a blind eye to any spiritual ramifications of why Rocky II didn't enjoy being set loose in Rocky I's favorite hamster ball). From the outset, people said they just wanted their guinea pigs (or terriers, or children) back, that they understood it wouldn't be the same, that it would be enough just to hold the new creation. And after all the emotional and financial investment involved, they were understandably hesitant to admit any disappointment. So they easily saw parallels that didn't really exist or that were universal across all species. "I still feel like we got 95% of Chance," Second Chance's owner told the press, after the second hospitalization. But even if that were true, that last five percent was crucial.

When human cloning became a reality, researchers undertook massive studies, subjecting the first clones to a grueling course of mental testing that lasted through most of their lives (generally up to the point when their Alpha had died). Nothing ever came of it. If a clone carried any residual memories of their parent DNA, it was hidden very, very well. Even so, scientists who had insisted it would not be possible for a clone to carry even a hint of memory embedded within their genetic code back when human cloning looked like a political if not scientific impossibility, were now first in line for grant money trying to prove the opposite now that it had become a reality. It had become the Holy Grail of both the cloning and psychiatric industries.

The hunt for a hidden memory bank wasn't just out of compassion for the grieving people who comprised the majority of cloning's customer base, though that was a part of it. It wasn't just another middle finger salute to the Pope on behalf of the scientific community, though that was part of it too. The idea that somewhere locked within a human mind could lie the key to another human's lifetime of experiences was just too irresistible to ignore. If a cloned woman could remember her predecessor's life—even if she could only recreate her thought processes—it would mean a breakthrough in everything we understood about how the brain worked. More than that, it could mean a potentially earth-changing development in the advancement of thought itself. If scientists could find a way to clone Einstein or Hawking at the height of his powers, then somehow trigger those memories within a new person with the same remarkable native intelligence, it could promise answers to all of the questions those geniuses left unresolved. The mysteries locked inside people's dying brains could be unraveled. Schubert's Unfinished Symphony would decisively come to an end. Edwin Drood's killer would be found. We would finally know just what the Mona Lisa thought was so funny.

For someone who thought for a living, it would mean immortality.

For Abraham Finkelstein, on the other hand, it meant someone was in for a heap of trouble.

21

HAROLD THUMPED ABE'S BACK, encouragingly. "You'll be fine. Just think back to all those Douglass debates."

Abe smiled crookedly, annoyed. He wanted to choke the clonologist. It had started already. T-minus five minutes. They were standing in the newly christened "green room" (what was it with Harold and these extra layers of theatricality? Calling things what they were didn't make artifice any less artful—or any more so. Especially not this particular artifice), which was actually the first of two connected rooms at the local Capitol Inn. Abe had hoped for something a little more dignified, or at least respectable, but Harold had vetoed him in favor of the slightly sordid but clearly patriotic Capitol. In all likelihood it was the best he could afford, though he wouldn't admit that. There was a certain fitness to it, Abe decided. This dumpy motel was no more the Capitol than he was President Lincoln. Hopefully somebody out there would make that connection.

Abe crumpled up his coffee cup, took aim at the trash can in the corner, running the commentary in his mind. "Finkelstein has the ball, two men on him, he breaks loose and goes for the three!!!" He looked both ways for imaginary guards, then hurled the soggy cup, missing by almost a yard. A brown dribble of humiliation leaked quietly into the faded carpet. Annoyed, he retrieved the cup and angrily lobbed it at the can from a foot away. He was already turned the other way when the cup bounced off the rim to land with a damp cardboard sigh on the carpet.

"Are you sure you don't want to wear the hat?" Harold asked. "The folks'll eat that up!"

"Yes I'm sure! Let it go already, I won't do it!"

"Hey, no biggie. It's your party."

It's my funeral, Abe thought, hearing his name—the Finkelstein part thrown away as inaudibly as possible—echoing across the front lawn.

Abe wasn't sure which assaulted him first—the glare of the klieg lights perched atop media vans, or the disorienting clickering of scores of cameras stopping and advancing, a spangled swarm of locusts all playing maracas. Harold had promised a giant turnout, but Abe thought it had been another example of the amazing smoke-blowing abilities of Harold's ass, and in no way a real possibility. Sure, he'd expected some style section reporters, maybe the New York Times and NPR would show up. But this was the real thing. There were at least as many big TV logos out there as you'd see at presidential announcements—maybe not so many as during a sex scandal, but certainly more than you'd get for those run-of-the-mill fiscal crises. The mix of people was what intrigued him the most: odd groupings of television reporters, news service stringers, bloggers and school paper editors all thrown together on the hot macadam of the parking lot, all watching him with the same expectant look and many already taking notes. His eyes kept returning to one young reporter in a neon-yellow version of a conservative suit, standing off to the side whispering intriguingly into a microphone in Spanish. What could she possibly be doing here, he wondered. But then again, what were any of them doing here? Himself in particular.

It was probably the wrong moment to start wishing he had dressed better, but steering his eyes down and away from the lights and the crowd, Abe accidentally got a clear look at his tie. He had successfully fought all of Harold's insane Lincolnesque suggestions (particularly that ridiculous stovepipe hat), but in a moment of guilt, ended up pulling out a red, white and blue tie as a compromise. He had wondered why Harold never commented on his patriotism, but now his inadvertent self-inspection revealed to him what many of the gathered crowd had already scribbled into their electronic notepads: it was actually only a white and blue tie, with some of the white embellished in the darker red of either Merlot or marinara. Well, he tried. Or at least he had intended to try, which ought to be plenty.

First Harold got up and said a few introductory words. How he was only the messenger bringing this tremendous historical miracle to the public's eye, and what an honor it was just to be present as one of the crowd. In order to repress the urge to curl up in a fetal ball, Abe went back to studying his tie, sending his mind back through dates and restaurants to try to identify the source of the patriotic reds. Cabernet sauvignon? Fra diavolo? Could it be blood?

Dr. Sanderson stepped up to the microphones next, giving a run-through of the facts of Abe's case. DNA diagrams, height and weight comparisons, the illegal process by which the Finkelsteins had been able to obtain their son from collected upholstery fibers stolen from Ford's Theater. From a scientific standpoint, this was fascinating stuff, but the audience was bored. Even the few science editors in attendance (most of the big media organizations had sent entertainment correspondents, some actually sent national news reporters) were fairly jaded; they had heard almost all of these facts before, years ago when it was new and fascinating, when the clones first started coming out. What was interesting about Abe's case wasn't that he had a case at all, it was Abe himself. Nobody cared about the strings of chromosomes. Not when they had the chance to meet him in person! But they all understood the role the scientist had to play; he was, in a sense, the carnival barker, pointing out the wonders they were about to witness. So they listened, half-heartedly, quarter-heartedly taking notes, until Dr. Sanderson's presentation was through.

It was blood, Abe remembered, and wine. He had been out with Sheila Fallon, they had gone back to her place, and he had tried to be suave with her antique corkscrew. In the act of opening the French wine she had brought out, had badly butchered his own hand and proceeded to go into just enough of a degree of hysterics over the amount of blood and possibility of needing stitches, to totally turn her off forever. No wonder he barely remembered the tie. He had shoved it way back in the rack for a reason. He studied his palm, looking for any hint of a scar. Any possible validation for his painful alienation of the beautiful Sheila. There was no sign of his ever having even been scratched. One of the tragedies of hypochondria is how little tangible evidence your suffering leaves behind. So the dark-red splotches carried a certain poignancy, Abe decided. Who knows—maybe Sheila would be watching this, wherever she was. Maybe she would see him with those bloodstains on his tie and feel sorry for him. Maybe all the girls who ever laughed at him would be watching and would see him with blood stains on his tie and finally realize—*Oh my God,* he thought, suddenly realizing how many people who knew him might possibly be watching—not to mention how many people who didn't know him—*What have I gotten myself into?*

Another slight push from behind, and Abe was at the rented podium in front of at least a half-dozen microphones, the smiling Harold hovering in the middle distance, trying to hide the worry-lines between his brows. Each interfering noise found its way to a stop like tumblers clicking into place, the camera shutters closed, the murmurs hushed. He was up, and everyone was waiting to hear what he had to say. No—much worse than that—waiting to hear what Abraham Lincoln had to say.

It would be so easy to give them what they wanted, Abe realized uncomfortably. His years of holding classfuls of disdainful high schoolers' attention had taught him that much. Just open with a joke, "Four score and seven years ago..." and they would be all his. Eating out of the palm of his pseudo-presidential hand. They would love him, he would fulfill the human side of their expectations without sacrificing the noble spirit of the original. He would be exactly what they wanted in an Abraham Lincoln. If Harold was right, he might even get rich. But he would never be free of them again.

Abe opened his mouth, then shut it again. So easy. Sell your soul in exchange for a much worthier one. "Four score..."

But he couldn't do it. He licked his lips, tried to make eye contact with the cartoon alligator on the billboard across the street so as not to get tripped up by any of the expectant live people in front of him, and said what he was thinking.

"Hi."

It wasn't a great start, but at least it was folksy. Had he stopped talking there, he could have gone right back into the motel room and might still have won everyone over. But he kept talking. "My name is Abe Finkelstein. I'm a history teacher. A high school history teacher. I don't know all that much more about Abraham Lincoln than you do. Possibly less than some of you. It's not my fault I'm stuck in the body of a dead president. To be honest..." he could almost feel the audience leaning forward—was he going to make an "honest Abe" reference or joke? He was not. "I'm not really sure why I'm here. And I really don't know what all of you people are doing here, either." You people? Did he really just say, "You people?" From that point on, he had pretty much no chance of redeeming himself.

Harold rocketed forward and tried to save him, his eyes searching the crowd for anyone sympathetic to make eye contact with. "What Abe means to say, is that while he realizes how important he is because of his heroic ancestor, he still wants to be appreciated for himself." It wasn't working. Nobody wanted to appreciate Abe for himself—"himself" being, apparently, a jerk. Abe could see a lot of hostile eyes dissecting him, and Harold's glib spin control only made his own treason more evident. Well, at least speaking his mind now couldn't make things any worse. He would try taking a positive angle.

"Abraham Lincoln was a great president, a great man. But I'm not a great man. I'm just this guy who works in a high school. Or used to, anyway. Look, there are all sorts of great books out there about Lincoln you can read if you want. Or Calvin Coolidge. He was pretty interesting, too. 'Silent' Cal..." And just like that, he made it worse.

There was a pause, as everyone silently rated him from 1 to 10 on a scale of how much they disliked him. Much too late, Abe smiled, hoping to defuse the tension. Again, Harold rushed in to try and save him. "Okay, folks, we're all ready to answer some questions if you've got any."

So many voices called out at once that it was almost impossible to distinguish one from another. Abe wondered what the protocol was for dealing with these things. Was he supposed to call on people? Or just let the loudest guys win? He pointed to a woman with what looked like a kind face. "Yes?"

"Mr. Finkelstein, have you ever had any flashbacks to your—Lincoln's—time? Any sudden memories?" Kind face or not, her question was nevertheless the least-favorite, most-loathed, most-often-asked intrusion that had tormented clones' existence since the very first clone had her very first therapy session. What was this woman, an idiot? Everyone knew that clones had no residual memories. They had known that since the very origins of cloning. Study after study had proven it. Did she think that somehow he would be different? Abe's mind weighed three possible responses, two of which depended heavily on the word "moron." He chose the third.

"No."

It wasn't an angry no, or a sarcastic one, merely a simple negative. But Abe leaned into the microphone a half-inch too far, and the word came out louder, sharper, ringing out with ear-spasming feedback. Even he was starting to hate himself. He twisted his mouth into a smile, trying to seem friendlier. "Don't go away mad, just go away now," was what his smile read. He gestured toward another less-threatening reporter.

"Mr. Finkelstein, do you see any sorts of parallels or co-incidences between your life and Abraham Lincoln's?"

Abe swallowed, leaned carefully into the mike. "Not really."

"Are you planning to grow a beard?"

"Did you ever think about running for public office?"

"Do you have any phobias about going to the theater, or are you okay if you just stick to the orchestra section?"

"Ever do your homework on the back of a shovel?"

"How about chopping down a cherry tree?"

"That was George Washington!!!" Abe exploded. There was a ripple of laughter, immediately cut through by an unsettling voice from the back.

"Mr. Lincoln, exactly how many of your friends are African-American?"

"Wha—I don't understand"

"Well, you claim to be God's gift to black people..."

"I what???"

"... Mr. Great White Hope, freeing the slaves and all that. You don't know the first thing about black people!"

"Me? I—I never said anything like that! Abraham Lincoln has nothing to do with me! For the last time, I'm just Abe Finkelstein!"

"That's a Jewish name, isn't it?"

"What?!?!"

However bad Abe had thought it would be, sitting and stewing on the motel bed just a half hour before, he had never dreamed it would be as awful as this. The heat from the klieg lights was starting to make his head swim. His stomach was hard at work making an ulcer out of the knowledge that whatever bad outcome came from this was all his own fault for agreeing to come out in the first place. And then it happened.

"What do you have to say about the biographers who claim that Abe Lincoln was secretly homosexual?"

"More power to him," Abe responded.

"So are you saying you're gay?"

"Is there a cloned Joshua Speed?"

Immediately, a wave of indignation surged inside Abe.

Not anger, not annoyance, but pure core-level shock, completely untempered and unstoppable.

"Now look, I never had any sort of ignoble feelings for Joshua Speed! Joshua was my friend—nothing more. The amity between brothers is quite a natural thing, a show of unaffected love between men of similar sentiments and sensibilities. We were as David and Jonathan—no less, but no more. For God's sake, he helped me with dear Mary when—Gentlemen, you are driving me to madness!"

Almost at once, the words had started to flow out of Abe's mouth in the powerful cadences of a born orator. If he had ever for a moment wanted the crowd's attention, he had it now. Not a throat cleared, not an eyelid wavered. Where had that language come from? It was as if a secret key had suddenly turned in a locked box long hidden inside him. A stream of unconscious thoughts pouring out of him. No, he thought, not thoughts. Memories. For a heartbeat's instant he could see Joshua, feel the warmth of his handclasp, his vague smell of raw tobacco and India ink. But how the hell did he know what India ink smelled like?

At that point Abe did the only reasonable thing a man in his position could do. He passed out.

It was clear the question and answer period was over. Dr. Sandberg and Harold grabbed Abe under the arms and ran, nearly wounding each other and cracking Abe's skull against the doorframe in their haste to be the first one back in through the motel room door. Practically airborne, Harold still remembered his role. "Thanks for coming, everyone! If you're interested in bookings, check the contact sheet— those are all my numbers!" he yelled, smiling graciously as he slammed the door shut behind him.

The first thing Abe heard as he regained consciousness, slumped against the bed frame, was Harold's grumbling voice.

"I still think you should have worn the hat."

22

WHEN ABE RETURNED HOME that evening, his phone was blinking wildly. More than a hundred messages. That couldn't be promising. He called up his voicemail, then changed his mind. He needed a shower. He needed a shower and then he needed something to eat and then he needed to crawl under the covers and die. The phone rang as he was adjusting the hot water. He picked up, reflexively, only to hear a voice he didn't know.

"Mr. Finkel-STINE, this is the—"

"Not interested."

Abe hung up the phone with a mixture of relief and disgust. Telemarketers had been illegal for as long as Abe could remember, but they still somehow found new loopholes that allowed them to barge their way through from time to time. And yet this voice didn't sound pre-recorded. Abe shrugged it off and stepped under the showerhead, turning on all the side jets to loosen up. As the steam rose around him and his brain finally started to relax, he heard the phone again. He would let the voicemail get it. If it was important, they would call back. From the shower, Abe stepped into his pajamas and slipped into a bottle of sleeping pills, then into the most welcoming bed he could remember in ages.

By the end of the night, they had called back eight times.

Abe awoke with the familiar dehydration and disorientation of a SleePerfect™ hangover, relieved himself at a slightly off-kilter angle, flushed without checking and headed for the kitchen. His coffee was brewed and waiting for him, which was a welcome relief. The automatic timer had been broken for weeks, but it must have started functioning again, maybe because of the cold. This too was good. One less thing he needed to take care of. Even after he tasted the deliciously unfamiliar coffee blend, he was still chalking it up to a lack of memory or surplus of luck, when he saw the shoes. Black, polished, conservative shoes that had nothing to do with a history teacher's life, let alone his salary. There were feet inside the shoes that were also unfamiliar to him, and there were two pairs of them, apparently attached to legs that were descending from his couch. Two of the feet were female. Working his way up their bodies, he soon found himself looking at two people he had never seen before, smiling what were clearly meant to be reassuring smiles. Reassuring under pain of death, perhaps, but still reassuring. Trying to find any sort of conclusions among the clutter of an already overloaded head, Abe quickly arrived at three truths. They were strangers, they were in his living room without an invitation, and they came with their own hazelnut-mocha blend coffee.

Abe was unsure which of these things was the most disturbing.

An hour later, now dressed and slightly more oriented, Abe had learned a few more facts about his visitors. Their names were Ed and Nita, they were affiliated with an unnamed major university, and they Didn't Work For The Government. He knew this last bit because they told him. Repeatedly.

It was not going to be a very long conversation, Ed and Nita assured him. They were unfailingly polite, and never for a moment dropped the air of reassurance with which they first greeted him. If they were the government agents which all of Abe's instincts (and all of their pre-emptive denials) told him they were, it was hard to tell which was the good cop and which was the bad. Ed gave off the air of a professor seeking tenure, his dark suit a bit tweedier, his necktie a bow. Nita seemed more like a lawyer—polished and upright. Abe looked for the gun-bulge. In movies, government secret agents always had gun-bulges. But despite his expensive-but-not-too-expensive suit and his air of complete comfort in unfamiliar surroundings, Ed didn't look like he'd ever held a gun in his life. Meanwhile, Nita looked like she never needed to. From the shine of her shoes to the sharp crease of her suit pants to the tight weave of her hair, Nita was poised like the business end of a cleaver. Should push come to shove, she was probably the bad cop. Probably. Abe immediately resolved to neither to push nor shove.

"How did you get into my apartment?" Abe asked, making one last attempt to be the one in control. Neither bothered to respond directly. They were there, Ed said, because they had watched the press conference on TV. They were intrigued by a certain comment—or set of comments—which Abe had made. Did he by any chance remember which comments they were referring to?

Of course he did, Abe thought, his stomach tightening just thinking about it. "I'm not sure. There were a lot of questions."

Abe's and Nita's eyes locked. She blinked first, but he gave a nervous swallow and blew his moral triumph.

Abe decided to meet them head on. "Joshua Speed."

"Yes. From studying the video of the conference, we were given the distinct impression that you weren't just answering questions. It seemed like you were actively remembering something from your past. What happened, Mr. Finkelstein?"

"Abe." He paused. He didn't know what happened. Even thinking back now, trying to remember exactly what happened, it was as if it had happened to someone else. Even if he hadn't been asked by two People Who Didn't Work For The Government, it still seemed terribly important that he remember, that he conjure up the same mix of emotions and knowledge and *memories*. But it was beyond him. He took a deep breath and decided to do something that would either be incredibly wise or impossibly foolish. He decided to trust them.

23

THEY HEADED OUT OF the house into the driveway, directly into the blinding late-morning sun. In tandem, Ed and Nita reached for and put on their sunglasses, in a beautifully choreographed Not-Working-For-The-Government maneuver.... so well choreographed, in fact, so perfectly timed in rhythm, that for yet another time in a series of times in a row, Abe had the distinct sense that maybe they did, in fact, Work For The Government. Abe's eyes watered.

"I need to go back for a second," he said.

"You don't need to go back," Nita replied.

"I just need to get my sunglasses. The sun..."

"The sun will be just fine," she answered, "without your sunglasses."

He tried to make eye contact with her, but it was useless. Even if he could focus through the glare of the sun without his eyes watering, he would have to contend with locating her eyes through the near opacity of her highly polished UV-protected lenses. Not to mention the complete opacity of her turned head, as she continued walking just behind him, suddenly interested in the remarkably uninteresting view.

Still, Abe wasn't ready to give up, even as she angled her body in that subtle way people angle their bodies to let you know that you are going to keep walking forward, without actually touching you and forcing you to acknowledge the conclusion as foregone.

"But how am I going to drive if I can't see through the glare?" As if on cue, Nita turned toward him. Apparently there were some glares you could see even through the darkest sunglasses. Lesson learned.

As if in answer, Ed called out from the end of the driveway. "We'll take my car. Whyever would we need two cars for just the three of us?" He laughed cheerfully. It was a strange laugh, defusing the tension like a kitten in a bomb shelter. Something wasn't right, but you still felt better.

Abe got into the back seat, with Ed and Nita in the front. It was an ordinary car, a late-model American sedan, ordinary ordinary ordinary. Not particularly clean, not particularly messy. There was a broken crayon on the floor under the passenger seat; apparently Ed had kids. The letters "crayo" and "periw" could be read on the side of the blue paper before it tore, the jagged edge of the break and the edges of the flat "end" were already worn smooth. This was a color that had gotten a lot of use. Ed's kid—he assumed it was Ed's kid—was probably missing it. He started to say something, then thought better of it and put the crayon in his pocket. You never know.

It wasn't until three or four miles later that he realized that the back seat had no door handles.

24

WHILE THERE WERE PROBABLY all sorts of logical explanations as to why a perfectly ordinary car driven by a perfectly ordinary person might not have any inside door handles, Abe couldn't think of any. This led him to two conclusions. Either this was not a perfectly ordinary car driven by a perfectly ordinary person, or... Okay. This only led him to one conclusion. Car was not ordinary, therefore Ed was not ordinary. Unless it wasn't Ed's car.

"So, um, is this your car?" Abe asked, hopefully. "Or just what you drive for work?"

"Little of both, really," Ed laughed. "It's a company car. But I own it. My wife and I sometimes use it for long trips with the kids. Little monsters." He winked at Abe. There was a lot in that wink. It was a wink that said *the back seat of this car has no door handles, in case you haven't noticed. Isn't that amusing?* It was a wink that said *There may also be a far more restraining seat inside the trunk. Which is also pretty amusing, when you think about it.* Abe thought about it.

Abe laughed along with Ed. "Kids!" Abe said, trying to sound lighthearted and one-of-the-dads, despite the fact that he didn't have any children. Doing everything in his power to telegraph *Please don't put me in the car seat—I swear I'll be good.* Despite his huge height, he suddenly felt very small. Deep down in his pocket, his hand wrapped around the bit of crayon and clutched it tightly.

"You got any kids?" Ed asked, jovially. The mood stayed light.

"You tell me," Abe said. He still didn't understand the game they were playing, but so long as it was a game, he might as well figure out what the rules were.

"Oh, okay. We know you don't have any kids. I was just trying to make small talk till we got there."

"Where's there?"

"Where we're going."

"Yes, I—Well, I was kind of wondering where that might be."

"Ah, you see? That's why small talk would have come in handy." Ed laughed.

Ed laughed a lot after he talked, Abe noticed. It was a hearty laugh, reassuring. In fact, it was a great laugh, almost perfectly calibrated to put someone at ease. Disarming, that was the word. As in, drop your weapons. Abe contemplated this, then refused to contemplate it. This was silly. He was a history teacher. This was a Buick. Granted, there were no door handles and he was going someplace they wouldn't tell him and they wouldn't let him go back for his sunglasses, but that didn't mean there was anything ominous going on. He was going out of his way to find menace for no reason.

He looked out the window. So far they hadn't passed anything he hadn't seen before. Themed mini-parks, Themed shops, Themed restaurants, all clamoring for attention.

At least he still knew where they were. The car came to a halt at the intersection of McDonald's and McDonald's. Not the streets, but the fast-food joints. For years, two nearly identical franchises had stood head to head in a wary stand-off across a busy roadway. In a flame-broiled experiment in class warfare that even the Montagues and Capulets might envy, they diverged in menus and décor, forcing the uninitiated traveler to take sides. To the north, the "ordinary" McDonald's, true to its roots across America, claiming to be untouched since the restaurant's inception but truthfully as updated with the times as every other franchise to meet the needs of yearly focus groups. Across the street to the south was the "updated" McDonald's, with table service, a healthier menu, and every item specially created for a new, more "upscale" clientele. And since neither one announced what made it different, most diners still chose the way they had from the chain's inception: proximity. As a result, both were a success. So long as people continued to travel north and south in equal numbers, both restaurants continued to thrive equally, and the experiment was either a colossal failure or a huge success, depending on how one looked at it. And so for years, McDonald's continued to look at it, and the standoff continued. A third, genuinely "original" McDonald's franchise had been discussed, its menu not just evocative of but actually identical to its 1954 original, but without a fourth idea for the fourth compass point to guarantee success, the idea had been scrapped. The novelty of originality, after all, was no guarantee against the proven novelty of novelty, which this town already provided in spades.

So he knew where he was, even if he didn't know where he was going. That was in his favor. He had his wallet and his cell phone, even if he had no idea who he could call for help. Or what he would say he needed to be helped from. Did he really need to worry about one and a half friendly people (after all, Nita still seemed half-friendly, Abe decided) who wanted to ask him some questions about something that frankly, he wanted to know the answers to himself? People who made him coffee? Hazelnut-blend coffee? So far Abe was the one who most seemed like he needed help, sure, but he didn't think the people who might come to rescue him would be any more to his liking than Ed or Nita. He was fine. Ordinary people, ordinary car. History teacher, regular car, going to regular place. Driver named Ed. What kind of bad guy was named Ed? Bad guys were named Edward, tops. Or Rocko. Or "The Professor." Abe forced himself to calm down. This wasn't a bad movie. This wasn't a theme park. This was real life.

Fuck. In real life, no one was named "The Professor." In real life, people were named Ed.

25

ENTERING THE COMPLEX, THEY were joined by two more People Who Didn't Work For The Government, much larger and less congenial-seeming, but still wearing ties. Their footsteps made all the usual echoing steps they make in similar hallways in all the bad movies Abe had finally convinced himself this wasn't, but the fact that this wasn't a movie, bad or good, suddenly wasn't quite so reassuring. They seemed to be in some sort of medical facility, or perhaps a science lab. The walls were painted a soothing but off-putting glaucous green, with all of the color's attendant mixed hints of comforts and illnesses and garden-variety heebie-jeebies. This was clearly not a good place to be.

His regular footing having been assumed by the large men, Abe aimed for any sort of mental footing. He took in every detail he passed, from the floors (Nev-A-Stain™ speckled linoleum), to the halls (many and long), to the signs on all the doors they frog-marched him past. There were nameplates on most of the doors, almost all of them indicating their occupants were doctors. He passed office after office of MDs, PhDs, and one disturbing DVM with a cute little picture of a ferret under the name. There were no signs anywhere. There were no water fountains or bulletin boards or colored lines on the floor to help you find your bearings. A person working here would have to know this building by heart. Though the use of the word "heart" in relation to this building was definitely a stretch.

The room they let him into was unmarked by any nameplate. The green of the walls was less soothing, more irritating. This was not a room you wanted to spend a lot of time in. There was nothing inside it but a small table, two chairs and a couch. All three seats were covered in some sort of thin moss-colored velvet embroidered with small frolicsome kittens and large fanciful cabbage roses. If the walls made you wanted to leave the room as soon as possible, the upholstery encouraged you to run from it screaming. There was no art of any sort, but one wall was taken up entirely by a large mirror—the kind that was never purely reflective. Abe waved at the mirror. He wanted whoever might be standing on the other side to know he was friendly. The two burly men stayed behind. But after the door closed behind them, he distinctly saw two similarly burly shapes silhouetted against the frosted window.

Faced with a choice between the chairs and couch, Abe opted for a chair. As his body sank into the cushion uncomfortably, he wondered if he had made the right choice. Especially when Ed and Nita remained standing. He couldn't remember if they told him to have a seat or not. He just assumed they had. What kind of people lead you into a room filled with lounge-type seating and don't expect you to take a seat? Was this some sort of test? Had he failed? Abe glanced at the mirror, then back at Ed and Nita. They were standing casually, as if waiting for something, not looking at him. Not looking at anything in particular at all. But decidedly not sitting. Feeling foolish, Abe stood up too. He decided to take a closer look at the mirror.

"Abe," Ed said, "do you mind taking a seat?"

Abe turned around. Somehow, in the 5 seconds it had taken him to walk halfway across the carpeting, Ed and

Nita had taken seats in each of the two chairs, leaving Abe the sofa. His instincts about preferring the chairs had been correct. This was not a happy couch. The springs made a high-pitched crunching noise in resistance as he sat down, almost as if there were real kittens inside, and he found himself tilting slightly to starboard due to some sort of imbalance in the stuffing. He wedged a pillow underneath his backside to right himself as best he could, hoping that any loss of dignity would be more than made up for by the fact that even at 6 inches deeper than everyone else, he was still a good 3 inches taller than anyone in the room. He sat up straight. Three and a half inches taller. He hoped whoever was behind the mirror was catching this. No wait, he didn't. He went back to hoping there was no one behind the mirror.

"If we could just start with a little formality," Ed began, seeming a bit embarrassed. "I need to ask you to empty your pockets."

Abe hesitated. Could he refuse? He figured it was worth a try. "I'd rather not, if that's okay."

"Well, you don't have to," Ed said. "But then I'd have to ask you again, and then if you said no again, then I might have to insist, and well, you know, it's just a formality right now, but since it's going to become an eventuality... let's just say informal is better." He laughed, that disarming laugh again, and Abe, seeing no other choice, allowed himself to be disarmed. One after another, Abe handed over all his means of escape—his cell phone, his wallet, his house keys, a handful of change. Seeing a hint of blue among the silver, Ed reached down and plucked the broken crayon out from underneath the coins. He studied it, then smiled at Abe as he pocketed it.

"Super—my kid was looking for this."

26

NITA SEALED ABE'S THINGS away into a small envelope, which she then locked into her briefcase, and took out two notepads, handing one to Ed.

Ed smiled congenially. "All right, Abe. Sorry about all the cloak-and-dagger stuff. Doctor's orders," he laughed. "Well, someone's orders. Anyhow, now that we're here I should probably ask you, are there any questions you want to ask us before we get started?"

"Who are you guys?"

"Oh, we can't tell you that."

"Well, what is this place?"

"It's a research facility."

"A government research facility?"

"Oh, no. We don't work for the government."

"We don't work for the government," Nita echoed, a little too quickly.

"So who do you work for?"

"We can't tell you that."

Abe sighed. Another dead end. "Okay. Well, what sort of research?"

"Scientific research."

"Are you going to answer any of my questions?"

Ed grinned. "Well, you could ask us the time."

Taking this as a hopeful sign, Abe did, after a fashion. "Okay. How long is this going to take?"

"Oh I don't know. As long as it takes, I suppose."

"A few hours?"

Ed looked at Nita. Nita looked at Abe. Abe suddenly realized it would be quite a bit more than a few hours. He blanched. "A few... days?"

"If necessary."

"That's really not going to work for me. I have to get back to work. I really have to be at school on Monday. I already took off work all week for that stupid press conference. I don't have any vacation left. If I miss any more, they could fire me."

"Oh, that's all taken care of. We've called your employer and they won't be expecting you back."

"But it's my job. You can't just do that!"

"Of course we can. I'm sure they've hired an excellent substitute."

"But why didn't you ask me? Don't I get a say in this? What if I don't want to be substituted?"

"You don't seem to understand," Ed said. "You've *been* substituted. It's done. And the new person is every bit as good as if not better than you were. To be honest, it sounded like they were relieved. Plenty of great history teachers out there. You're interchangeable."

"I'm—what? This isn't about how good the substitute is, Ed—this is about me! How could you give away my job?"

"Ahhh," Ed said. "Now, if that's the troublei—f you don't mind my saying so—you're making a huge fuss over peanuts. It's just a job. You had no right to it in the first place. From an existential perspective, you were substituted a long time ago."

"What?" Abe said, still not understanding.

Nita spoke up. "Your current employment 'substitution'

is irrelevant. Your DNA, on the other hand, was never yours to substitute. You shouldn't exist."

"But I do exist. I'm still a person," Abe managed, dumbfounded.

"Oh, it's nothing like that," said Ed. "Of course you're a person. You're just not legally permitted to be alive."

"So what am I supposed to do?" Abe asked. "I mean obviously, I am alive, right?"

"Not till we say you are," Nita responded.

Ed leaned in. "Look. If you're having Lincoln's memories, you're not purely biologically a clone. As it is, since you're not registered as one, your legal status is automatically in question. Your social security number is invalid. The legal you died in 1865. So legally speaking, the current you doesn't exist. We need to figure out who you are. And until then..."

It was Nita's turn to lean in. "You belong to us. We own you."

27

IT'S NOT WELL KNOWN how often the original Abe Lincoln chewed tobacco. At this moment however, Abe Finkelstein was particularly grateful for not having picked up the habit himself. Because if he had been one to chew tobacco, there is no doubt that at this moment he would have swallowed it. Nita couldn't possibly have said what he could have sworn he just heard.

"What do you mean, you own me?" he asked, not sure whether to laugh at the ridiculousness of the statement or allowing even for a second the possibility that she was serious. Not that she seemed to possess a funny bone. In fact, he suspected if any part of her anatomy ever dared to allow itself be called funny, her other body parts would shoot it. "Are you saying I'm your sla—" But well before his lower lip even began to make contact with the tips of his upper teeth to form the V, he realized that what Nita lacked in sense of humor, she more than made up for in lack of sense of humor about slavery. He shifted his question to, "Am I under arrest?"

"We're not cops," Ed said, in his irritatingly reassuring voice. "We don't work—"

"Yeah, I know," Abe interrupted him. "You don't work for the government."

Ed smiled. "We're just..." he paused, looking for the right words. "...very *interested* in you right now. Surely you must understand that you represent a unique case in the history of—well, of modern history. As far as we know, there's never, ever been anyone like you before."

"I beg to differ." Abe's mouth was dry. "I think I could argue pretty persuasively that there was someone exactly like me. Even more like me, because he might actually know whatever it is you wanted me to tell you. Is there any way I could get something to drink?"

"Later, Abe. First, if you don't mind, could you tell me—us—sorry, Nita—exactly what was going through your mind at the press conference?"

Abe thought about it. He thought about how they showed up in his house without knocking. He thought about how Ed's car had no inside door handles. He thought about how they said they owned him. He thought of an option that he was surprised he hadn't thought of before. "I want to speak to a lawyer."

Ed smiled again. "You bet."

Abe blinked. He expected more resistance than this. He looked around, feeling incredibly stupid. Should he get up? Was it that simple? "Okay," he said. "I don't have one, but I can get one if you can just let me have my phone." He fidgeted. He started to get up, but Ed stopped him with a hand on his knee.

"Where are you going?"

"I thought..." Abe said. "I was going to..." He was missing something. Once again, the point when things decided to start making sense had been and gone without him. He struggled for the right words, but lost his verbs. "Lawyer. Phone call." Adding, hopefully, "Drink of water, maybe."

"Oh. No." Ed said, again with that godawful civil-servant-bearing-bad-news laugh. "You misunderstood. Of course there's no problem with your talking to a lawyer if you'd like. No problem at all. To be honest, I'm surprised you didn't ask sooner. The fact is," Ed leaned in, so close that Abe could clearly see his pores, so clearly he could even count them if he wanted to, "I'm a lawyer!"

Ed grinned at Abe as if this were the biggest stroke of luck in the world, at the same time nudging his elbow into Abe's ribs jovially, in a way that was just the tiniest bit too hard to be entirely convivial. It was clear that Abe was supposed to laugh along. Abe laughed along. It was clear that Abe was supposed to laugh along some more. Abe laughed along some more. It was clear that Abe was supposed to stop asking to talk to a lawyer. Yep. That was pretty clear too. Defeated, Abe wondered if he asked again for a glass of water, whether Ed would claim to be one of those too.

28

HABEAS CORPUS NICELY DISPENSED with, Ed leaned in toward Abe and flexed his hands forward in a back-to-businesslike manner. "Let's try again, Abe," Ed said. "The press conference. What happened?"

"I don't know," Abe said. "It just happened."

"What just happened? You remembered things?"

"No—I just suddenly knew the answer to the question, and I answered it. I didn't even realize what I was saying until I had said it. I don't know what happened."

Ed started to write things down on his notepad. Abe tried to see what he was writing, but Ed's arm shielded it from his view. He tried to tell from Ed's face whether he was pleased or displeased with his answer. After a moment, Nita began taking notes too, though from the way her pen moved, her annotations were less substantive, terser. Or even had nothing to do with what he was saying at all—from the looks of it, she could just as easily have been making a shopping list. *Eggs. Cat food. Armor-piercing bullets.*

"Was it a memory? A flashback?"

"Not exactly. It wasn't a real thought at all. I was just talking. It was like I *was* him. I mean, I wasn't Abraham Lincoln. He was me. I mean, I knew the answer to the question because that *was* the answer to the question. It wasn't a memory. It was just the truth. I don't know what I'm saying. Does that make any sense to you?"

Ed's writing had become a maniacal scribble, too fast to possibly be legible. "Did you get that?" he asked Nita. She nodded and grinned, and continued taking her own methodical notes. *Bag of oranges. Cyanide suppositories.* "Did you get that?" he called out to the mirror, then coughed and turned to Nita and added "...uh, Nita?" in an approximation of the same loud tone, then looked at back at Abe as if to somehow pretend he hadn't just talked to people behind the mirror and was actually asking Nita again. She rolled her eyes and nodded again. Abe wasn't sure which was the bigger insult—that Ed felt it was a lesser evil to insult his intelligence and try to make him think that Nita was hard of hearing, or that he was still pretending Abe wouldn't know there were people behind the mirror in the first place. Did he really think he was that stupid? Well two could play that game. Abe waved at the mirror, gave it the thumbs-up. Then at the moment Ed saw him, turned it into a clearly faked hair-combing gesture. The score was tied.

"So you 'were' Abraham Lincoln?"

"No. Yes. Maybe. I don't think so. I was just, well, *channeling* him, I guess would be the best way I could describe it. I was him without ever actually being him. Or he was me? He was in me, maybe. I don't know." Abe was more confused than ever.

"And then what?"

"And then the next thing I knew, I was back in the hotel room."

"You passed out," Nita said.

"Ah, right," Ed said, and jotted that down too. "That's just amazing." He sat for a moment, just looking at Abe. Abe fidgeted. He had now officially told them everything he knew. He was tired. He really really needed something to drink. But he had done what they wanted. Aside from the mirror-waving thing, he had cooperated fully. He thought for sure that they were done—but Ed still wasn't done asking questions.

"I'm getting sort of dehydrated, Ed. Could I just have some water?"

"In time, in time, Abe. So has this ever... happened to you before?"

"Once when I was on a class trip out in Arizona," Abe said. "We were visiting Montezuma's Castle. I left my canteen on the bus so I guess I didn't drink enough, and the next thing I knew I was seeing these floaty spots and some weird old guy was standing over me asking who I was and if I was okay."

"And who was that?" Ed asked, practically breathless with excitement. "The old man? Andrew Jackson? Ulysses S. Grant?"

"What? No. I don't know who he was. Just some old guy."

"But some old 'guy' from the nineteenth century? You actually saw him?" Ed half rose out of his seat again with excitement.

"What? No! A regular old guy. In Bermuda shorts. From Duluth. What are you talking about?"

"What are you talking about?"

"The last time I passed out. That was the only other time that I can remember. When I was 12. At Montezuma's Castle."

"No, I asked you if your Lincoln channeling episodes had happened before."

"Are you sure?" Abe asked. "Because I know I remember Nita telling me I passed out. And then you asked me if that happened a lot. And then I remembered Montezuma's Castle. And how I passed out because I got dehydrated because I didn't drink enough. I could really use a drink of water or something," he added hopefully.

Ed refused to take the hint. "So now that you know my *real* question, Abe, have you had other occasions when..."

It was Abe's turn to ignore his hint. Well, not his hint, his pointed question. His possibly gun-pointed question, but so long as there wasn't a visible gun, Abe was resolved to keep stalling on the bigger questions whenever he could. He had told them everything he knew. Anything he didn't know that might lead to a further line of questioning and a longer stay here could only make things worse. And remembering the field trip had reminded him of something else that he suddenly realized needed to be said. Something he used to teach during one of his history units, back when he used to have a job.

"You know, the funny thing about Montezuma's Castle is—the Aztecs abandoned it around a hundred years before Montezuma was even born... it had nothing to do with him."

"Abe—" Ed interrupted.

But Abe didn't stop. "The first white settlers just jumped to the conclusion that it had to be Montezuma's because he was the only Aztec guy they ever heard of. Also, it wasn't a castle, it was a whole vertical city, but you see, they didn't know vertical cities, and a castle sounded much more romantic, so when they named it, they threw the facts completely out the window, if they were even called windows."

There was a simultaneous concert of phlegm, as both Nita and Ed cleared their throats. But Ed spoke first. "That's fascinating, Abe. Now if you don't mind..."

But Abe wouldn't stop. "And the funny thing is that now, even though historians know it's something more special and older and far more unique than anything having to do with either Montezuma or castles—even though everybody who knows any history knows this—they still call it Montezuma's Castle, because people would rather believe they were seeing Montezuma's place because they've heard of him, he's famous, than some no-name Aztec guy's vertical city. It's just marketing. Do you get where I'm going with this? All people care about, really care about, is the famous name."

"Abe. That's not important right now. Let's get back to what it was like when you were, as you called it, channeling Lincoln. What did it *feel* like...?"

Abe sighed. Clearly, Ed did not get where he had been going with it. He would never be a no-name original again. Then again, maybe he never had been. He wondered if there was a way to channel a drinking fountain into the room.

29

THE AIR WAS DAMP, but the rain had ended for the night, so the voicemail recording said the meeting would go on as scheduled. Apparently Normalyn meetings never met on rainy nights, at least not in Florida, because too many of the Marilyns had shoe issues. Norma hated that she understood this and hated even more that she was secretly grateful for it. She wanted to wear a pair of beat-up sandals in defiance, just to show how little she was one of them, but she didn't own a pair of beat-up sandals. She didn't own a pair of beat-up anything. Even her flip-flops were well maintained.

And the truth was, she wanted to look good for whoever would be there. She wasn't sure she wanted to go, or whether she belonged there, and she was perfectly ready to turn around and go home if nothing sparked for her in the first five minutes. But she couldn't just show up looking like she didn't care. Not when she knew that by definition every other woman in the room was going to be drop dead gorgeous. She needed to make as good of an impression as possible, just for her own sense of self-worth. She had chosen another of her mother's castoff vintage sundresses, a pair of open toed slingbacks with kitten heels, and put her hair back in a loose ponytail, gathered at the base of her neck. It was a lovely, old-fashioned style that she knew she looked good in, but that Marilyn Monroe would never have been seen in, in any of her incarnations, having been born several decades too soon. She was willing to let every single woman there tell her she looked nothing like the blonde bombshell. She just hoped that someone else there would tell her that she was prettier the way she was. Wasn't that the point of support groups?

The Orlando meetings were held in a dance studio in an out-of-the-way strip mall, surrounded by a collection of non-touristy shops and closed storefronts: a computer repair company, an Indian restaurant, a business that made signs for other businesses. Despite the presence of this neighbor, the space itself had no sign at all, so Norma had to check the address twice to make sure she had the right place. She leaned against the glass doors, enjoying the feel of the cool metal of the handle where it made contact with her skin. The door wouldn't budge. She leaned harder, putting her full weight against the door, but still it wouldn't move. She knew she had the right day, the right time, the right address... she pressed her face against the glass, but the windows were tinted and she couldn't see a thing. Stepping back, puzzled, she finally noticed a small button to the left of the door and pressed it. A buzzer sounded.

Confident, she pushed the door again. Again, it refused to move. As the electronic lock on the door continued to buzz, she heard a faint crackling noise as an intercom speaker came to life to her left.

"Pull the door, dear," said the voice.

Norma pulled the door. It opened smoothly. On instinct, as the door shut behind her and the buzzer ceased, Norma tried it again. It opened instantly. It had never been locked. It took an immense strength of will for her to turn around and face the room behind her, and not flee the scene immediately. Fortunately, the main doors opened into a foyer with a second set of doors, so whoever it was who had witnessed her initial confusion was a solo gatekeeper, and she wouldn't be subject to the mass humiliation she was afraid of. Unless the front door was projected on a video intercom onto a screen in a main room somewhere. Norma pulled the next door open (no problems this time) and went into the room.

The meeting site seemed as if it had once been a beauty salon, but now was clearly used for small groups of all descriptions. A circle of folding chairs took up the center of the room, with more against the far wall, which was mirrored from floor to ceiling. Other walls were arrayed with yoga and gymnastic mats, a ballet barre, film projection equipment, and most incongruously, a trio of hair-drying chairs. A few women, all around her age (though who could tell?) were gathered already in a small clump, next to a small table where small bottles of mineral water and some cookies had been laid out. All of them held bottles of mineral water and it looked as if the cookies had already been pillaged. But they were all remarkably thin, remarkably gorgeous, with glowing clear skin that no chocolate chip could ever threaten. Norma knew the type. Hell, she was the type. She knew that all of them would regret every bite of those cookies, and would look in the mirror and think they could literally see each mouthful reflected in cellulite on their bodies (and exactly where)... and she knew that all of them were looking at the others and thinking what she was thinking: "How come you can eat twelve of those and stay so thin, while I eat just one and I look like a cow?" And she glanced from the women to the table, and she saw that they had those oval fudgie things with the chopped pecans on top, and she *loved* those, and she knew that more than anything else in this world, she needed a cookie.

Crossing the room, Norma was shocked by the various women's reactions to herself: besides a brief glance across the room as she walked through the door, there was no reaction at all. She was used to all sorts of sizing-ups as she walked across rooms—appreciative stares, jealous sidelong glances, long gazes and dismissive ones, even the defiantly contemptuous looks of the people nature had been less kind to. But on days when she made an effort to look her best, she was never ignored. Even on those occasions when she barely paid attention to how she looked, she knew that others always did. She never thought of herself as vain about her beauty—if anything, she always assumed she felt somewhat burdened by it. That if she woke up one day and looked only as pretty as the beautiful girls she worked with at Lord's, or just "conventionally pretty," whatever that meant, or even ordinary looking, not pretty at all, it would almost be a relief. At least that was what she always told herself, her way of compensating for allowing herself to indulge in vanity about her looks. She had often secretly wondered what it would be like to be average-looking, to blend in, to be the human equivalent of a pocket tee. Well, now, just by virtue of walking into a room with this unique handful of women, for the first time in her life she knew exactly what it felt like.

She didn't like it one bit.

Especially when looking at two of them looked just like looking in the mirror, and looking at another one of them looked like what she used to look like looking in the mirror, back when she was fresh out of college and she really liked what she saw. And three others were like looking at the loveliest version of herself she ever saw, the version that everyone in the whole world recognized and dreamed about and wanted to take home to bed and never to Mother. Her pale reflection in the dressing room mirror, only more so; better makeup, better bone structure, better posture. It took her breath away.

In her mind, Norma always saw the post-op platinum-dyed plucked-and-teased Marilyn Monroe as a larger than life nightmare, the female fat Elvis, too iconic to even walk straight. She visualized every bad impersonator on television, and every over-the-top sexpot performance, and always that glassy-eyed Warhol image, repeated ad infinitum. It was a horrible vision, clownish and plastic and unreal. "Marilyn" had become such a mass-produced industry that it had become impossible to remember that there really was a Marilyn, and she really was breathtaking. The artifice she had used to transform herself from Norma Jeane Baker wasn't something she did in order to make herself into a whole new person... it was a step by step process she employed to turn the beautiful woman she already was into the most desirable woman on earth. Now, faced with the flesh-and-blood reality of what Marilyn really looked like, Norma finally understood what drove these other women to want to go through the transformations when they could choose to live in obscurity. There was more to it than just that costumes and playing dress-up. Before, she rejected coming because she thought it was stupid. Now she was beginning to wish she hadn't come for a more ominous reason. She could never want to become conspicuous, to be clearly marked as a clone like that. But oh, those women were so lovely, and when she looked at them long enough, she could see her own features reflected in their faces like a gorgeous promise...

"It's amazing, isn't it?" said a Spanish-accented voice behind her. "We're all so alike, and then the Marilyns are such an inspiration." Norma turned, and was shocked to find herself facing not the expected doppelganger, but instead a shorter, tanner version of herself, dressed in a spot-on perfect replica of the white halter dress from The Seven Year Itch. Besides the slight height difference, which in a room of such complete uniformity was immediately jarring, there was something even more disturbingly different about this particular twin. Beneath the white crepe pleats and the high heels, under the platinum blonde waves and the iconic birthmark, the woman who stood before Norma was, well, undeniably male.

Meeting her eye with a friendly look that seemed to contain as much of a challenge as a welcome, the stranger smiled. "I'm Vee."

"I'm Norma."

"Babe, we're all Norma here. Except for those of us who are Marilyns. I'm Marilyn, in case you haven't noticed." And without pausing the flow of her conversation for even a second, she simpered and twirled, her full skirt billowing around her as it was clearly designed to do. "So obviously we can't go by first names here. Much too confusing." She pointed to her name tag, where a large capital V was printed in a flourish of black ink, bursting with curlicues. "First letter of your last name, if you please, unless you have a nickname. Unless your nickname is 'Sugar.' Or 'Lorelei.' Some girls think they're so original." She rolled her eyes.

Norma couldn't resist smiling. For the first time, she stopped regretting she'd come. Still, she helped herself to another couple of cookies, for emotional support. She caught V's eyebrows silently tracking their motion from plate to hand in a smooth sardonic upward sweep, but she didn't care. The staccato clicking of high heels on hardwood interrupted their silent showdown, as yet another painfully beautiful twin (triplet?) joined them.

"V," she sighed, "You know better than to terrorize the newbies." Dressed in a simple pair of jeans and a simpler black sweater set, and an incredible pair of leopard spectator pumps, the new girl was every inch a Marilyn. "I'm M," she introduced herself. Of course she was. "Don't worry about V. She's harmless. Just don't lend her any of your shoes." She pushed her hands apart in a stretching motion, grimacing.

"You're just intimidated by my true inner Marilyn," V sniffed, and walked away, casually picking up a water bottle from the table with two fingers as she passed like she was making off with a Lieber minaudière. True Marilyn or not, she had style.

"I'm Norma—I mean G," Norma said, filling out her own name tag. "If that's okay."

"That's great," M said. "We don't have a G yet. By the way, I love your dress."

"I love your shoes."

And just like that, despite all her efforts, she fit right in.

30

So, Hon, what brings you here?" They were all seated in a loose circle. The speaker, L., was one of the older women, somewhere between a "Norma" and a "Marilyn"— bleached blonde hair and it looked like she might have had some work done, but she didn't dress particularly provocatively and her hair was pulled back into an almost matronly updo at the back. From the intonation, Norma thought she recognized the voice she had heard through the intercom over an hour before.

It had been an interesting meeting. After the cookies and chitchat, the group gathered on the folding chairs for a combination of group therapy and cosmetics workshop. They talked about their romantic troubles, and their search for a good cosmetic surgeon who didn't charge through the new nose. To a woman they had all had the same orthodontic work when in their teens, to a woman they all fought the same mental battle over whether and how much to alter their faces. A young woman named H talked about getting her rhinoplasty as a bat mitzvah present and never looking back, which drew a chorus of approval from the similarly sculpted Marilyns, while causing a set of hands—Norma's included—to involuntarily drift upwards as if to check that theirs were still intact. Noses that were lovely to begin with, it had to be said. In fact, it had to be said for several minutes.

Norma soon realized that that was the main problem with this group—it was nothing like most support groups, with a goal to be met, where the place you started was necessarily seen as less good than the place you ended. Alcoholism is bad. Overeating should be curtailed. Drug use must be overcome. One day at a time, carefully following the same steps, until you can look back and separate from your former self. Marilyns Anonymous, on the other hand, was serving a split personality. Those women who wanted to change themselves into someone they weren't needed to be encouraged to celebrate their new identities, while at the same time, those women who wanted to hold on to their identities needed to be reassured that they were perfect just the way they were. So which was it?

And so when one woman mentioned a problem with dry skin, another two would immediately rush in with solutions—not always their own, Norma noted with amusement, but some that were nearly a century old. Marilyn used Nivea Skin Moisturizing Lotion. Marilyn removed her makeup with olive oil and lanolin. Marilyn slept in a face mask she made from Vaseline. And when another woman mentioned troubles with men, the help she received was a combination of stories from the women's own lives, and comparisons to "that time with Joe DiMaggio…"

It was hard to tell how much wisdom there was in the room, and how much of it was actually a joke. On the one hand, V stood out like a sore thumb, with the barest hint of a five o'clock shadow concealed beneath her otherwise exceptionally good makeup, but she was sucking up every word like it was gospel, and was one of the most active contributors. And then there was a particularly well put-together woman called A, who perched on the fringes and rarely spoke, and then only to make snide comments. Norma wasn't sure whether she came for the makeup advice or the food, or otherwise saw it as just a big social gathering, without any real purpose. She threw out the Marilyn references louder than anyone, but it seemed more with the intention of baiting the more gullible among them. She spoke up fairly early in the meeting, to hand out some business cards for a guy named Harold who got work for celebrity impersonators. The cards were mostly rejected. She described it as easy money, but the general viewpoint was that it was a step above stripping, and that it should be left to out-of-work actors and drag queens, a reference V pointedly ignored. Norma took the card out of politeness, not seeing a way to outright refuse an overture when she was the newcomer in the room, but let it settle to the bottom of her purse without a glance. Being asked to impersonate Marilyn Monroe was precisely her problem. Whoever this Harold was, he would have to miss out on someone who had both the credentials and the wardrobe handy. If he had sent A here on purpose, this just wasn't his lucky day.

And now it was Norma's turn to talk. What brought her here? Hoping she wouldn't start crying again—hoping they would understand without her even mentioning her dressing room breakdown that morning—Norma slowly pulled the birthday dress and wig out of her bag and held them up. "My boss wants me to wear these to work," she whispered, and felt the tears running down her face all over again.

Their reaction was not exactly what she was hoping for. While a couple of women did gather around her for a hug—soothing her with the uncomfortable comfort given by strangers which never quite consoles but at least never quite disappoints, the way that a parent's hug always does once adulthood sets in—most of them were far more interested in running their hands over the costume. Like the shiniest new toy on Christmas morning, it was passed from hand to hand, spread out over many laps, held up to the lights more than once to be admired. And a chorus of voices all began asking her—almost demanding of her—whether they could try it on, a set of queries that quickly devolved to an argument over which woman had asked first. And the obvious objection Norma would normally have reached for when turning down someone rifling through her wardrobe, simply wouldn't apply here. With one minor exception, there wasn't a single woman in the room that the dress wouldn't fit.

"I can't," Norma said, "they'd kill me," and there was a shift of mood throughout the room. Something in the tone of her voice told them that more begging might succeed, but that her emotions were so fragile that it wouldn't be worth the price. They had all been in that state at one time or another, and knew just how fragile a state it could lead to—for some of them a stint at AA or various rehabs, when it came right down to it, and they all remembered other attendees who used to show up, only to break down and then vanish... Once again the dress was passed from hand to lingering hand, and once again it was shoved sacrilegiously back down into Norma's bag. "At least wrap it in tissue paper," one of the girls whispered, but was hushed at once.

"It's just... It's not me," Norma started again, and again felt the tears welling up. Five monogrammed handkerchiefs and a box of Kleenex were immediately pushed her way. "I've gone my whole life rejecting her—no offense–"

"None taken," M replied.

"—And now they just want to throw me out there like this—they don't even know, and I put the dress on, and I..."

"And you hated it because you don't want to lose your identity? That's really normal." M put her arm around

Norma's shoulder comfortingly.

"No—that's the thing. I loved it." Norma started crying again. "I just felt so sexy and so powerful. For the first time in my life I felt like I knew who I was. And it scared the crap out of me." She was truly sobbing now, almost gasping. It felt so good to let it out, to the only people who might actually understand. "I don't know who I am."

Just then A piped in, her voice cutting through all the sympathetic cooing spreading around Norma. "Oh that's just a garden-variety existential crisis. Go do some shopping—you'll snap out of it."

Surprisingly enough, it was V who came over to Norma and provided what she realized she most needed to hear. "You're as Marilyn as you want to be on the inside," she said, waving her hand around her head as if sweeping cobwebs away. "Everything else is just accessories."

31

THE NEXT MORNING, IF that were possible, was even worse. Abe had spent a bad night. After what felt like several more hours of pointless questioning along the "How did it feel?" line, Ed had finally let Abe take a break for lunch. Across the hallway from the sparely furnished questioning room was an even more sparely furnished cafeteria. If you could call it a cafeteria. It had three molded fiberglass picnic-style tables, and a long aluminum steam table against one wall. Disturbingly, there was yet another large mirror over the steam table. Were they going to monitor his eating preferences, too?

Standing behind the steam table was a largish apple-cheeked woman wearing the odd combination of an oversized apron, a hairnet, and a lab coat. She beamed at him as she opened the lid of each warming tray and put food onto his plate. The food, like the woman herself, was pure Middle America. Turkey with gravy. Mashed potatoes. Peas. The cutlery was all plastic. Clearly they were taking no chances.

From the way that Ed looked at the food but didn't take any, Abe had the distinct feeling that there was far better food provided for the staff than there was for the... guests? Research subjects? Prisoners? What was he? How long was he going to be here?

Still, he was too hungry to start worrying about that then. He gulped down nearly a pitcher of water before turning to his food. That's when he first realized there was something wrong with his turkey. It didn't look unappetizing, only—well, odd. The colors were off. The aroma was different. Was it something that wasn't actually turkey that he was supposed to think was turkey, just to see if he could tell the difference between a real poultry and a synthetic one? What did eating real turkey feel like? His head spun. The same was true of everything on his plate. The potatoes were starchier. The peas weren't the right green, and they were shaped strangely, more bulbous than round. He poked at them. Were they drugged? All he knew was, they weren't right. Suddenly he wasn't hungry anymore. He looked up. They were watching him. Every single one of them. Ed, Nita, and the woman in the hairnet, were all watching him.

And watching him.

And watching him.

And then, Ed did something Abe hadn't seen in over thirty years. He lifted an imaginary fork to his mouth and made chewing motions and nodding. This was ridiculous. They couldn't force him to eat. Out of all the disturbing things that had happened to him that day, out of all the half-threats and menacing hints and ominous environmental clues that he kept picking up, nothing had been so unsettling as this. Was Ed going to do here-comes-the-airplane next? Abe wondered. He waved at Ed with his fork and gave a half-smile. Ed smiled back and made more chewing faces. Hairnet lady looked at him expectantly. There was no way out of this nightmare but through his stomach.

He took a bite.

It was the most delectable not-turkey he had ever tasted.

All of it was delicious. He wasn't even certain anymore that it wasn't real. If anything, it was more real. It didn't taste like anything he had ever had before, the textures were all wrong, and they didn't really taste the way he had always identified as "turkey," "potatoes," "peas," but now that he had eaten these, he was ready to be told that they were the way that those foods were supposed to taste, and that the foods he had always called by those names were actually pale copies. Clearly they had to be drugged. Or the water was. It was all he could do not to lick the plate.

Without even looking away from his plate, he could tell that Ed, Nita, and the steam-table woman in the hairnet were wearing ear-to-ear smiles. Well, Ed and the steam-table lady. Nita just cocked her head to the side an extra two degrees in satisfaction.

Ed spoke up, "Not bad, right? That's the real deal. Genetically-sampled cloned specimens direct from the late nineteenth century. Lincoln's time. No pesticides were used, purely organic soil, the turkey was even fed historically correct genetically cloned grain. These are the way that those foods are supposed to taste, Abe. The foods we've always called by those names are actually faint copies."

Abe shuddered. Had he read his mind?

"Jog any memories, Abe?" Ed asked.

"What? No," Abe answered.

Ed looked disappointed. "Well, it was worth a shot. They've been breeding these over in the horticultural wing for a few years now, and I thought it couldn't hurt to try. Cost a small fortune." He took away Abe's plate and dumped it in the trash. A pair of cafeteria workers had already begun clearing away the contents of the steam table out of the room. Abe sighed as he watched them go.

"We could always try again..." Abe suggested, hopefully, watching them leave the room. He wished he had licked the plate. Or at least asked for seconds.

"Yeah, well, I wouldn't get my hopes up."

"So wait," Abe said. "Am I here to tell you about what happened to me? Or to try to make it happen again?

"Well, both," Ed answered. "We believe that someplace inside you is the clue to how the real Abraham Lincoln really thought and felt and, well, *was*. We're trying to get to him."

"All because I blacked out for two seconds on national TV."

"Well, all because of what happened before you blacked out, yes."

"But what if I was making it up, just to get attention?"

"Were you, Abe?"

Say yes, Abe, Abe thought, willing himself to say the magic words that just might let him go home. *Say yes, say you were making it up. Say you did it for an endorsement deal, or to get some girl's attention, or because Harold dared you. Say yes and maybe this will be the end...* He looked Ed in the eye, trying to look as sincere as possible. He had Abe Lincoln's unfailingly honest grey eyes; he could do this.

"Were you really making it up, Abe?" Ed asked again

Their eyes locked. He opened his mouth, the lie right there on his tongue, ready to save him. The turkey decided to speak first.

"BUUUUUUUUUUURRRP!"

So much for that.

32

I F THE MORNING'S DISCOMFORTS of Ed's inane repetitive
questioning and Nita's unspoken menace weren't fun, the
indignities of the afternoon were even less of a joyride. The
two silent-but-beefy shadows rejoined them at the door
of the cafeteria, appearing to be no more congenial with
the knowledge that he was now well fed and they weren't.
"They were extremely small portions," Abe found himself
telling them, trying to deflect any ire. They simply linked
their arms through his once again, and continued their walk
onward. At times, their speed was such that Abe could feel
his feet being lifted off the ground when he didn't keep up.
This was not a good sign.

The series of Not Good Signs that followed were like
the ending to a fireworks display—one followed another in
such a spectacular succession that you almost couldn't remember the last, you were so busy being bowled over by the
one that followed. There was a large wooden chair parked
just outside the room, directly opposite the door, in which
one of the large men took a seat. Bad sign. The room itself
had no windows. Bad sign. There was a doctor's examining
table. Bad sign. There was a hospital gown neatly folded on
the examining table. Bad, bad sign. He also noticed that this
room had no large mirror. Which at first he took for a good
sign, but then realized was possibly a very bad sign because

if no one was watching, anything could happen. Bad, bad, very bad sign.

One of the large men looked at him and nodded toward the robe suggestively.

Abe looked back at the man, nodded toward the robe, then shook his head no.

The man looked back at Abe, nodded toward the robe, and decided to use his right hand to see what it was he had brought with him in one of his inside pockets that Abe now noticed was bulging.

Abe looked toward the man and picked up the robe with a meek smile.

The man smiled back, and nodded again—toward the table, making the sequence of events clear to Abe. It was the smile of a man who understood the meek, and didn't hold a lot of stock in the whole "inherit the earth" thing. He did understand the earth and the meek's place in it in the here and now, however. And that place was on the table, in the robe.

Satisfied, the man left the room.

Abe picked up the robe. He held it up. It was a typical hospital gown, powder blue and imprinted with "PROPERTY OF." Thrilled to finally get a clue to where he was, Abe searched to see whose property the robe belonged to. But maddeningly, whoever had constructed the robe must have printed the identifying marks directly onto the fabric before the garments were made, because in a wholly inexplicable coincidence, every single "OF" led directly to a seam. At least he assumed it was a coincidence. For someone to be so diabolical as to purposefully make a "Property Of Anonymous" robe, knowing that its wearer would be driven insane with the mystery... It was a gown tailor-made for an asylum. Literally.

Or for a person without an identity.

Or, okay, Abe thought, calming down, for a place that didn't want to be identified.

He put on the robe. Mercifully (thank God for small blessings), the cotton canvas strings were long enough and the gown itself sufficiently large that he could tie it around himself without any unnecessary posterior display. This was a tiny Good Sign. And just in case, he had left his boxer shorts on underneath. Nothing in his huge escort's pantomime had in any way suggested "boxer," "shorts" or "off." There, finally, was something positive to be said for silent but deadly.

There were no chairs in the room, and the only counter was covered in random standard medical equipment, so he folded his clothes and tucked them under the table. This was a bit of a relief, as it felt almost like he had hidden them. And even though they would immediately know where they were, at least it would make it harder for them to take them away. With no chair to sit on, he perched hesitantly on the table. The protective paper cover crinkled under him. Why there was a need for a protective paper cover was beyond him, but it was still reassuring. They cared for the sterility of the room. Therefore they cared for the sterility of the patient's nether regions. Here was another Good Sign. He tried not to think that it was there as a protective sheath to prevent whatever happened to patients from staining the chair. Still, the Good Sign was screechingly downgraded to Neutral. He had to stop looking for signs.

He waited on the table, but no one came. Which was another good sign (stop it, Abe), another good indication that no one was watching him. He thought about putting his clothes back on and trying to make a run for it, then remembered the second bodyguard in the chair outside.

Not to mention the first one, who was probably not much farther away. Still, with no one around, there had to be something he could do. He got up and looked around the counter hopefully. Other than the large machines, he could see nothing he could make any use of. It was all standard physician's-office stuff. Tongue depressors. Cotton balls. Gauze. If he'd had a jar of paste he could have built a little arctic fort like in second grade, but that was about it. Not very helpful.

He went back under the table for his clothes. Was there anything there he had missed? He checked his pockets again for anything he could use—a house key, some money, a remaining piece of that crayon... a business card...

He had a business card? What was he doing with a business card?

Cursing his luck that the only thing that had managed to stay in his pocket was also the one thing he was certain he had absolutely no use for, he pulled out the card and examined it.

It was worse than he thought. It wasn't even a business card. It was some sort of perfume sample card. Probably part of some practical joke from one of his students that hadn't come to fruition. Maybe he could still use it as a weapon. He could papercut them to death. He examined the card again. It featured a hologram of a wisp of smoke that became a woman's torso. There was something very intriguing about it, and incredibly sexy. Even crumpled and worn with some age, it still smelled nice. Really nice. The fragrance was called *Illusions*. He quickly ran through a mental tally of all his female students who might have slipped him the card, either as a joke or as a come-on, but none of them seemed the type. Or at least he hoped not, seeing how every last one of them was jailbait. Not that jail might not be a step up from wherever he was now, but still—he crossed his students off his list. That left—Nita? He looked at the shifting female silhouette on the card with its seductive fragrance and tried imagining Nita slipping it into his pocket in one of their closer, less-threatening moments. But he couldn't imagine it. If Nita wore any perfume, it was probably squeezed directly from the skin of other women.

He turned the card over, expecting to see the same image repeating. Instead, he found a blank surface. And across it there was scrawled a name and phone number in decidedly female handwriting. Someone named Norma TransAmerica. It was the strangest name he had ever seen. He didn't know any Normas. And what kind of last name was TransAmerica...? It sounded like it should be the name of a bank, or an insurance company, not a person. Wait. In a rush it all made sense. It—she—the invisible woman. The beautiful invisible woman who hit his car with her dress. Of all the things in his pockets he had been forced to surrender, the one thing he had managed to save was a miracle. A completely and utterly useless miracle, but still a miracle. Not as miraculous as a knife or a pen or his cell phone to call anybody, including her, but it still gave him a sense of hope. Norma. Whatever they were going to do to him, if he ever got out of here, he had one thing left that they couldn't take away. Someplace out there was a woman named Norma, who had hit him with her car, and if they ever let him make one final phone call, it would be to her. She would probably hang up on him, because after all, she had hit him with her car, but he wasn't going to split hairs. He knew her name. He knew her number. He knew what she smelled like. He knew her insurance company.

He knew someone was coming into the room. Before the door handle finished turning, he had stuffed his pants back under the table. But he slipped the card underneath the protective paper on the table under him. Just in case.

33

THE DOOR OPENED AND Abe was surprised to see a pleasant-looking woman come in wearing a long doctor's coat. She was tall, nearly as tall as he was, dressed in a simple turtleneck and skirt under the jacket, her look completed with a stethoscope and pocketful of standard physician's tools. She had long straight hair and wore sensible polished loafers. Everything about her radiated calm professionalism. She introduced herself as Dr. Butcher. So much for feeling 100% calm.

"Just try to relax, Abe, I'm only going to take some standard tests. I'm here to make sure you're in good health before the real tests start." She put her hand on his wrist and began measuring his pulse.

"Um... what are the real tests?" Abe asked, trying not to show any alarm but guessing from the expression on her face that his pulse had sped up already. She was making notes on a chart. He could see some notebook papers sticking up out of the file. Were those Ed's notes? Nita's? He wondered if there was a way to get his hands on them. Was there a way to ask that would get this doctor to tell him? She was the first person he had interacted with who seemed at all considerate in her treatment of him, who did not seem in any way menacing.

"Oh, just tests. You're lined up for an MRI next, which is again probably just routine, but after that I can't really tell you anything about them." She took a sphygmomanometer down from a hook on the wall, and started rolling the sleeve of his gown up, fastening the cuff around his arm. "I don't work for the government."

She opened his gown just enough to slide the bell of the stethoscope in against his heart. The cold of it made him wince. Either he hadn't realized how warm the room was, or he was more stressed than usual, his body temperature higher than normal. Maybe he was running a fever, he thought hopefully. Maybe that would be enough for him to mark on his chart that he wasn't in good enough shape for the "real" tests. The cuff quickly tightened around his upper arm as she watched the gauge.

"So..." he said, "if you don't work for the government, does this mean that this is a government outfit that you're not working for? Ouch!" She had tightened the rubber cuff far beyond a normal amount of constriction before letting the pressure release.

"Sorry about that." She sounded sincere, but answered a half-second too late to be completely believable. "I meant I don't work for the government. Say aaaah."

"Aaaaah." She held his tongue down and looked into his throat, then took a culture. The rest of the session continued in a similar way. She went through every standard test he could ever remember having gone through as part of a standard physical. Height, weight, ears, nose, throat were checked. Blood was taken and labeled. She was as devoid of nonsense as his first impression had suggested, and she was certainly thorough.

"You kept your shorts on," she reproached him, pulling aside his robe. "Didn't they tell you...?"

"They didn't say anything. I didn't think I needed to... You don't really have to..."

Unfortunately she did really have to, she said, pulling on a pair of rubber gloves.

34

THE MRI ROOM WAS just across the hall, a larger room than the exam room, but which seemed even more claustrophobic from the oversized machinery filling its space. Looking something like a cross between the hero's spaceship on any sci-fi TV series and a giant gaping mouth, the MRI unit gawped open, quietly menacing in the way that only the most impersonal things can truly menace. When someone hated you, it was personal. There was passion behind the emotion, even in a negative way. When someone—or especially something—didn't care about you in any way, it was hard not to feel intimidated. At six foot four inches tall, Abe didn't feel small very often. Next to this MRI machine's vast blank surfaces, though, he was dwarfed.

A technician in scrubs stepped out of a side chamber and held a hand out to shake. "Hi, Abe, I'll be doing your scan in just a moment, but I need to ask you some questions first." Abe noted that the man knew his name but hadn't given his own, but otherwise couldn't find anything particularly threatening or even unsettling about him. Expecting yet another round of "What does it feel like" explorations, Abe was surprised by what came next.

"Do you have any prosthetic limbs, metal plates in your body, any surgical screws?"

"Not last I checked," Abe said.

"Pacemaker? Ear implants?"

"No, nothing like that."

"How about any piercings we might not have seen?"

"No... Frankly, at this point I don't think I even have any body parts left you haven't seen."

The technician chuckled appreciatively at Abe's joke. "Well, just the one. Hop on up there." He motioned to the white cushioned table perched at the edge of the scanner's open maw. Abe half expected to have his mouth opened and checked for fillings, but either they wouldn't be a problem or the tech forgot to look.

The technician handed him a pair of headphones and smiled reassuringly. "You won't feel anything, and it shouldn't take more than about a quarter of an hour or so. It gets pretty noisy though. Try to tune it out. Hope you're not claustrophobic any."

Abe wasn't, but that didn't make him less apprehensive. He climbed gracelessly up onto the table and lay down, putting the headphones over his ears. Stirring orchestral music played, heavy on the horns and piano. He didn't recognize the piece, but wondered at the choice—surely a brain scan would call for something more relaxing? He shut his eyes and merely felt, rather than saw, his head and upper torso disappear into the machine. Then the noises started. No wonder they had chosen loud percussive music—anything softer wouldn't have stood a chance of breaking through. It was remarkable that a machine that looked so glossy and sleek could emit such gothic clanking sounds. If he hadn't been warned, he would have been convinced something was wrong—that a gear was loose in the works, or something more sinister. As it was, he tried to tune out the noise and focus on the music. Then he heard the voice.

It was a quiet voice, a woman's, placed at regular intervals that almost but not quite blended within the rests within the music. He could barely register the words over the music and the clanking, but when he was finally able to focus he recognized her speech within a few words. She was reciting the Gettysburg Address. After this there was a pause, and then she was reading nursery rhymes: Mary Had a Little Lamb, Humpty Dumpty, A Tisket, A Tasket. And then one he didn't know, very odd, that sounded something like,

"For Reuben and Charles have married two girls,
But Billy has married a boy.
The girls he had tried on every side,
But none he could get to agree;
All was in vain, he went home again,
And since that he's married to Natty."

A longer pause, and then the Emancipation Proclamation was read. This continued for some time. He couldn't always follow the words, and wasn't sure whether he was supposed to focus on them or try to tune them out. The readings seemed to be alternating between passages closely associated with Abraham Lincoln and expressions with no association to him whatsoever. Another pause, and she was reading something that sounded more like a letter, something about growing a beard. There was another pause, followed by a litany of words he didn't understand. It didn't have the cadence of prose, or the rhythm of poetry. Was it even English?

It was names, he realized, hearing the familiar syllables that made up "Mary Todd."

"David Derickson,"

"William Seward,"

"Sarah Bush,"

"Ann Rutledge,"

"Joshua Speed,"

"Joshua Fry Speed,"

"Mr. Joshua Speed."

Abe laughed out loud as he heard the familiar name repeated in several more variations and intonations. So that was their game? Really? He wondered what his brain imagery was showing. If they had been hoping to trigger another reaction, they failed, unless the reaction they wanted was amusement.

More names followed, then place names. There were some paragraphs that Abe didn't quite place, but was fairly certain came from the debates against Stephan Douglass. And finally, the stirring Springfield speech that included the stirring passage "A house divided against itself cannot stand." At these words, Abe felt his heart beat more strongly. It had always been one of his favorite quotes—possibly because it so perfectly summed out how he felt about the dichotomy of his own house—his body, his self—which the circumstances of his birth split open.

The clanking stopped, and he was left with the music as the table slowly rolled out from inside the scanner. He felt tired, drained. He wondered what they had seen. The technician helped him up and took back the headphones.

"See anything interesting?" Abe asked.

"Not my place to say," he responded. He opened the door, revealing Doctor Butcher waiting as if she had been there the entire time.

"Hi again." Abe said cheerily. "Miss me?"

35

"YOU DID GREAT," THE doctor said, after another forty minutes during which Abe had run on a treadmill, blown into a tube, ridden a stationary bike and recited tongue twisters while she looked on. "You're really in excellent shape for your age. I still have to run these samples to the lab, but between you and me, they're not really necessary for what they're doing. It's more to cover our asses. Pardon my French." She smiled, revealing a beautiful set of teeth.

Hopping off the table, Abe reached for his clothes so he could begin covering his own ass. Doctor Butcher, who had up till this time been gathering together his charts and throwing out the detritus of the various testing kits, turned at the sound of rustling fabric. "Don't change yet, Abe. The important tests are coming after this. In fact..." she went back and pulled out the sheet of notebook paper that Abe had seen sticking out of chart, reading it through. "Yes. I'm supposed to take these." She reached out and took Abe's clothes. "See?"

She held up the sheet of notebook paper. Instead of revealing the long list of notes in Ed's handwriting that Abe had been hoping to somehow abscond with, all there were were ten discouraging words: "Remove test subject's civilian clothing from examining room after physical." Under those nine words were two more even more disheartening: "Including underclothes."

"Sorry about that." She scooped the pile from out of his arms. "I'm sure they're just taking them for cleaning or something. You can keep this if you'd like." She offered him the piece of notebook paper. He considered taking it, then changed his mind. He had no pockets, no pen, no need for a reminder of this final humiliation.

"Will I see you again?" he asked.

She shot him her most sympathetic look yet. "I don't know, Abe. But I'm a medical doctor. You might want to hope not."

36

THEY HAD FORGOTTEN HIM. Abe was alone in the examining room, with no clothes, and they had all forgotten him. There was no clock on the wall, so he had no true way to gauge how much time had passed, but he was certain it was at least twenty minutes, probably longer. The room was starting to get colder, and he could feel goose bumps beginning to form beneath the thin gown. He hugged himself, trying unsuccessfully to squeeze himself back to warmth. They could at least have left him his socks. Or a magazine. Or some of that turkey, even. His mind wandered back to the incredible turkey, and he felt his stomach growl. Had enough time passed that it was already time for dinner? And would they feed him dinner? He wondered again what constituted the "real" tests. When another ten minutes had passed with no sign of anyone coming, he decided to try the door.

Slowly, quietly, on tiptoes even though there was no one in the room, Abe crept over to the doorway, turning the knob by infinitesimal degrees until he heard the bolt slide open. He pulled the door open a crack, peeking out around the corner. Maybe if it had been an outward-opening door, he would have been able to see a bit more, but as it was, he didn't have a chance. By the time the door was open wide enough for him to see out, he could already see Big Man

#2 looking in at him, making full-contact eye contact. He slowly pushed the door back shut and sat back down on the examining table with a papery crunch. He was just going to have to wait.

As it turns out, it wasn't a wait at all. Ed came right into the door, holding a stopwatch, which he happily showed to Abe—though too quickly for him to get a good look. "Forty-eight minutes!" He announced triumphantly. "You're a very patient man, Abe. Very trusting. I thought you'd cave before thirty, but Nita had you pegged—she said you were good for at least forty-five. She's a great judge of character. Always knows who's going to run and when. You'd think I'd learn not to bet her." Ed chuckled and shook his head at his own defeat.

Abe felt distinctly uncomfortable sitting here with nothing between himself and Ed but his hospital gown. Noticing his discomfort, Ed opened up a bag he had brought with him into the room, which Abe hadn't noticed before. The waving stopwatch had distracted his eyes away from the vinyl garment bag, which Ed had meanwhile draped over the head of the examining table behind him. "These should all fit you just fine. I'm sure you already know what they are." Ed grinned conspiratorially, and Abe realized that he did indeed know. "You may have some trouble with the fastenings. Zippers weren't invented until 1914, you probably know. Anyhow, give a holler if you're stuck and someone'll come in and help you out. Or help you in." Ed laughed that laugh again, along with the expectant look which encouraged Abe to join in, but he just didn't have the heart to do more than smile weakly. Yesterday he might have appreciated the pun a tiny bit, today there was nothing about the word "stuck" that he could find even remotely risible.

Ed left him alone with the bag of clothes. Knowing full well he was being given another visceral history lesson, Abe expected to smell the odor of mothballs, but there was nothing of the sort. As he took out the gabardine pants, plain cotton shirt and string tie, he said a silent prayer of thanks that he hadn't been born from the cloned embryo of Molière, or Sir Walter Raleigh, or anyone else who regularly wore ridiculous tight-fitting leggings or ruffled collars.

Having done this once already for Harold in a far lower quality wardrobe, Abe was able to master the indignity of being dressed like Abraham Lincoln more quickly than he would have several weeks ago. Still, it was humiliating. He had never before appreciated the importance of elastic, or of Lycra fabric in general. Or of fabric softeners.

But he had one good thing to say about this suit. It had a pocket. Before anyone could come back into the room, Abe slipped the perfume card out from under the table protector and into his new jacket, next to his heart. The absence of a two-way mirror in the room had once again joined the ranks of solid positives.

A double knock on the door, and before Abe could get to the "in" of "Come in," Ed was already in the room. "You look great!" he said, genuinely admiring the effect. "Very Presidential. How does it feel?"

"Itchy," Abe responded.

"Well, it's old wool. And the thread is original too. Everything was made exactly the way old Abe would have worn it. So you should feel right at home. Lincoln must have thought his suits were itchy too. That's a good bit of research you're already yielding us."

"How long do I have to wear this?" Abe asked.

"Oh, I'm not sure I have the answer to that yet. Though of course we have a whole set of homespun pajamas waiting for you for after hours—wouldn't want you to sleep in your daytime clothes, of course."

"Of course," Abe sighed, dejected at this new proof that they had no intention of letting him go home anytime soon.

"We did make a hat for you too, if you want it, but we felt it wasn't necessary, since you won't be going outside. And there was no way we could do the wooden teeth, obviously."

"That was George Washington."

"What?"

"The wooden teeth. And Washington didn't really have them either."

"Huh. Well, we couldn't do them. Not without pulling your teeth out. We decided it wasn't worth it."

"Good to know."

Ed shepherded him out of the room and back into the hallway, where Nita and the two unshakeable chaperones were again waiting for him. Even with his "forty-eight minutes of lead time" (what did that make him—a sheep? Abe could kill himself for his mindless complaisance), they still didn't trust him to take three steps without attendant goonery. Where was he going to go?

Though truth be told, if he knew he could get away, he still thought he might just make a run for it. So maybe they were justified. The lights in the corridor seemed dimmer somehow, and Abe realized that it was because the few rooms that had windows were now unlit by any natural light. Evening had set in. His stomach growled again. But they passed by the cafeteria without stopping.

"Where are you taking me now?" Abe asked. "Don't worry, I'm not expecting an answer."

"You ever hear of a Mnemonic Device?" Ed asked, winking at Abe.

"Sure," he responded.

"Well, we're hooking you up to one."

37

THEY PASSED THROUGH WHAT seemed like an endless number of connecting corridors before they reached a pair of double doors that were unlike any of those they had passed before. For one thing, they stretched from floor to ceiling and took up the entire breadth of the hallway. For another thing, these doors had a sign. The sign said "KEEP OUT—AUTHORIZED PERSONELLL ONLY" carefully hand-lettered in multiple colors of magic marker. Even more unusually, underneath the words, the sign was decorated with a magic marker illustration of a chase scene of a stick figure trying to run through a pair of giant floor-to-ceiling double doors, while being pursued by a number of scary-looking stick figure guards with guns. The fleeing stick figure was bleeding out of many, many bullet holes. A speech bubble coming out of his mouth said, "I should of read the sign!" Sure enough, in a touch worthy of the finest postmodernist minds, on one of the hand-drawn doors was a tiny rendering of the same "KEEP OUT" sign, stick figures and all. What was this place?

Ed paused while punching in the combination into the keypad next to the door to open the lock, and nodded toward the sign. "Every month we have a contest," he explained, answering Abe's silent question.

Abe noticed that the burlier of his silent guards was beaming like a proud parent. "Your kid did this?" Abe asked, thrilled at the opportunity to gain some points. He then watched in horror as the grin disappeared from the man's face and the grip on his shoulder tightened. Abe couldn't imagine what he had said wrong. And then he imagined it. A smarter man than Abe would have stayed quiet at that realization. Unfortunately, Abe was not a smarter man than Abe.

"Of course a kid couldn't have done this. I don't know what I was thinking. They could never have captured all the nuances this sign conveys. It's a great picture. Really telegraphs 'Keep Out.' Really really communicates 'Obey the sign that says 'Keep out.' And the consequences for not. Keeping out."

The hand that was slowly relocating his shoulder to somewhere south of his ribcage began to relax. Abe decided to continue. "And it's very creative. Particularly the orthography. It really does stand out."

At that Abe distinctly heard Nita cough in what he could have sworn was not laughter.

The electronic lock chirped and the right-hand door swung open, letting them through. It closed with a whoosh of air as soon as they were all on the other side. For a big door, it moved quickly. Had any of them taken a second longer, their clothes might have been caught. Ideally their clothes. In a best-case scenario, their clothes. But pretty much anything that stood out or otherwise dangled. Having two much larger people behind him suddenly seemed like not such a bad thing after all, Abe thought.

In constructing a building, architects create hallways as a way to pass from one room to the next without having to pass between subsequent rooms. When asked to describe or draw a hallway, most people would draw or describe a long space with doors spaced along it, which the hallway connects. After all, that's its job. Connecting rooms. This was not that sort of hallway. This was more of a runway. A long narrowing corridor that led to nowhere. Like a gallery, but with no artwork on the walls. In fact the walls were starkly, painfully white. So white he kept looking down at his feet, fully expecting to see that his bare feet had somehow left scuff marks. It was a space that said there is only one destination, and that is directly ahead of you. It was essentially shaped like an arrow, with a far broader tip. And Abe was being walked down the shaft.

Only when they reached the far wall did Abe notice the doors recessed into its white surface. They had no handles, no hinges, no visible hardware of any sort. And it was hard to say how many of them there were, now that he was only just noticing them from a one-foot distance. Perhaps he had been passing them all along. Ed stepped up to the large rectangular space where a door was delineated, and placed his hand on it, pushed, touching it with his fingertips first, followed by his palm. From somewhere within the wall a mechanism chimed electronically, then the door sprung open like a kitchen cabinet. Abe became aware that he hadn't exhaled in almost half a minute. He could hear his heart pounding in his chest.

"That's all we need," Ed said, and the two bodyguards who had been Abe's constant companions turned and headed back down the long hallway. Having them perpetually there behind him had been alarming, Abe now realized. But not needing them had to be worse.

Abe followed him into the room, only to be shocked at what he saw. It was the same room they had been in originally. Same irritating green walls. Same large not-purely-reflective mirror. Same frolicsome kitten couch. They had only approached through a separate entrance he hadn't seen before, hidden in a side wall.

"It's not the same room," Ed said. "It only looks the same."

Abe couldn't believe it. Why would they have two identical rooms like that, and in such horrible taste?

"We find it gives test subjects a calming sense of familiarity that helps inspire a positive intellectual frame of mind. Revealing that it isn't in fact the same room then creates an unsettling psychological effect, which provides an even more effective mental enhancement. Then again," he added, after a pause, "it could be the same room."

Three people entered the room to join them. Nita, soon followed by an older man with a large briefcase, and a nervous-looking young man, probably in his early twenties. The older man sat in one of the comfyish chairs, indicating to Abe that he should sit in the one facing it. Nita and Ed sat on the lumpy kitten couch. Abe felt this was progress.

The older man introduced himself as Dr. Lamb, following it up in a practiced way with, "But you can call me Steve." The other, younger man he introduced as "Brian, my intern." Brian reached out to shake Abe's hand, then stopped at a look from everyone who wasn't Abe. Seeing that all the chairs were now taken, Brian sheepishly sat down on the floor. "For God's sake, Brian," the doctor sniffed, "Get off the floor. Get yourself a chair. Harvard," he said to Abe, rolling his eyes, as if this was sufficient explanation. Brian left the room humiliated.

Dr. Lamb began opening the suitcase. "So, Abe, I suppose you know what we're here for by now."

Abe shrugged. Why should he make this easy for them?

The doctor continued, "I'm a therapist. A psychotherapist."

Abe countered with a dead-on impersonation of himself at the press conference. "You think I'm some crazy person who thinks he's an important dead president, and you're here to cure me?"

"Well, not crazy, just recalcitrant. Or maybe blocked. So I'm just here helping you jog your own brain a little bit. You don't have to participate if you don't wish to. So far, from what I understand you haven't wished to. So I brought a brain jogger to do it for you." Abe forced himself not to allow himself think what that meant. Instead he imagined a group of brains in track suits, jogging around a mall. There, that was better.

Dr. Lamb opened the suitcase fully to reveal a set of steel odds and ends that were every bit as disturbing as the instruments in Dr. Butcher's examining room had been unsurprising. It was like going from a doctor's office to a... well, like going from a doctor's office to a freaky room with a mad scientist doctor where you didn't know what they were going to do with you and you wanted to run screaming away. Exactly like that analogy, in fact.

Another rubberized cuff was put on Abe's forearm, only this one was connected to a spiral cord like an old-time telephone. An identical one was strapped to his opposing arm. A miniature cuff was slipped over his left index finger and squeezed tight. The doctor—if he even *was* a doctor, Abe reflected—next removed a pair of tiny balls, also attached to spiral cords, although much thinner ones. It looked a lot like a pair of portable ear bud headphones, but without the foam guards that gave plastic things the illusion of comfort.

"This might feel funny at first, but you'll get used to them," Dr. Lamb said, leaning forward with the earphones. Only they weren't earphones. In a move too expert for Abe to flinch in time, Dr. Lamb took both small balls and popped them into Abe's nostrils. His reflexes kicking in too late, Abe snorted for air, but his blocked nasal passages only caused him to cough convulsively. Abe gasped to inhale, which would have been easy enough given that his lung-mouth connection was still perfectly clear, but having foreign objects in his nose somehow made it a bit more difficult to remember that other means of respiration existed.

"You might want to breathe through your mouth," Dr. Lamb said, not at all helpfully.

All of the cords were then plugged into a small box with a track pad and a four-inch square screen, which fit neatly within the briefcase. Dr. Lamb looked at the screen, made a face, and wiped it with his thumb. He looked at it again, scowled, and wiped it against his jacket cuff vigorously, inadvertently pulling Abe's head forward for the rocky ride. He checked it again, tried wiping it with the palm of his hand, shook his head, and shrugged.

Then Dr. Lamb reached down into the pocket of the case and pulled out a small metal box. He opened the box and checked inside. Abe could hear its contents rattle before he saw it open. Then the doctor held the open box out in front of Abe. It was filled with small white pills. He shook the box slightly, indicating that he wanted Abe to take one. Abe clenched his fists and sealed his lips, prepared for a fight. Whatever it was, they would have to force it into him. But he hadn't been strapped down in any way, and the mood was still calm. "Abe?" the doctor asked.

Abe shook his head vigorously. "No, thank you."

"Suit yourself." Dr. Lamb shrugged. He turned to Nita, offering her the box. "Mint?"

She reached over and took one, popping it in her mouth. Dr. Lamb helped himself to a couple and closed the box, tossing it back into the briefcase with a small clunk. Abe could feel his mouth watering as a hint of a peppermint smell wafted toward him. Yet again he felt like an idiot. He swallowed, only to feel his ears pop from the pressure of his clogged nostrils.

Brian the intern came into the room then, wheeling a heavy desk chair with one caster that kept turning the wrong way and squealing as he forced it to right itself. The noise was grating, and they all winced with every squeak. Abe could see Brian wincing even more than the rest, clearly cowering under his inevitable dressing down and equally inevitable public disgrace, but it didn't come. Apparently he, Abe, was going to be the only victim in the room. After what seemed like an excruciatingly long time, Brian wheeled his chair to a place in the room that he clearly believed to be a suitable distance for him to watch the proceedings without being intrusive. He got out a notebook and a pen.

"Okay. Let's start." Dr. Lamb began. "What we've hooked you up to is called a Proustometer. It operates on the theory that all memories are grounded in the physical world, and can be reached through corresponding mental stimuli. We've found stimulating the olfactory nerve to be the most effective noninvasive method." Noninvasive? Abe wondered what constituted an invasive method, considering that he was already being nasally raped.

"Brian, can I see that pen?" Dr. Lamb reached over and snatched Brian's pen away from him, leaving the hapless young man with only a notebook. Abe could see the intern checking his pockets and looking around the room feebly, but he was stuck. And the door was far away, clear on the other side of the room. Brian sat looking at his notebook impotently. Then he caught Abe looking at him and straightened his posture, trying to still seem professional. Harvard, Abe thought, echoing Dr. Lamb, and snickered to himself.

Dr. Lamb held the pen up and waved it slowly in front of Abe's eyes, back and forth. "Now I'm going to try to put you into a light hypnotic trance. Watch the pen." Abe tried to watch the pen, but he could see that Dr. Lamb's other hand was fiddling with the track pad, and a warm sensation was flowing through his index finger, and he could feel a tingling sensation in his temples, and more disconcertingly, in the soles of his feet. A warm smell, like a wood fire and pipe tobacco, and maybe a summer breeze, lingered in the air.

"Watch the pen, Abe." The pen moved back and forth. Abe had to admit it was a soothing sensation. But there was nothing at all hypnotic going on in his mind—it still stayed clear. Maybe the device only jogged his memories if there were any memories there for the jogging?

"Are you watching the pen, Abe?"

"I'm watching the pen."

"Okay. It's 1864... You're in your own bedroom at the White House... tell me: What do you see?"

"I see a pen."

"Don't look at the pen. Ignore the pen. What do you see?"

"But you told me to watch the pen."

"I want you to watch the pen, but don't think about it. I want you to tell me what you see with your *inner* eyes. I'll start again. You're in your bedroom at the White House... The Lincoln bedroom... your bedroom... but the year 1864... now tell me: What do you see?

"I still see a ballpoint pen. Looks like it came from a bank."

"Abe." Dr. Lamb's impatient sigh could have shuffled papers. "Please cooperate."

"The government lets you steal pens from the bank?"

The justificational explosion came from all sides.

"No!"

"That's classified!"

"It's not from a bank!"

"We're not from the government!"

"It's not a pen!"

This was better than he thought. Abe decided it was time to play along. "So I'm not supposed to see the pen?"

"Forget the pen."

"In that, case, I don't know what I see. I don't see anything."

"Abe, work with me just the tiniest bit. You have to concentrate."

"But there's nothing to concentrate on. I don't remember anything because there's nothing to remember. You know clones don't have residual memories—it's physiologically impossible. And every scientific study they've ever done has proven that. The case was closed decades ago."

"No, every study they've ever done has been inconclusive. There's a big difference. That's why we're here. The scientific case has been reopened, Abe. Like it or not, you reopened it two days ago. There's a new ongoing study in past-life memories in clones. And you're in it, right now. You are it, in fact. Because you had one."

"I don't know what I had. It was a fluke."

"Maybe. But we think it was a memory. Which makes it one of the most important flukes in recent scientific memory. Pardon the pun. So it's our job to do what it takes to recreate it, Abe. Or figure out why it happened. Besides, just think how exciting it would be if you were the first one who actually turned something up."

"I'm sure I could hardly contain myself," Abe said, flatly.

"Well, in that case, we would contain you," Dr. Lamb replied.

Abe added that to the list of things he was determined not to think about. It was getting to be a very long list. "And if we can't figure anything out, if there's really nothing there, can I leave? I'd really like to go home."

"Home? Which home? Springfield? Washington? Backwoods Kentucky?" Dr. Lamb asked hopefully.

Abe found it very difficult not to go on a flailing spree, knocking down whatever he could between himself and the door. But the door itself appeared flail-proof. And he still didn't know who—or what—was behind the mirror. If he had learned anything over the course of the day, it was that any sort of escape plan would be a losing battle. Like Bull Run. Or Manassas. His lip twitched. Oh no, Abe. Not that. Don't giggle, Abe, please don't giggle, whatever you do I beg you please don't even give the tiniest twitch of a hint of a...

Abe giggled.

Dr. Lamb leaned in, immediately interested. "You find something funny?"

"No. The machine made my foot tickle."

"Abe, don't you see that if we could just explore your past, we'll be taking that one step closer to unlocking the future?"

"Lincoln's past is not my past!"

"Calm down, Abe. But I'm going to ask you again to co-operate. Everyone has been very patient with you. *I've* been incredibly patient with you. Let's start over." He touched the track pad again, and Abe could feel the warm tingling in his finger again, and the heat at his temples, and the hint of wood smoke. Watching the pen was doing nothing for him, but the heat at his forehead was off-putting. It didn't seem to be doing anything for his memory. But it was starting to make his head throb.

"Now, Abe. Tell me about the first time you ever met Martha. What can you remember...?"

"Who?"

"Martha—your wife..."

"That was George Washington!"

Dr. Lamb scrambled, checking his notes. "Right. I meant Mary Todd. That's what I meant. What can you tell me about her? Jog any memories?"

Abe could feel beads of sweat starting to form on his forehead as the heat pulsed through the machinery attached to his body. But no thoughts. "Nothing."

"Are you watching the pen?"

"American Federal."

"Stop watching the pen."

38

WE'RE NOT GETTING ANYWHERE," Ed cut in unhappily. "I say we call it a day."

"You want me to take a turn?" Nita asked. It was the first time she had spoken all afternoon, and her rich deep voice cut through the room like a knife through small intestines. Abe did not want her to take a turn. Fortunately, Dr. Lamb didn't want her to, either. "Nah, you're not trained. This isn't as simple as it looks."

"Well, it looks like it's not working," said Ed, testily.

"It's only the first day," said Dr. Lamb. "But you're right. He's resisting too much. And everything's probably too new for him. He needs to settle in a bit."

Ed's mood seemed to improve immediately with that suggestion. "Right. Settle in! He hasn't even seen his new quarters. Of course he needs to get accustomed to them before we'll make any progress here. His clothes probably don't even fit like his own yet. I can't believe I didn't even think of that!" Dr. Lamb shot him a veiled look that seemed to say, "I respect you too much to roll my eyes."

"You know," Ed went on, "you've been doing this all wrong. We shouldn't even have brought him in here. The whole process should have taken place in his living quarters—we need to move the device in there from now on. He can't possibly remember the past surrounded by so much of this modern—" he waved his arm, to indicate their inelegant surroundings "—well, this uninspiring environment."

"Ed, he pulled his past-life recall in the middle of an international press conference. I don't think the décor is the issue. And if your guys hadn't kept hijacking the budget, maybe we could get some decent furniture."

"Hey it's not my guys doing the requisitioning here—your people are the ones stealing pens from the bank."

Nita cleared her throat, and just like that, the argument ended. Abe wondered what caliber throat Nita had that she could achieve such a powerful effect with so little effort, and whether she had to go through any sort of mandatory waiting period before obtaining it. Abe's respect for Nita was growing with every new piece of information he was gleaning from her, if you could call her intimidation techniques "information."

No, not respect for. Fear of. But there was a certain comfort in knowing that she seemed to have the same effect on a lot of people. Not working for the government must be a great job for someone like her. Not working for the Mafia would have been another. If she could somehow be harnessed into not working for the IRS, the U.S. could probably gain a fortune in eradicating tax fraud.

"Brian, give me a hand here," Dr. Lamb ordered, and the intern bounded up, nearly tripping over his own feet. The two of them together unhooked and unstrapped Abe from the various cups and wires binding him to the little plastic box. Abe could still feel their slight weight and tingle for a while after they were gone, like a host of tiny phantom limbs. But he was glad to be rid of them.

The foursome paused outside the door of the room, and Abe expected to again see his favorite pair of moving brick walls with heads, waiting to take him on another forced march down yet another long and winding series of confusing corridors. But instead, as Dr.-Lamb-you-can-call-me-Steve and Brian-my-intern headed off down the empty white widening hallway and into the distance, Ed simply paused by the recessed rectangle he had originally stopped at before they had entered the room in the first place. Again he placed his hand on what Abe now knew was another door, the electronic lock chimed and unbolted, and the door slid open.

What Abe saw inside was simply astounding.

39

IT WAS A LOG cabin. They were standing in a doorway inside the sterile, almost futuristic 21st-century blank white corridor, and somehow, somewhere in the 1850s. Abe had to shut his eyes for a few seconds, his senses were so completely overwhelmed.

"Amazing, isn't it?" Ed said, grinning.

And it was. Abe walked in, slowly drinking in everything. He couldn't believe he was still in the same century, let alone the same building. The attention to detail that had been paid in constructing every square inch was literally breathtaking. The walls were made of square-hewn logs, from floor to roof, which somehow rose upward to a point. They were so cracked and uneven in texture that they looked like they came from an even older century than the 1800s, almost slapped together, as if thrown together in a hurry by someone who had never heard of the concepts of a plane or sandpaper. The floor was nothing but dirt. There was a wooden bed with a handmade quilt, and a beautiful turned-leg desk with an upright chair that looked like the most uncomfortable thing he'd ever seen in his life. All together it looked like a cross between an L.L. Bean catalog and a crazed mountain hermit's shack—the crude and the beautiful thrown together incongruously without any rhyme or reason. There were kerosene lamps and tin candleholders mounted on the walls, and rows of shiny metal jugs covered with muslin and tied with burlap rope. Wood-plank shelves lined one wall, stacked with earthenware plates and cups he longed to touch. In fact, he longed to touch everything. The mix of such rough, handmade and homespun objects with what must be priceless antiques was a bit jarring, and seemed like a bad judgment call, but everything still was so clearly *old*, so *real*, that he didn't care. It was more real than the turkey he had had for lunch, more real than the rough woolen trousers he was wearing which in the past hours had started to feel far more at home and comfortable on his body. If any of this was a re-creation, he didn't want to know it. He longed to take his students here.

He ran his fingertips along one wall, feeling a groove between two cracked boards. It was wood. It was real wood. "It's real wood," he said, unable to help himself. Without even realizing it, he had wandered well inside the room. The others were still standing outside.

"You expected some sort of polyvinyl fiberglass?" Ed asked. "But that would defeat the purpose. We want you to feel at home here. That's the point. Most of it's genetically sound, too, grown from original seeds or refurbished antiques. The rest we had to reconstruct. Hopefully your subconscious mind won't be able to tell the difference too much. We thought about bringing in original bedbugs, but decided that too much discomfort might increase your resistance." Ed laughed his most annoying laugh. "Just between you and me, Abe, we're not happy with your resistance. Well, just between you, me, and Nita."

Abe tried to work up a corresponding response to the muted threat. But he almost didn't care. The cabin-room was too seductive. It was exactly the sort of thing that drew him into becoming a history teacher—into studying history—in the first place. The hidden call of the past. And he wanted to laugh, too—but not with them. Of all the ways they could have devised to get him to cooperate in their ridiculous plan to exploit his clone legacy, this was without question the least likely to succeed. Surrounded by so much tangible, visceral proof that there was a past time when an actual Abraham Lincoln had lived and slept and breathed, how could he not know to the bottom of his bones that he was anything but a pale twenty-first century copy? The dusty floor under his feet felt delicious because it was not polyurethaned, the heat from the wood stove in the corner was wonderful because he compared it to the kind that came out of his vents. And wondered how much air-conditioning the facility must be running around the outside of the room so that he could enjoy a wood stove.

Ed seemed to sense Abe's distraction, though without realizing its significance. "Anyhow, goodnight, Mr. Lincoln," he smiled. "We'll let you get settled in. One of us will be back for you in the morning."

"Ed will be back for you," Nita corrected him. "This place gives me the creeps."

The door shut and left no sign of its opening. Abe walked over to where he knew it had been, but there was no lintel, no hinges, practically no evidence of there ever having been a doorway there of any sort—even the logs themselves seemed to have rejoined themselves into long boards. Only by the closest scrutiny was Abe able to see where the planks had been cut to make way for the doorway. They must have used a laser to make such a precise cut. Somehow they had managed to disguise the exit utterly. He knew that was a violation of fire codes, but somehow he didn't think that pointing that out was going to help him any. Still, if this was a prison, it was the most wonderful cell he could ever imagine. He scanned around the rest of the room, and saw that there was another door set into one wall, a real door, which he had taken for granted. He walked over to open it. It was locked. Actually, he realized as he tugged on it, it was probably not made to ever open. It had the encumbrance of a door without any mounting hardware, as if it was actually sealed to the walls around it—if not actually bolted to additional load-bearing walls behind it. No matter how real it was on its surface, it was still there for decorative purposes only. He should have realized that their definition of reality had its limits. And he was trapped within them.

And that's when he noticed the window.

For the first time all day, Abe had a window.

He looked out, but all he could see was the black of night, and what looked like trees. He had no idea if it was a real window, leading to the real outdoors, or a simulation to make it feel like the real outdoors. He couldn't believe that they would give him an actual window when they wouldn't give him an actual door. It had curtains—cornflower blue with a red and yellow gingham pattern which also looked like they had just been ordered directly out of any number of Maine country catalogs, except that they were clearly handmade, somehow more substantial, and tied back with more burlap ropes. They had thought of everything. He put his hand to the window glass (real glass, he thought), and it was cool to the touch. Just like a real window on a cold night. But it was thick, wavy glass, and if the exterior of his chamber were air-conditioned, the cool temperature would be meaningless. He would have a better idea of what lay outside by morning when the sun rose.

The idea of spending the night there raised other associations for Abe. He was hungry. But Ed had said they would get him the next morning. What about dinner? Were they really not going to feed him? Or was he supposed to wait for someone else to come and escort him to yet another meal? Suddenly he felt more like a prisoner than ever. All day he had been walked from place to place, had been poked in places only he should have the right to poke, and had been asked questions he couldn't stand the sound of, they had been repeated so often, but nothing seemed quite so dehumanizing as knowing that he was dependent on unknown forces to supply his food. And didn't know when, or whether, or in what shape they would come. He might have to go without food for the night, all because he was completely at their mercy. Nothing could be worse than that.

Almost nothing could be worse than that.

One thing could be worse than that.

There, peeking out from under the bed, he saw the chamber pot.

40

FTER SPENDING SEVERAL MINUTES staring in dismay at the little china bowl painted, disturbingly enough, with flowers that he was pretty sure were supposed to be (oh the irony) forget-me-nots, Abe tried to return to his earlier joy at this field trip into the past. He opened drawers and poked at things that stood out. He found a loaf of bread, some blackberry preserves, and a jug of whole milk, plus a large pitcher and basin of water that he knew was for washing but he thought contained enough surplus that he could drink from it too, should the need arise. This, then, was to be his dinner.

It was incredibly delicious, every bit as much as he had hoped after his lunch hours and hours before. But the events of the day, coupled with the adrenaline rush of his fears, made him far hungrier than a simple meal of bread could satiate. On the other hand, he realized—thinking again of his new little porcelain friend—less in, less out. And he was all in favor of less out, at least until he could go back to modern conveniences. Whenever that would be.

He sat at the desk, played with the pen and ink and the intriguing wooden spool that served as both inkwell and penholder, then looked at the books on the shelves. They were all law books, dated in the 1800s but with new leather bindings in what he was certain were historically (and probably genetically) accurate leather. But while they were interesting as historical artifacts, they were as boring to him as dry toast. As dry twenty-first century toast. He sat in the chair, finding it even more uncomfortable than it looked. He wondered whether the lack of sufficient food and material comforts (and even the heat from the wood stove was feeble) was some sort of psychological tactic. Possibly a brainwashing technique to break him down and get him to divulge the information that he kept telling them—that he knew—he didn't have. And if that were the case, he was almost afraid to test out his theory on the mattress. Parasite-free or not.

As it turned out, his suspicions were correct. Instead of a box spring, the mattress rested on a web of more of those all-purpose burlap ropes. It was stiff and lumpy, not like a board was stiff or a sack of oatmeal was lumpy, but more like a mugging victim's body was stiff and lumpy. And it had an odd smell to it, not the way things you're not used to always have an odd smell to them, but the way that makes you wonder if you stepped in something earlier and accidentally rubbed it off there and now you'll never be clean again. And so began a very unpleasant last few hours. After much internal debate, he decided to change into the nightshirt they had left him, carefully hung upon a peg set into the wall next to the bed. There was a nightcap too, but he couldn't bring himself to put it on. As the night grew colder, and his counterpane not quite long enough to pull over his tall frame, he began to see the logic behind wearing it, but his vanity still won out. Like that insidious stovepipe hat—which incidentally they had left for him and was sitting mocking him on another peg by the fake front door—he would not ever stoop to putting it on. No hats. Not if his life depended on it. Well, maybe then. But not until then.

But right now, all that was at stake was sleep, and the longer he tried, the harder it was to get there. He tried counting things, and recounting things that had happened, and trying to come up with escape plans, and nothing had helped him. And tepid, room-temperature milk, he found, by no means worked the same soporific magic that warm milk was rumored to do. The lamps had burned down hours before, and they had left him no means to refill them, so reading was out of the question. In the darkness, stretched out on the hard bed, he let his eyes try scanning around the room, seeing if he could actually do what they had hoped for him here: try to feel as if he had traveled back in time.

There was a soft smell of wood coming from the stove. From the faint glow of moonlight (real moonlight?) coming in through the window, he could vaguely make out the shapes of the desk, the torture-chair, the shelves. The pitcher and basin. And up high in a corner, tucked behind one of the eaves in a chink between two of the logs that must have been improperly joined with whatever it was they used to join them, he saw a red dot.

But there was no reason he should see anything red in the dark.

Unless it was glowing.

Like an LED bulb.

Abe nearly flew out of bed with the realization of what that meant. Of course they had a camera. Of course they were watching him. Maybe they wanted to know whether the real Abraham Lincoln slept on his right side or his left. Or whether he snored *(did he snore?)*. Or how much he drooled on his pillow. More realistically, they wanted to know if the fake Abraham Lincoln had any intentions of making a break for it. For all he knew, the cloudy silver looking glass on the wall was a two-way mirror as well. How could he have been so stupid? He had to get out of here. He tried not to stare at the dot, not certain whether a person was monitoring him even then, or whether it was all being fed into some digital recorder to be studied later. Whether they had a zoom function, and could see him staring. Whether it was better for them to know that he knew they were watching. In which case, should he wave? Write them a sign with their pen and ink? Put on the damn hat so he could tip it? He remembered their repeated hints that they were unhappy with his refusal to cooperate with their testing. Their veiled and not-so-veiled threats. And he was relatively certain at this point that whoever they were not, they most certainly were not Not From the Government. Too much money had gone into this setup. And at the same time, too little planning. No one seemed to know exactly what to do with him. Ed seemed to be at cross-purposes with Dr. Lamb about the immersion element, which Dr. Lamb clearly thought was unnecessary. Dr. Lamb seemed to be a slave to his device, which as far as Abe could tell did nothing at all. And Nita? What was her role, other than to intimidate the crap out of him?

Okay. Even if that was it, she was very, very good at it.

He wondered whether there was any way that he could exploit their differences of opinion for his own benefit. It would buy him some time, at any rate. The room was growing colder and colder, to the point where it was becoming almost unbearable. Abe wondered what time it was, but they had left him no timepieces in the room of any sort. He decided to risk the greater chill outside the blankets to see if anything could be done. He resisted the urge to look up at the little red light as he got up, and tried to walk normally as he crossed to the stove. He hadn't remembered there being any kindling underneath or next to it, but maybe there had been a pile or a bin of some sort that he had overlooked.

Sure enough, on closer scrutiny there was a small woven twig basket filled with logs and strips of paper tucked into a nook beside the stove. He opened the door of the stove carefully, using the corner of his flannel nightgown wrapped twice around his hand so as not to burn his skin, and peered inside. Maybe there was something he could poke deeper toward what was left of the flames. Not that there was a poker, but he would worry about that once he discovered what there was in the way of pokee.

But the point was moot, he discovered as he looked in. Deep inside the stove, a fire was still glowing merrily, the flames dancing brightly behind a black mesh screen. They were red, orange and yellow silk, flickering upwards on the breeze of some hidden fan, and lit from below by a red 20-watt bulb. Some sort of aluminum foil streamers gave it a hint of extra dazzle. A small air-freshener pumped the now-familiar wood smoke aroma out through a vented fan. The rest of the interior protected a glorified space heater, which was now apparently set to low.

Furious, Abe cursed and kicked the stove, then yowled in pain as his bare foot made connection with the extremely real cast iron. He slammed the door of the stove shut and hobbled back to bed. He yelled again, another primal yowl, and punched his pillow hard. A mix of feathers started to burst out of one side, clinging to his face and hair. Exhausted, Abe curled up into a tight ball, lay down onto his now much flatter pillow, and finally fell into a deep sleep.

41

A BE WOKE UP IN shock the next morning to the sound of a rooster crowing. Lost in the tangle of his unaccustomed surroundings, his back aching from the slablike mattress and his head still spinning from the trials of the night before, it took Abe some time to recognize the noise or what to do with it. A child of the suburbs his entire life, Abe had never heard a real rooster crowing before. The word "rooster" sprung into his mind, and he knew instinctively that it was right, having heard the sound often enough in movies and on TV, but he couldn't ever remember having come in contact with the real thing. And was he hearing one now? Or was it a recording—another fake, like the fire in the stove?

He could feel his toes throb faintly in sympathy with the memory. The stove still gave off its heat, much warmer now, as if in mockery. Maybe they hadn't been watching him last night. Maybe he wasn't supposed to have noticed the thermostat going down, the classic symptom of Florida's over-dependence on climate control. He got out of bed gingerly and walked toward the window. Would he see the chicken outside? If it was even outside, he corrected himself. If the entire scene outside his window wasn't artificial. Already, from his vantage point across the room he could see trees. Where was the bird? He felt as if his entire day were going to rest on whether there was a chicken outside or not.

Standing with his face practically pressed against the glass, Abe gaped. It must have been just after dawn; there was some reddish sunlight to be seen on the horizon, but much of the sky was still dark. In the early morning light, though, he could still make out that his "cabin"—for he already felt it to be more than simply a room, the longer he spent in it—was surrounded by a thicket of trees. And not just any trees, but oak trees, maple trees, buckeyes... trees that had no business in Florida. And birds flying between them that were nothing like the fanciful wetland birds that high-stepped through Orlando. He thought he saw the red flash of a cardinal, or possibly a woodpecker's head, but it was gone as soon as it came. The whole scene was impossible. Which of course made it unreal.

But it *seemed* real. The sun looked and behaved just like the sun. The birds were absolutely real birds. And only God can make a tree, Abe said to himself, hopefully. He couldn't remember the last time he had wanted anything as much as he wanted those trees to be real. It was like believing in magic. He would cooperate with the project; he would try to find the ghost of Abraham Lincoln buried inside of him even though he knew he wasn't there, he would write long florid love letters to Joshua Speed if it only meant that he could go outside his windows and try to climb those trees, if they were real.

Ed was so proud of his achievements in "reality"—everything was original, or grafted from the original hosts, or genetically spliced. So those could be Lincoln's own trees, somehow made to grow in Florida soil. And if those trees were really Abraham Lincoln's oak trees and ash trees and maple trees, then this really could be Abraham Lincoln's log cabin if he wanted it to be, and who cared what lay beyond the wood if he could just wander into it and feel it—feel what it was really *like*.

He realized he was suddenly thinking like them. Was their project working, or was he losing his mind? He realized that he didn't care.

He remembered the rooster. Where was it? The rooster was the sign. If a rooster appeared, then the forest was real. No rooster, no forest. They wouldn't have gone to all that trouble to plant a real forest, stock it with real birds, and then microchip a chicken. It wasn't possible. He looked down at the cleared ground outside of the cabin. The outside was made of logs, and from their thickness he was convinced they were the same logs that comprised the interior walls. There was a pile of firewood and an axe (Abe groaned at the sight of them), and a water pump, but no sign of any livestock. He couldn't hear any clucking or other animal sounds either. And the cock's crowing was never repeated. He watched and watched, burning the negative image of the dirt ground into his retinas, but no rooster appeared. Finally, he gave up and returned to face his still dark room, and began to dress.

As he pulled on his single pair of undergarments, he sighed. The idea of wearing them for a second day in a row was not a pleasant one. But he had no choice. He smelled them before putting them on, then blushed, remembering the camera. It could have been worse, he supposed. But he couldn't help lamenting that fabric softener would not be invented for another hundred years. He pulled on his trousers and shirt, fastening on the collar while looking in the cloudy mirror. He wondered if anyone was looking back at him. His suspicions weren't allayed any by the fact that the second his last button was fastened, Ed arrived.

It was a strange moment, worthy of a science fiction movie. First, there was the distant sound of a pure electronic chime. Then, where there once had been a solid log wall, a tall rectangle of white light suddenly appeared. The white light spread, until it opened into a doorway, revealing a completely white corridor behind it, with Ed silhouetted in its center. Abe hadn't realized how completely he had been immersed in the world of the nineteenth century over the past several hours. But when he saw Ed before him, his modern clothes looked jarring. Ed came in, holding a large basket.

"Good morning, Abe. Hope you slept well."

"It was okay," Abe answered. Despite his moment of revelation just minutes before, all his hostility had returned. "The bathroom left a lot to be desired."

"Ah," Ed said. "Well, we won't hold you to that. Not if you help us get what we need in return."

"Ed, look. I don't know how to help you. I don't have any memories."

"Didn't the room spark anything?"

"Not yet."

Ed lit up at this. "Ah—not yet! Well, just think if there's anything that can help with that, and if it's within reason, maybe I can pull some strings. Maybe a little more food?"

Ed opened up the basket to reveal more bread and preserves, with butter this time, more milk, some cheese, and more than that —

"Eggs." Abe exclaimed.

"Yep. Fresh eggs. Laid this morning."

"From an 1860s chicken?"

Ed beamed. "You guessed it! 1840s, actually. Wait till you taste them! You know, once you've had fresh-laid eggs, you can't go back to store-bought. You just can't. And these..."

"Show it to me." Abe's tone was flat, almost harsh.

Ed held up an egg, quickly. "It's hard-boiled."

"No." Abe said. "Show it to me. The chicken."

"I don't under—"

"Show. Me. The. Chicken!"

"What?"

"Show me the chicken! Show me the chicken! Show me the chicken!!!" Yelling now, Abe lunged for Ed's throat. Immediately a klaxon sounded and out of nowhere a team of people he had never seen before came rushing in and pulled him off of Ed, restraining him. He felt a needle entering his arm and everything went spinny, then calm. The room went black.

Abe awoke alone in the room again with an awful headache. The uncomfortable chair had been removed from the room, as had the wooden bedstead. His mattress was now on the floor. From the sunlight streaming in through the window, he guessed that it was hours later.

The breakfast basket was gone. In its place was a grilled chicken.

42

NOT LONG AFTERWARDS THE wall's innards chimed and the hidden door opened again. This time the two heavyset guards accompanied Ed, who looked nervous. Clearly he was taking no chances. His eyes went warily over to the table, where there was little left of the chicken carcass. He smiled wanly. Abe, gnawing on a last drumstick, managed a half-smile back. He was starving. Any symbolism the bird represented could take a flying leap out the phony window.

"Come on," Ed said. His voice was tired. The morning's excitement seemed to have sucked all the joy out of the log cabin experiment.

"I'm feeling really good, Ed," Abe said, realizing it was true. "Something about this room is really... inspiring."

"Oh yeah?" Ed's face lit up briefly.

"Oh yeah. I think it's definitely working. Especially the chicken. You have any more of those?"

"I could look into that." Ed sounded unsure.

"Good." Abe smiled, a dangerous smile, and handed Ed the denuded drumstick. Ed looked at it, unsure what to do with it, then put it back on the desk with the rest of the bones.

"Oh yeah, just put it there," Abe said. "Unless you think I'll use it as a weapon later. You know, maybe I'll keep it."

"Come on," Ed said. He linked his arm through Abe's and headed out of the room. With the two bodyguards standing only a couple of feet away from them to make sure Abe wouldn't flee, Ed placed his palm on the panel of the next door room, and half-led, half-pushed Abe inside. The door shut behind them.

Dr. Lamb, Nita, and Brian the intern were already in the room waiting for him, all in the same places he had left them the day before. It was almost as if no time had passed. He had a seat in the chair, and proffered his arms for the various straps of the device. This time, however, something new was added. Once he was fully strapped in, before he had the chance to see what was going on and possibly put up a fight, another needle was inserted into his arm and another shot injected.

"What was that?" He asked.

"Oh nothing," Dr. Lamb answered. "Just a little something to try to make you more cooperative. Since your response to hypnosis was so unsatisfying."

"Let me guess. You lost the pen," Abe said.

"To be honest, Abe, your almost phallic fixation on the pen was a bit alarming. If it weren't for its possible significance in light of the Jonathan Speed memories..."

"You've got to be kidding me. Sometimes a pen is just a pen, Steve."

"I'd rather you call me Dr. Lamb from now on."

As it was the first time Abe had called him anything, and as Dr. Lamb had been the first one to initiate the idea of Steve-calling, Abe debated whether the downgrade was something he should worry about. But it didn't make much difference to him. Exchanging one name for another seemed more than arbitrary here; it was meaningless. Abe didn't know who these people were or whom they worked for. The doctor's name might or might not be Steve Lamb to begin with. There was no way to know whether the "doctor" meant an M.D. or a Ph.D. or a chiropractor or just a word that went with his seniority in the system. He wore a white coat and was called "doctor" by others; therefore officially he was a doctor. So it stood to reason that so long as they continued to exclusively call him "Abe" or "Mr. Lincoln," and kept him wearing Lincoln's clothes, they had no doubts he would eventually produce the past-life recollections they were looking for. If Abe asked for a swimsuit and bathing cap and insisted on only being called "Esther Williams," in time he might convince them he had synchronized swimming flashbacks instead. The threads of DNA that tied him to the original Abraham Lincoln were the reason that brought him here. But he was starting to feel certain that it was only blind faith in appearances that was keeping them from letting him go.

The shot didn't make Abe feel any different than he felt before he received it, but he wasn't sure it was supposed to. The cuffs and cups were giving off the same warm tingle they had the day before. The warm woodsy smell was softer, more inviting.

"Let's begin, Abe," Dr. Lamb announced. "It's a sunny spring day, June 1842. You're in Indiana, in your boyhood home. Looking out, you see the family chickens. Tell me about the chickens."

Abe snorted. Then he started to feel the effects of the injection he had been given. While he could find the question hysterical, he couldn't fight it beyond a certain point. He wasn't certain that he had been given a truth serum—but he did feel compelled to cooperate. "I don't see any chickens. There are no chickens."

"What happened to the chickens, Abe? Can you remember?"

"I have no idea. I'm not getting any memories of any of it. I don't have any memories of anything. You're barking up the wrong—chicken." It was hard to make the joke. The diodes in his finger and temples actually burned. But it still felt good to resist.

"Was there an important chicken at the White House, then? Or during the Civil War? Perhaps at Ford's Theater?"

"Was he calling Frederick Douglass a chicken?" Brian the intern piped in. It was the first time he had spoken in the entire session. All heads turned to look at him. "Never mind," he corrected quickly.

"No—no—no," Abe insisted. "I wasn't having any chicken flashbacks. I swear."

"So why did you attack Ed? What was the importance of the chicken?"

Abe felt himself compelled to answer, though he tried to keep the full answer as much to himself as he could. "I needed to know if the trees are real."

There was a long pause as Dr. Lamb looked at the screen of his little box, and Ed looked at Dr. Lamb. Dr. Lamb looked back up and shrugged. "If it's an act, he believes it."

Nita stood up. "I told you your experiments were silly and unlikely to work. Now it looks like he's becoming mentally unstable because of them. I can't let this continue. You've had your fun. You've had twenty-four hours. We're taking him upstairs and having him cracked open to see what's really there."

"Nita!" Ed protested.

"Don't be so hasty," Dr. Lamb said. "Twenty-four hours is nothing—and we only just started. I haven't had *my* twenty-four hours."

"We were supposed to have a week, Nita," Ed added.

"You heard him," she responded emotionlessly. "Chickens and trees? He's delusional. We're getting nowhere and possibly moving backwards. And you've already spent a fortune in taxpayer money. I can't allow it."

"Taxpayer money?" Abe cut in. "I thought you didn't work for the government."

"Who says we work for the government?" Ed said, grateful for the change of subject.

"You did. She did. She said taxpayer money. Taxpayer money means you work for the government. You lied to me." He looked Nita in the eyes.

"So we're from the government. That gives us the right to lie." She shrugged.

It was the most he had heard Nita speak since meeting her the day (could it only have been one day?) before. And the more she spoke, the more he understood why everyone feared her. The unspoken menace she exuded was apparently only the dainty lace trimmings on the leather overcoat of her true outspoken menace.

Then the fog of his thinking cleared up just enough to let through the jist of her first statement. "And what do you mean, have me cracked open?"

"She doesn't mean anything," Ed said. "Just work with us here, and we'll see if we can't come up with all the answers we need right here. We don't need to do anything invasive."

Dr. Lamb corrected him. "We don't want to do anything invasive prematurely, certainly. But until we know for sure we can't get there, we really shouldn't rush to drastic measures. Think of the loss of historical information..."

"There's no information," Nita replied curtly. "He keeps telling us it was a fluke. Obviously some synapse snapped or something. That's all they care about anyhow. No one upstairs cares about the 'historical' loss. They just want to know why his brain did what it did. You know that."

"Hello?" Abe said. "Third person in the room here! Who can hear you!"

"Um... fourth person...?" Brian said, waving his hand and attempting to correct him, then lowering it as he felt the comment made as little impact on the room as his presence.

"Abe," Nita said, looking at him dead-on, "at the press conference. Did you remember anything, or was it a fluke?"

This question again. After twenty-four hours of insisting that he hadn't, that it was impossible, that there was no conceivable way for anything resembling a memory to have taken place. But he could see both Ed and Dr. Lamb standing behind Nita, both making desperate yes-faces, and he knew that more than just historical verisimilitude was at stake. He didn't know how to reverse course though. And even though he wanted to, he couldn't. His body—or whatever they had injected into him or the device attached to him or both—wouldn't let him. All he could do was dance as closely to the answer he wanted to give without it being a lie.

"I don't know. I've never felt like that before. I was him. Somehow. I just knew the answer to the question." Was that the right answer or the wrong answer? It wasn't admitting to a memory. But it was agreeing that something had happened in his brain—would that shore up her argument that he needed to be "cracked open"?

"Right." She responded. "And since you've been here, have you had any memories again?"

Again he saw the almost desperate looks on the faces of the two men. But he couldn't say what wasn't true, no matter how much he wanted to. He held out saying anything for as long as he could. He tried to make it look like he was thinking back, trying to remember, replaying the events of the last twenty-four hours in his mind. And in a way he was, though more from the perspective of one long inner primal scream.

"No," he said, finally. She nodded. Her case, it seemed, was closed. And then he had it—a possible way out. "But —"

"But...?" she asked.

"But...?" Ed echoed

"But?" Doctor Lamb asked immediately afterwards.

"But early this morning, looking at the trees out of the window... I almost felt I *could* get there... somehow. Maybe if I had more time."

"You see?" Ed said. "He just needs more time. Let him have the week settling in. You'll see."

Nita closed her eyes briefly, then opened them and eyed Abe with suspicion. "No. No week. He goes upstairs tomorrow for the exploratory. I can let you have tonight. They need that long to prep the surgery anyhow. If he comes up with anything earth-shattering between now and then, you can write it up and we'll let the guys upstairs make the call. Deal?"

They looked at each other. It was a long look that took a lot of the air out of the room with it. Or at least Abe wasn't breathing while it lasted, he was so busy waiting for Ed to say "no deal," to fight, to do anything that would either get him more time to hide under the mattress or make that word "surgery" sound less like "cut him open" and more like "drive him home."

"Deal," Ed said. And then he laughed. "Wow—you are tough! I am never playing cards with you."

"No one ever does," Nita responded, smiling.

Abe couldn't believe it. Just like that, they had bargained down his fate, and were now cracking jokes. The same as if he had been a box of surplus office supplies. Or a lab rat.

"Well, I guess my work here is done," Dr. Lamb half-joked, as he began unstrapping Abe from his machine. He seemed genuinely crestfallen. Brian bounded up to help him, but as soon as he reached his hand toward the finger cuff, his hand touched his superior's and was rudely swatted away. Then the doctor backhanded him across the shoulders for good measure.

"Dammit, Brian—Just stop getting underfoot."

"Sorry," he muttered, dazed.

"Well, I didn't say just stand there and do nothing!" The device fully detached, Dr. Lamb practically threw the case at Brian and stomped out of the room, leaving him to wrap the cords and put everything in its place. Abe wanted to feel bad for him.

But he was still too busy feeling worse for himself. "Um... if it's okay for me to ask..." he said. "What's this surgery you keep talking about?"

"It's nothing," Nita said.

"Don't worry about it," Ed added. "Maybe you'll have all sorts of flashbacks before morning comes and the whole thing will go away."

"Please tell me—what's this surgery?" Abe was doing everything he could to control his voice, to maintain the calm he knew he needed to get them to answer the question. If anything could get them to answer it.

"It's nothing. You'll be sedated," Nita reassured him, if you could call it reassurance.

"They're just going to examine your temporal lobes and dissect a section or two to see whether any pieces of them are bigger or shaped differently or unusual in some other way..." Brian began, his head still buried in the briefcase as he continued winding and rearranging the device's cords.

"It's a pretty standard research technique." He was so completely absorbed in that he didn't realize he shouldn't have spoken.

"You're going to cut out my brain?" Abe yelled.

"Abe, calm down." Ed said.

"Calm DOWN? How am I supposed to calm down when you're going to cut out my brains? I NEED my brains!"

Ed gave another of his Brian's-an-idiot conspiratorial glances. "You're overreacting. No one's going to cut out your brains. We're not monsters here."

Abe felt his heartbeat start to return to something approximating its normal levels. But only approximating. He had still heard what he heard. "But the surgery...?"

"Totally routine procedure. They just need to take out some tissue from various *parts* of your brains. It's no big deal. Maybe fifteen, twenty percent tops. Spaced out all over—you look at an x-ray, I bet you won't even know the difference. So to speak. Not you necessarily. Anyhow, I hear they've had tons of success with this on mice, monkeys— even dogs!"

"Oh, even dogs?" Abe's heart rate had stopped approximating normal, and was now bearing a much closer resemblance to that part in the middle of the song "Wipeout" where the drums go airborne.

"Well you know they're the closest biologically to people in a lot more ways than monkeys, or so I'm told. And this is a top-notch facility you're dealing with. We're not just talking mutts, Abe—they use Golden Retrievers."

Once again, Abe took a flying leap toward Ed's throat. Ed made a high-pitched squeaking noise, almost like a piglet, and ran out of the door to escape his grasp. Just as the door was closing, he called out again, "Don't worry, Abe!"

Nita meanwhile, was putting her own things away and paying him almost no attention at all. Was she really that convinced that he wouldn't run? Or only that certain that he'd never get away?

Brian had the briefcase all packed up and his back turned, and Abe knew he had to go for it if he was going to. Torn between the first door that led to the white corridor and his log-cabin room, and the original door that would lead him (he hoped) back to the ordinary hallway and maybe the parking lot, he chose the latter. He yanked on the door handle as hard as he could—and ran straight into the arms of one of the giant guards.

"There you are," Nita said, still smiling. "He's just going next door for now. I can take him from here. But we'll need you back here at eight tomorrow morning."

As he was being led back to his room, Abe stopped and looked at Nita. It was the first time he had been alone with her. Surely she couldn't be as hard-edged as she seemed.

He touched her on the arm, then grabbed her wrist. She stiffened, then relaxed when she saw that he meant no harm. Abe again scanned the room for any way out he hadn't found yet, and continued to not find it. His options were limited to violence and giving in. His eyes pleaded with Nita's, hoping to send the message as one of the meek to one of the clearly stronger, that he really was hoping to inherit his tiny share of the Earth just a bit sooner.

"Come on, Nita, please—you can't let them do this to me," he begged. "Please. Don't let them cut my head open. You have to help me."

"Oh for Pete's sake, Abe," she said. "Haven't you been paying any attention? I'm Bad Cop."

43

ABE TRIED TO COUNT the seconds, the minutes, anything to keep him from thinking about whatever it was that was lying ahead. He needed to form a plan, but what sort of plan could he possibly form when he was faced with such a widespread government monolith that had clearly been mapping out every step of his journey since they had forced him into the car so few days ago. Hours ago, really—though they had stretched into such a mass of time that it might as well have been months, years, even the century-plus they had told him to bridge. He couldn't have been more trapped if they had thrown him backwards through time and thrown away the key to getting forward again.

Though at least that would have kept him safe from the scalpel. He tried not to think about it all over again. Amazing how much effort it took not to think about something.

His only hope, if there was any, was to play their conflicting motives against one another. To try, somehow, to get them to keep infighting over what to do with him while he was still conscious and able to be done-with. So what did they want?

He crossed Dr. Lamb off the list immediately; he was clearly a charlatan and was probably already off the payroll and would never be heard of again. Or at least he would make himself scarce until the next subject came along for him to test another harebrained device on. So he was out.

Nita wanted whatever the government wanted, which in this case was a speedy conclusion. Was there a way to change what the Government wanted? Probably not in the next six to eight hours. Four hours? Ten? He knew he had until 8 a.m., but without any clocks, there was no way of knowing how soon that would be. Yet another in the long list of questions he realized he should have asked them, if he hadn't been so busy screaming. Though if he had the chance to do it all over again, he probably would have done the same things he did do, only possibly tried a little less hard to fail.

Ed wanted him alive, that much Abe knew. But Ed's voice had been effectively silenced. By Abe. No, Abe thought. By his project being boneheaded and stupid and my not playing along. So is it too late to play along? Abe mulled it over, feeling a glimmer of hope. What if he suddenly remembered all sorts of details? Gay romps through the woods with Joshua Speed, if they wanted, or pillow fights in the Oval Office with Mary Todd, even a torrid foot-fetishizing affair gone wrong with John Wilkes Booth... whatever it would take if it bought him some extra time.

But Abe had a feeling it wouldn't fly. Even if Ed believed it, and he might, by bringing in Dr. Lamb and his gimcrack Device he had by this point lost all credibility with the others. They couldn't have made it more clear. And besides that, they weren't interested in history. They were interested in biology, in genetics. Even if Abe turned up genuine memories, it would probably only increase their desire to find out which of Abe's neurons were firing abnormally in order to make it happen. Four score and seven tissue samples. There was no way a schlemiel like Ed could stop that train.

The fact was, they already were at cross-purposes with one another, and the end result was that the wrong side had won. If that was going to buy him any time, it had already done so—five to ten glorious moments of time, which he had wasted on making jokes about a pen.

The memory jolted Abe, nearly causing him to sit up in bed. The kid who came in with the pen in the first place— Brian. What was he here for? What did he want? What was in this project for him? Abe racked his brain. Brian was young, meaning this was a college internship, or maybe grad school, which meant his clock must be running too. He needed something to put on a resume, possibly to write a paper about, possibly something for a grade. Abe remembered the intern's subservient attitude toward Dr. Lamb, which never let up even while he was being treated with complete disrespect. How he ran to do his bidding like a puppy chasing a boomerang, all wasted energy and disappointment with everyone else in on the joke. Obviously he needed a recommendation, so he had to stay on Lamb's good side. But if he needed to write a report of his own, too... Abe thought back to his own college years, and the students who competed for high-powered internships, seeing them as stepping-stones toward higher-powered careers as soon as they left the university. Kids who would do anything to succeed if they thought it would get them a step higher up the ladder. It was possible that Brian was just such a student. After all, he was here—wherever "here" was. If he was willing and eager to play a part in the furthering of Science, thinking it would help in the furthering of himself, then maybe Abe would have no problem exploiting him.

And in the wee small hours of the morning, if anyone was staying up watching the video monitoring screens into Abe's "cabin", it would have to be Brian. However dedicated to research the others may have been, none of them would possibly be motivated enough to stay round the clock. Not when they had families, and cell phones. And especially not when they had an overeager intern on call.

Abe lay in the lumpy bed trying to formulate any kind of plan, but the soft crackling of the artificial woodstove kept distracting him. If only he could find a way to silence it, but the electric (or gas, or oil) element that ran it was far too cleverly hidden for him to discover, especially at nighttime. Or if only he could use it to—Wait. That was it.

He would just have to convince Brian (or whoever was watching the monitors, but it was bound to be Brian) that he was Abe Lincoln, that he was honest Abe and therefore could be trusted.

Abe began to toss and turn on the bed, moaning slightly. He kicked at the covers, doing his best not to overdo it. For a growing amount of time he feigned uncomfortable sleep, finally sitting up and bed and pulling at his hair. "Two days..." he murmured aloud, quiet enough to seem like a soliloquy, but hopefully loud enough to be picked up by whatever microphones might be hidden within the room. "Two days they have denied me tobacco!"

He walked to his desk and rifled through its contents, searching until his hands clasped around the pipe he remembered seeing from his first day. "And all the while they mock me with this," he said, doing his best to let his voice take on what he thought would be convincing 19th-century cadences. "Why provide the instrument if you do not provide the wherewithal to use it? This is torture!" This was good stuff! "Torture!" He repeated for good measure, and put his head in his arms on the desk.

He felt rather than heard the crack of the hidden door in the wall opening. Could it really be that simple? He looked up, thrilled to see Brian standing silhouetted in the door-frame, the now-darkened blank hallway behind him. He was still in the same clothes as he had worn earlier that evening, now far more rumpled-looking, and he looked tired, but there was something more in his eyes, too. He looked like he had won a prize—and Abe knew that that could only mean that he fully believed what he was seeing.

"Mr. Lincoln?" he asked, still hesitating. His voice was almost a whisper, deferential to the office of the man of the past as well as to the possibility of breaking whatever spell it was that somehow brought him back. Abe looked up, doing his best to assume a faraway look. Was this how he had looked that day at the press conference? At the time he didn't feel any different, only pissed off and hot under the lights, and then overtaken. Now he was totally putting on an act. Was it enough to give the kid what he wanted to see? Or was he running the risk of overdoing it?

"Yes, son?" he tried, going for it.

"You wanted something?" Brian asked.

Abe put the pipe down in front of him, lifeless on the desk, an unspoken message.

"You want to smoke? You need tobacco?" He talked as if communicating with a monkey, or with a very slow foreigner, all slow words and high inflections. What's that, Lassie? Timmy fell down the well? Smart one, that Brian.

Abe only nodded, a long-suffering smile he remembered from countless portraits displayed on his face.

"All right—okay, I don't know if... All right. Just hang on a second." Brian practically ran from the room, knocking over a coat stand in the journey. For a brief second Abe thought he would leave the door open, but he was mistaken. Brian might have been hapless, but he still followed the protocols. Several minutes went by, long enough for Abe to be convinced not only that Brian wasn't coming back, but that the next time the door opened Nita would be there with a tire iron there to help her explain why he shouldn't be talking to Brian again.

When he finally saw the lighted rectangle of the door magically appearing again, he couldn't help holding in his breath for a second, waiting to see who would be on the other side. But there was Brian, almost triumphantly holding an oddly decorated tin can.

"Here you go, Mr. President," he said, presenting the can to Abe as if it were an Academy Award, which frankly, at this point Abe deserved. With some effort, Abe popped it open. Inside were some extremely pungent flakes of what he could only assume was pipe tobacco, along with a smaller tin box holding sizeable number of white-tipped wooden matches. Jackpot.

Trying not to show his excitement, Abe looked up at Brian and smiled. To his dismay, Brian had settled himself on Abe's bed, watching his every move, fascinated. Abe was at a standstill. Did Lincoln even smoke? Abe had no idea. He supposed he must have, seeing as how the pipe was here in the first place, and how (just as he suspected) they actually did have some historically accurate tobacco and matches on-site for Brian to dig up. But Abe did know that he, Abe, had never smoked anything in his own life, especially not pipes, and he didn't have the first clue how to go about it. He had to get Brian out of there.

Then he realized that there was something more that he could take from Brian, and that Brian was in the perfect position to give him. He stood up, and sat next to the intern on the bed. He could hear the rope support system creaking in protest at their combined weight, as the homespun quilt puckered between them. He sat very close, and put his arms around him, in a way that used to be called manfully.

"Thank you, Joshua," he said, his grey eyes looking penetratingly into Brian's, "my bosom friend." He pulled him in close for a second embrace. Pulling back, he could almost read Brian's features making the mental calculation of how much it would be worth it to him to ace the internship, weighing whether the slam-dunk grade he would receive and the stellar peer-reviewed journal article he would certainly get would in any way counter the actual experience of whatever man-on-man 18th-century ex-President-on-intern sordidness that Abe was hinting at. And deciding that no, he would much rather settle for pretending that the interchange had never happened. He shot up from the bed so quickly it knocked Abe backwards, practically leaving skid marks on the floor in his haste to exit the room.

Alone again, with things finally beginning to look brighter, Abe chuckled. Whatever Lincoln's true relationship had been with Speed, it certainly was useful.

44

ABE DRESSED QUICKLY, FUMBLING with the still-unfamiliar armholes and fastenings. He hoped that Brian would take his time before returning to surveillance mode, or at least that he wouldn't notice that Abe had changed. For the millionth time, Abe triple-checked the inner pocket of his long jacket to ensure that the small cardboard rectangle was still tucked inside. He picked up his socks and shoes, put them down again, then remembering his late-night encounter with the corner of the wood stove, picked them up again and put them on. Then he picked up the jar of tobacco and matches, and headed to the desk.

Abe wondered whether he should bother filling the pipe with tobacco, and decided against it. He didn't know the first thing about how to smoke a pipe, let alone fill a pipe, and the room was dark enough that he hoped he could get away with mimicry. So he opened the tobacco can and pretended to put some in the pipe's bowl, tapping it down with his thumb. That seemed realistic enough to him. Then he reached for the law books and took down a few, as if preparing for a late-night study session. He took the kerosene lantern down off the wall shelf, though he was certain it was empty of fuel. A careful shake confirmed his guess. A second, more careful shake sent it flying across the room, smashing against the wall over the bed. He tried to look concerned about this, to make it seem as accidental as possible. But he knew his time was limited, and wasn't about to waste it play-acting in the dark.

He opened first one law book, then another, carrying them to the bed and creating a small paper village. He took the writing paper and wooden inkwell and dragged the chair over to the bedside. He picked up the basket of kindling and logs stacked ornamentally next to the fake stove and tossed all of it on the bed as well. Now he was ready.

The first match failed to ignite, and broke in half in the process. He tucked the broken pieces inside the nearest law tome, and reached for another. The second flared up instantly, with a strong phosphorous smell that reminded him of the Fourth of July. Fitting, he thought, as he dropped it into the box containing the other matches. The entire box caught light in seconds, and Abe wasted no time in scattering them over the contents of the bed. As he had hoped, the antique books and wood were not only incredibly historically valuable, they were also incredibly contemporaneously flammable. Carefully, so as not to accidentally snuff out the flames through overzealousness, Abe added other dry-looking things to the pile—the rickety chair, the burlap twine curtain tiebacks, and then the curtains themselves, the rag rug.

The history teacher in him was appalled at what he had done—what he was doing—at all the gorgeous, horrific waste. But the young boy that was also still inside him watched the flames rise and consume the pyramid of antiques, and could only think "Coool."

The response was slower than he thought it would be, though still came extremely quickly. A klaxon horn sounded, and a robotic voice echoed around the walls through a remarkably good sound system, calling "Fire! Please make your way to the nearest exit and await further instructions!" over and over again. Hidden electric lights illuminated the room. Best of all, far better than anything Abe had anticipated or even hoped, the wooden door to the cabin—the sealed wooden door that he assumed had been permanently nailed shut—popped open and an electronic "Exit" sign was projected over top of it.

Abe took a last glance around the cabin, now virtually unrecognizable as the wood walls were slowly consumed with flames. The smell was wonderful—there was nothing plastic in the room, nothing inorganic to interfere with the pure scent of fire doing what it does best. Almost as an afterthought on his way out the door, Abe took down the stovepipe hat from its nearby peg and tossed it into the flames. He was free.

Abe ran quickly through the cabin door and out into the woods. He would have loved to take the time to examine the trees, looking for roots or gathering leaves to see if they were real or not. But he knew that the fact that he had already made it so far without being apprehended was a small miracle, and he wasn't about to press his luck. He ran through clumps of trees, tripping over roots that were real enough to catch his toes (fortunately he had decided to put his shoes on after all), even if they were only fiberglass, and kicking up very real dirt. He scanned in all directions for the telltale red glow indicating that once again federal safety regulations had trumped verisimilitude. He caught sight of a distinctive red gleam in the middle distance and headed that way—sure enough, it slowly formed into the word "Exit," hovering over a well-disguised door. He threw his weight against it and it opened wide, out into the humid Florida night. The dirt underfoot gave way to asphalt, but here again Abe was incredibly lucky—there was still not a person in sight. Even better, the exit had taken him within a quick sprint of the parking lot—and because of the lateness of the hour there were very few cars to choose from.

None of the cars looked like an obvious choice—he scanned window after window looking for any sign of a crimson H—the dead giveaway to end all giveaways of a college decal. But no such luck. Fortunately, there were other ways to find what he was hoping for. He reached into his coat with a grin and pulled out the set of keys and cellphone he had lifted from Brian's pocket during their brief intimate embrace. A quick push on the keychain's button and a Volkswagen chirped into life at the other end of the lot. Abe ran for it, jumping into the car and starting the ignition just as the first people began making their way out of the various building exits. He could hear the distant sirens of fire engines on their way. Abe gunned the engine and zoomed out of the complex.

45

NORMA STARED INTO THE dregs of her wine glass, wondering whether it was worth hazarding another. She hadn't intended to be the designated driver, but after watching Shosha down two beers in short succession while she was still nursing her initial Chablis, she realized that someone was going to have to take it easy. Her plans for the evening, meanwhile, had gone down the hatch faster than Shosha's Coronas.

If Norma had to make a list of her favorite options for spending a weeknight, going out for drinks with her boss wouldn't even crack the top one hundred. In fact, she had studiously avoided it for years, ever since Shosha stopped just being her boss and began her campaign to become BFFs. It wasn't that there was anything wrong with Shosha; under different circumstances, the two of them might be—well, not friends, but certainly casual acquaintances. Neighbors who signed for each other's packages? Something friendly but low-impact.

It was just that Norma had learned the hard way that becoming close with your boss never worked out for the best for her. She was too easy to take advantage of, too greedy for approval. She wasn't a pushover; she knew how to say no and stick to it, but it always left her feeling guilty. Which led to something almost worse than being taken advantage of: offering up herself unnecessarily, just to be liked. The price she paid for skipping Shosha's birthday night out was a week's worth of extra shifts, all volunteered for by Norma without being asked, just at Shosha's hint that she could really use the time off. The time Norma said no to Shosha's "Girls Only Weekend" at some spa resort on Key West, she made up for it by offering to spend that weekend watching Butch, the largest and foulest-tempered tabby cat she had ever met, who "doesn't like to be alone." Butch proceeded to spend the weekend whetting his nails against Norma's vintage settee, while blunting them again on all her throw pillows. The coup de grace came at the end of the weekend, when Norma had finally successfully coerced the cat into his carrier for the trip back to Shosha's apartment, only to find that sometime during the past few days he had thrown up in her Jimmy Choos.

And yet, if she had to do it all differently, she knew, she still wouldn't have said yes to the weekend with Shosha and her friends. Even a peep-toe full of cat vomit seemed preferable to joining in with whatever Shosha did for fun, knowing that it would be followed by more invitations, photos of the pair out together all over SocialEyes with the sophomoric comments Shosha thought witty, and the pitying looks of her fellow perfume girls, who all had lives much better adapted to turning Shosha's social advances down. Despite everything, the truth was that Norma liked Shosha. And knowing her any better could only jeopardize that.

But the day Shosha walked in carrying that *Illusions* box, it all changed. She had to find a way to convince her boss that she would do anything, wear any costume, take any extra work on she had to, to get out of being trapped inside that golden dress and platinum wig every day. So: Operation Butter Up Shosha.

She'd brought the costume along with her inside her bag for backup. She decided she wasn't above putting the wig on backwards or otherwise messing it up to make it look less appealing on her and more like the mistake she knew it was. The problem was, Shosha didn't seem to need any help self-buttering. As soon as Norma brought up the subject of the costume mandate, Shosha stopped her cold. "I never talk about work outside of work," she said, downing her second bottle and waving toward the bartender for a third. "Plenty of time for that when the time clock's running. Outside of work is for being ourselves. Let's talk about you."

And that was that. All her well-laid plans, laid well to rest, and replaced by everything Norma was hoping to avoid. She tried to get the subject back on board by steering there through fashion, or celebrity gossip, but neither tactic worked. As soon as Norma as much as mentioned the costume, once even "accidentally" letting the wig begin to tumble out of her bag as she reached for something inside, Shosha just wiggled her index finger in a mock disapproving way, shook her head no, and changed the subject right back. It was no use.

"Hey, girl," Shosha said at last, as Norma wistfully reached for her car keys for the umpteenth time. "I think I'm drunk."

"Yeah, Shosha, I think so too," Norma sighed.

"'Sa funny word, drunk. Because I drunk... so much drink." Shosha curled in on herself in a fit of snorting giggles, nearly toppling out of her seat. Norma grabbed her arm to steady her, and left out some cash for the tab as she helped Shosha to her feet.

"No—no," she waved at the table. "It's on me." She made two failed attempts to get into her purse, then gave up. "I owe you," she slurred into Norma's ear, her breath hot and moist against the skin. "Don't forget."

Not for quite some time, Norma thought, but managed to keep herself from saying aloud.

"Say, Norma?" Shosha looked up, doing her best to maintain eye contact. "I think maybe I could use a ride home. Could you do that for a pal?"

"Sure thing, Shosha," Norma sighed.

It took some doing, but somehow she managed to maneuver Shosha into the back seat of her convertible, not expecting her to stay upright through the ride but praying she would at least maintain equilibrium. Butch's vomit had been enough. Shosha would just have to deal with her own car in the morning. Norma had the feeling it wouldn't be the first time.

Halfway home, Norma's boss was fast asleep in the back and snoring loudly. Norma could have kicked herself. Living the wild life again, she thought. Could this night have gone any worse?

Which is, of course, when her phone rang.

46

PLEASEPICKUPPLEASEPICKUPPLEASEPICKUP... JUST WHEN ABE thought the phone couldn't ring any more times, when he knew he was about to be shunted to a voice-answering system of some kind and certain recapture, he heard a click. And then a voice.

Her voice. A bit confused, and more breathy than he remembered, but definitely hers. "Hello?"

"Hi." Abe knew he needed to tell her his name, or what he needed, or beg for help, or anything, but her voice—that breathiness, the scent still lingering on the card... he felt like he was back in high school, trying to figure out how to ask a girl out. He didn't even know this woman. He had only seen her once. His *life* was at stake at this point, and he was so afraid he would blow it that he waited for her to talk first. Idiot.

"Hi." Norma waited. She knew from the voice on the other end that it wasn't a salesperson, that he wasn't reading from a card. Not at one in the morning. Plus, no one reading from a card said "Hi." And the long pause and the caught breath meant it was someone who had met her before, probably someone who liked her a lot. It felt a bit like when boys used to call her back in high school. She liked how that made her feel. It was a seductive feeling that made her toes curl a little. She let the pause linger, for him to say someone else. Maybe tonight would have a bright spot after all.

"Hi," he said again.

This was not Abe's finest hour.

Another, longer pause.

"Um—who is this?" she asked.

Abe knew without having to be told that she was going to hang up on him if he didn't say the next thing exactly right. He needed to be casual, not desperate. But he also needed to be commanding. She had to understand that he wouldn't take no for an answer. That she had to meet with him.

"This is Abe Finkelstein. We met the other day. You crashed into my car."

So much for the bright spot. She hung up.

Abe looked in all directions. There was no one coming. He was still safe. Roughly half an hour had passed since he had fled from the complex. He had tried going home, but a quick look down his block revealed an unfamiliar nondescript sedan parked across the street and another at the end of the block, both parked in front of the homes of neighbors who he personally knew would never have anything to do with nondescript sedans. If his home was unsafe, then he had to assume his school would be as well. There was next to no chance that the goon-types who had dogged all his previous steps were not already alerted to his disappearance, and therefore likely to arrive at any minute—especially if Brian's car had any sort of GPS. Abe ditched the car at the corner of the dueling McDonald's, left the keys in the ignition, and took off at a run, finally ending up in a new suburban division of identical mock Spanish Colonial villas. Each house unique from its neighbor in ways only the homeowners themselves could differentiate—begonias instead of geraniums, a garden gnome in favor of St. Francis, the grass a quarter inch longer in the front.

Abe didn't know how long he would have until the cellphone, too, was traced. He knew he could only afford another one, or possibly two, more phone calls. Was it really worth trying her again? He ran through everyone else he could think of that the FBI wouldn't have thought of already. His students. His old college roommates. The guy who used to walk his parents' dog, back when they would go to the Keys over the holidays—well, he would certainly be safe. There was no way the FBI would think of searching for him there. But there was also no way for Abe to reach him. He had no idea what his number was, or where he lived, or even his last name. Even his cell phone had had him listed under "B," for "Bob The Dogwalker." Besides, none of the people he could think of had Norma's—such an awful name for such a gorgeous woman—had her lips, her shape... her phone was ringing again please pick up please pick up...

"Hello?" It was her voice again, but less sultry this time, more edge to it. She knew it was him. "Do you have any idea what time it is?"

"No," Abe responded, honestly. He had no idea. "I'm sorry it's late. It's an emergency. You were the only person I could think to call. It's not about the car. Forget the car. I need to see you. Please. Please."

"Now?"

"Now. Please."

The third please won her over. Who says please three times? And he hadn't even asked it, not like begging, only a request, as if they had known each other for years. He had a gentle voice. Even more than the second please, though, was the "forget the car." Up till then, she had forgotten the car, had thought the whole thing had gone away, but in a sudden burst of understanding she realized that his insurance company wouldn't. There was no doubt the accident had been her fault, and if he hadn't forgotten about it, if it hadn't gone away—well in that case, if now he was suddenly telling her that he was willing to forget the car, she should definitely meet him to get it to stay gone away.

"Sure." She named a coffee place a couple of miles from where she lived. It was almost a twenty-minute drive from where Abe was hiding. "See you there?"

"I'd love to," Abe said, breathing out in relief for what seemed like the first time in hours. "But can you pick me up? I have no car."

No. Norma thought. There is no way I wrecked his car. The accident wasn't that bad. "I thought you said this wasn't about the car," she said, suspiciously. Her voice regained its hostile edge.

"It's not—it has nothing to do with my car. I have nothing to do with my car. Just pretend I have no car." He tried to hide any hint of exasperation, or desperation, or any other -peration he was feeling from his voice.

"Why would I go out with a guy who has no car?" Norma teased, immediately regretting she had asked it.

"Okay—just pretend I had a car, and you crashed into it and wrecked it, and I want you to pick me up and meet with me instead of calling your insurance—"

He could hear his words petering out into dead silence. Had she hung up on him again? Both of them weighed their options in the momentary standoff, both of them understanding that he needed her. Intrigue over what his reason could be kept the line tethered at her end.

"I thought you said," she finally said slowly, "this wasn't about your car."

"It's not about my car," he replied, just as slowly, his eyes still darting around him, looking for any passing vehicle that might look out of the ordinary—or in the case of Steve's car—very ordinary. "Except in the sense that I can't get to it right now, and you're the only person I could think to call to rescue me, and if you can't come pick me up soon, there might not be a me to pick up. I know that sounds nuts. I promise I can explain that part. And I only mentioned you hitting my car again because of the guilt factor. I won't do it again. I promise."

"You really do sound nuts," she said, but there was something about him that still kept her on the line. She tried remembering back to the day, the dress, the frenzied rush, the other driver... what was it about the other driver? There was something about him that had caught her attention at the time; she remembered having thought that. That he was unusual in some way? That he was dressed funny, maybe? Did he have an accent? No, of course not; she was talking to him now. He was tall, she remembered that. Very tall. And he had kind eyes. And she thought she had met him before.

And he was cute. That was it. Really tall and shy-guy cute.

"Okay," she said finally. "Tell me where you are, and I'll meet you there. But I'm going to need you to help me with something first."

He scanned the street signs and gave his best guess as to his neighborhood based on what he had seen on his dash from the McDonald's. Fortunately for him, the one landmark he had seen—a giant fiberglass cow in a matador outfit advertising some attraction—was one she recognized. That wasn't a given. In this town, giant fiberglass anythings tended to vanish in one's memory banks as quickly as they appeared, as lost to the eyes as a single neon sign in Las Vegas. A real cow would have had far more of a chance of drawing a crowd. She estimated it would take her about twenty minutes. Abe could feel the impending time stretched out in front of him like the achingly long line for a new rollercoaster snaking out in a twisting mile. His stomach clenched in a knot with a combination of nausea and excitement and fear. He didn't know how long it would be before they discovered he had escaped and wasn't hiding on the premises—didn't know whether there was already a tracer out on Brian's car, or on this cell phone...

"Look," he said, "You'd better not call me back. And if anybody calls you after this and asks about my calling you, tell them it was a wrong number. Even if—especially if they tell you they're from the government. Actually, especially if they tell you they're not from the government."

"What?"

"I'll explain later."

"I hope so. This is starting to sound really exciting. I'll see you soon."

"I can't wait." Abe said. "I mean, I really can't wait."

He really couldn't. He tucked and rolled under a nearby RV and prayed the roving sedan with tinted windows that approached and slowly passed by didn't see him.

47

NORMA COULD HAVE KICKED herself as she slid her convertible onto I-4, immediately caught up in an unexpected snarl of late-night tourist traffic. Why was she always allowing "cuteness" to be a factor when it came to making crucial decisions? She could see herself caught up in a bank holdup, asked to turn the gun on an innocent fellow hostage to allow the robbers to get away. Captured by the police, and asked to defend her actions, she would only be able to say of her abductor, "He was yummy."

It would never stand up in court. Not even if the robber in question looked like Michelangelo's David, though if that were the case, with enough women or gay men on the jury she could possibly get a less severe sentence. Especially if he wasn't wearing many clothes. But she knew it was a self-destructive tendency. She knew it verged on being completely irrational, that so many things counted for more than looks, especially when it came to making personal judgments that had nothing to do with dating. But time after time, from the moment her hormones first started to allow her to differentiate between the boys who ate paste and the ones who used it to better define their cowlicks, Norma had an unfortunate tendency to think with her pituitary gland.

So here she was, at one in the morning, on her way to rescue—did he say rescue?—a man she didn't know beyond the fact that she crashed into his car, all because he was tall, dark and cute. Not even handsome. Tall, dark, and handsome she could understand. Who wouldn't jump into their car at a moment's notice for tall, dark, and handsome? She didn't even know if the guy was single or not, though something in the way he spoke to her told her that he was.

And she still thought she knew him from somewhere, though she couldn't for the life of her figure out where. Had he dated one of her friends? She hoped not. Nothing soured the possibility of a new relationship like the knowledge that a guy wasn't good enough for one of your girlfriends. Especially since that girlfriend was inevitably going to tell you why. Or worse, tell everyone else why. Followed inevitably by, "But if she doesn't mind it..." with that half-pitying smile of smug superiority. Then again, going out with a man who had dated and dumped one of your friends was even worse, because the fact of his caddishness was bound to be discussed and rehashed over and over again, as a warning sign that you couldn't possibly want to waste your time on such an obvious bastard. And if the worst-case scenario followed—if he wasn't a bastard to you, only to your friend—well, that had never happened, but she imagined the aftermath of that would be appalling.

The traffic was much worse than the time of night warranted. The theme parks had all closed, and for all the after-hours attractions out there catering to the drinking-age set, Orlando was still predominantly a kiddie town. The cars were a mix of kamikaze drivers attempting greater and greater feats of creative cutoffs out of the idealized belief that all the cops were in bed, and overcautious types hoping that if they stayed just under the speed limit, no one would notice their failure to stay completely within their lane. Though she was in no hurry, Norma still tried to drive at a safe medium pace between careful and reckless.

The fast speed helped her focus. Thinking about how best to maneuver through the maze of barely licensed retirees and out-of-state looky-loos was far better than planning a romantic future with a man she hadn't even met other than to exchange insurance information.

Then again, daydreaming about a mystery man beat thinking about the concrete reality. Another night out drinking with Shosha would be the end of her. Her other girlfriends, her actual friends, were always there for her when she needed them, but they had all started pairing off, getting married and having babies and generally finding perpetual excuses to be unavailable. There was Stuart, the Frog Prince from the other night. He was a real winner. He had called a few times, all of which she had managed to just barely entirely avoid picking up. As in, she saw his name, thought about it, rolled her eyes, decided to let it go to voice mail, panicked that he was still better than nobody, changed her mind, made a last-second dive for the phone, and in the nick of time said "Hello" into the mouthpiece just as the screen said "Missed." And felt relieved at her rescue. And never called him back.

And besides Stuart, there was... who? No one, really. Her last few boyfriends had been one disaster after another—no sense in reliving past history. And sure, there were the usual number of men who chatted her up at the perfume counter "for their girlfriends," then slowly revealed that they didn't actually have girlfriends. Duh—guys with girlfriends talk to the counter girls, not the spray girls... the spray girls were there specifically to lasso in the unattached and otherwise unmoored. The loser types who could be flirted into making an unnecessary purchase, and who always gave her their cards. In other words, No, thank you.

But other than that, how did you meet people? How did anyone meet people? She used to ask her friends to fix her up with guys, but it almost always backfired. No matter how many times she told them not to, when asked enough times "What does she look like?" by prospective dates, they would always blurt out some hint of her Marilynity. So the guys would arrive prepped, and from then on everything was downhill if not doomed. They were either disappointed that she wasn't the blonde bombshell they were expecting, or that she wasn't interested in becoming just a little blonder, or just that she wasn't what they expected. She was too plump for some of them (well hell, Marilyn was full-figured, what did you expect?), and not plump enough for others (well, dammit, I look better in a size 6 and if I can diet my way into one I'm going to if it kills me). And then the less shallow ones had issues that she didn't particularly care about: the suicide vs. homicide thing, or the JFK thing, or whether she was a good actress or just a great performer. Rita Hayworth once said, "Men go to bed with *Gilda,* and wake up with me." It was the same thing for her, except they never made it as far as the bed. No one wanted her to be Norma. No one wanted her to be herself.

And the worst irony of it was, they all knew it was skin deep. They knew it was. They all apologized and fell all over themselves apologizing and tried to redeem themselves afterwards. Well, not all of them, but the good ones did. They recognized it, and tried to recover from the *faux pas,* and changed the conversation. Asked about her, about her job, her family, her dreams. Listened. Treated her like a date should. But it was too late for her. Because she would always know that they still saw her for who she wasn't, and always would. And that they would always know she could be that surface, if she only wanted to.

People only say "beauty is only skin deep" when they don't have it. Or when they want you to pretend it doesn't exist. But if you had a choice to make do with only the beauty within, or have that inner beauty and still get the beauty on the outside too, there isn't a person alive who wouldn't ask for the twofer. With any man who had looked forward to meeting her as a Marilyn, she could never, ever, ever feel wholly herself.

So maybe that was why she was rushing headlong (at 47 miles an hour) to meet a promising stranger. It was a rare and enticing opportunity to be a promising stranger herself. And it wasn't every day (let alone every middle of the night) you get called to take part in what was clearly an adventure.

And then there was that other matter, currently conked out in her back seat. She could definitely use help with that.

She nearly called off the adventure when she reached the development and saw what was waiting for her on the other end. She wasn't sure what she was expecting, but she was absolutely certain it hadn't been Abraham Lincoln.

48

NORMA KEPT HER CAR doors locked as she slowed to a halt beside Abe, rolling the passenger side window down just enough for conversation. It was too weird. She'd thought Abe had looked familiar, she'd had had a feeling she had known him somewhere before—it just never occurred to her that the first time she had seen him had been in her elementary school history books. No wonder she'd thought he seemed honest.

"You're that guy," she said, realizing who he was an instant later. "I saw you on the internet."

"Yeah, I guess it would be hard to pretend otherwise," Abe sighed, indicating his outfit. He wished he had taken off the long jacket back when he abandoned the car. He felt like a complete idiot.

"So you've gone full-on Lincoln now?" Norma asked.

"It wasn't my idea. I promise you—it was the absolute opposite of my idea."

Norma knew how he felt, having been thrust into the exact same situation only days before, thanks to Shosha. Speaking of which. "Okay. I'll give you a ride. But I need you to do me a favor first."

"Sure," Abe promised, trying not to show how impatient he was to get into the car and get the heck out of there. He knew that showing impatience now would send her off towards the horizon forever.

It must have worked. She popped the automatic door locks to let him in.

Abe slid into the passenger seat and shut the door behind him with a thunk. "So where are you headed?" he asked.

"Well, that's the thing," Norma answered. She gestured with her head toward the back seat.

Sprawled across the seats was the most strangely dressed little man he had ever seen, snoring peacefully. "Your boyfriend?" he asked

"What?" Norma looked bewildered. Then the penny dropped. "No, it's my boss. I need your help getting her home. She's had a bit to drink."

Abe snuck a second look. That the passed out passenger was female explained the outfit—all leather and metal and a pair of glossy boots tall enough to keep a pirate dry in a squall. But what role she was expecting him to play in whatever was going on here was beyond him. Was it some sort of kinky sex thing? After all he'd been through, he truly wasn't up to some sort of kinky sex thing.

He really hoped it was some sort of kinky sex thing.

Abe rolled down the window and hoped Norma wouldn't notice as he quickly threw his cellphone out the window. It bounced several times, then landed under someone's plumeria bushes. Good enough. "Let's go."

When it turned out that all Norma wanted help with was helping her inebriated boss into her house, up the steps and into bed, he felt a strange mixture of disappointment and relief. But at least it was easy work. Though her outfit probably added fifteen pounds to her weight, she barely came up to Abe's shoulders and it didn't take the two of them long to get her lying down and comfortable, once they got past the huge and malodorous cat that was perched just at the turn of the stairs.

Norma seemed to already be familiar with the beast. "Watch your ankles," she warned him, as they stepped carefully around the defiant tabby. "And your shoes."

As he was laying Shosha down, her eyes opened briefly, taking in Abe with a look of bewildered fear that quickly turned to mirth. "I know you!" she said in a friendly voice. "You're that guy! The one from the nickel!"

"Actually, that's Thomas Jefferson," Abe said gently, unable to just let it lie. "I'm the one from the penny."

"What do you know," Shosha mused, burying her head deeper into her pillow. "Thomas Jefferson." She relapsed into senseless snoring.

He almost wished he could be there when she woke up, just so he could hear about what exactly she thought she had dreamed.

49

S O WHERE ARE YOU headed?" Norma asked as they got back into her car, still unclear whether continuing on with him in was a good idea. She had watched him carefully throughout their time in Shosha's house, and he hadn't tried anything remotely funny. Well, except for the Jefferson joke. Which was sort of a hoot.

Abe shrugged as he slid into the passenger street. "Anywhere. Just drive. I'm assuming we can't go to your place?" he added hopefully.

Norma shot him a look.

"Right. Of course not. Anyplace, really. I'll explain as we go."

Norma was intrigued, but stayed quiet. She assumed that he would explain at some point. For now, she would sit back and enjoy the intrigue. While Abe's outfit was definitely off-putting, he still didn't strike her as being a creep. But where should they go? She headed out onto the highway, occasionally glancing at Abe's face for clues. He didn't seem to be sending any. She wasn't going to take him home with her, for obvious reasons. But at one in the morning, where could they go?

"So, seriously. Where do you want me to drop you?" she asked at last, hoping that by using that final phrase he would make it clearer exactly what sort of evening he had in mind.

"I don't know," Abe answered, noticing her turn of phrase. So she was only agreeing to serve as his taxi service, then? In that case, how could he make it a long trip? "I know this sounds ridiculous, but I may be being followed. It would take forever to explain. I just need to find a place I can lie low for a few days while I work out a plan."

A few days? This was worse than Norma thought. "I don't..." she stared, "I can't..." What was there to say? She was still driving vaguely east, still with no destination. "How low do you need to lie? Can't you just go out into the boondocks somewhere and hide?"

"If the people looking for me are as powerful as I think they are, they'll already be in the boondocks somehow. Besides, where am I going to hide?" Abe asked, thinking back to the interchange in her boss's home. "My face is on money."

He had a point, Norma thought. But still, where did he expect her to take him? "Maybe you'd better tell me the whole story."

And so he did.

They ended up pulling in to an all-night fast-food joint disguised to look like a fifties diner. Norma only looked slightly incongruous amidst the T-birds and mini-juke-boxes; even without the jacket, Abe looked like he had wandered onto the wrong movie set. Over stale coffee and a shared order of fries, Abe told Norma everything, from the first time he met Harold to the press conference, to the strange research facility and all the tests. He left out the part involving the rubber gloves. He had a pretty good idea of her limitations.

Norma was fascinated by his story, then horrified. She thought she had it bad as a Marilyn Monroe clone—it never occurred to her that being an anomaly that everyone knew existed could be other than a bad thing. Now it turned out there was something worse: being a unique clone who everyone wanted to know better.

Her own relative lack of private history suddenly seemed like a much more positive thing. No one cared all that much about the Marilyns. There were so many of them out there now, you could get away with being a private person. And the Norma Jeanes all had a certain degree of anonymity, at least with the majority of the population. But imagine if she had been the only one. And with Lincoln being known for wisdom and leadership and—well, and America itself—no wonder Abe was on the run. For all the times she had debated getting plastic surgery, it was never to look less like her forebear. She couldn't imagine having to consider going under the knife just to look more generic.

Not that it would work for him if he tried it. He was well over 6 feet tall. It would take more than a nose job to disguise his origins. That he managed it for so many years was astounding to Norma.

For Abe, the amazing thing wasn't the questions Norma asked, it was the ones she didn't. She was the first ordinary person he had met since coming out as a cloned president, and he was naturally expecting an onrush of all the questions he had been dreading, the ones which had kept him in the closet his entire life. But she didn't ask them, not any of them. It didn't seem like she didn't care, or wasn't interested—it was almost as if she already understood. Or maybe she didn't care and wasn't interested, but was just very very good at pretending with men. It would certainly go with her looks—really beautiful women often had a way of seeming to be whatever it was you wanted them to be, until suddenly they weren't. But he didn't think it was that. Whatever the reason, it was an unexpected relief. He had been through enough questioning already—enough to last his entire lifetime. For almost a full hour Abe felt like he did before the whole incident had begun; like a person, rather than a persona. Interesting for himself and not his DNA. It was a welcome reprieve.

It didn't last, of course. Abe had just finished recounting his role in the fire when the door of the diner opened and a couple of men in suits entered. There was nothing noticeable about them, except that it was Orlando, it was the middle of the night, and they were wearing suits. Maybe they were businessmen taking a late-night excursion from some convention, out on the hunt for non-room-service pie. But it was far more likely—and Abe was pleased to see that Norma seemed to share his apprehension—that they also didn't work for the government.

Before the men had the chance to spot them, they left cash on the table and made a run for it, two fives gazing up after them with Lincoln's honest visage as they made their escape out into the night.

Back in the car, Norma drove as fast as she could safely manage, away from the diner and back toward the highway. Had those two men been out looking for Abe? He seemed to think so as much as she did, but it was entirely possible they were mistaken—between the late hour and the cloak-and-dagger suspense of Abe's story, it was easy to see bad guys lurking in every dark corner, menace in every set of headlights reflected in her rear-view mirror.

"Were those the guys?" she finally asked.

"I've never seen them before," Abe admitted. "I guess I just panicked. But they could have been."

"They could have been," Norma agreed. "They looked suspicious to me."

"Really?" Abe asked. "I only thought they were suspicious because they looked so normal."

"I guess that's what I mean," Norma replied. "Normal doesn't make sense this late at night. If they were trying to look inconspicuous, they would have been wearing souvenir t-shirts and fanny packs—that's it!"

"Fanny packs?" Abe was confused. What was a fanny pack? It sounded vaguely unwholesome. He sort of hoped it was.

"No—I just had an idea. I know where we can go where you can lie low for a while. I just have to make a quick phone call."

"Don't tell them—"

"I won't tell them anything about you. I just need to get them to let us in."

Abe was thrilled by the word "us." That sure sounded like she meant she was planning to spend a bit more time with him. But he didn't want to force her to. "You can just drop me off if you'd like," he said. "There's no need for you to stick with me if you'd rather not. I'm already in your debt."

"What I'd rather doesn't really matter any more," Norma replied, matter-of-factly. "If those guys were the people looking for you, they're probably after me too by now."

"What makes you think that?" Abe asked.

"Abe," Norma sighed, "Mine was the only other car in the parking lot."

Abe's stomach knotted up, but his heart soared. She was stuck with him. No matter how much worse the morning might be, the night just kept getting better.

50

YOU KNOW, I'M REALLY not allowed to do this," Stuart said, swiping his key card through the slot at the wide double doors leading into an enclosed courtyard. They walked through the courtyard to a complex of identical concrete block buildings, staying tightly together as he led them to one disconcertingly topped with a fake thatched roof and several gables. It was like looking at a beautifully vanilla-frosted brick.

Stuart caught their perplexed glances. "In case anyone catches sight of it from the monorail. They can't see the bottoms of the buildings, but they might see the roofs. Can't ruin the overall mood by showing the staff bunkers... would kill the 'magic.'" He rolled his eyes. "Come on. I can't get caught with you. This is so against the rules it's not even funny. If they find out I let you in here I will be so fired. Even if they don't fire me they'll fine me who knows how much... or worse, make me wear a head."

Abe, unsure what to make of this as a form of punishment, started to ask a question, but Norma shut him up with a look. "I'll explain later," she whispered. They headed down a long corridor that Abe was surprised to see looked like—well, a high school. Scores of remarkably young people milled about, bulletin boards everywhere proclaimed tryouts and lost and found items, and down every hallway were mundane rooms with small chicken-wired windows that for all intents and purposes looked like classrooms, a cafeteria, possibly rehearsal studios. "What is this place?" He finally asked.

"Fantasy World Pre-Prep B," Stuart said with a shrug. "It's just a big break room. Come on, we don't have time to stare at people—they might stare back."

"But shouldn't they all be in school?"

"They're all in their twenties. Or older. They're just short. Mouse's orders. Cast members have to have an approach-ability factor—makes it easier for the kids to identify with them. That's code for a height restriction. You must be at least this tall to hug." He held his hand out at a low head height, posing like the cardboard characters at the front of ride lines. "They don't actually say it, but you can tell. We also think it keeps the costumes cheaper. Saves thousands of dollars on fabric." He looked up at Abe. "Guy like you would be instant gift shop. And even then, they'd probably make you stand in a trough or something."

Abe shook his head, but looking around he started to notice that no one seemed as young as he originally thought. Only smaller, and preternaturally cheerful. He assumed that was another corporate mandate. The three of them arrived at a pair of doors marked "Men" and "Women," each with a silhouette of an approximation of a mouse in simplistically gender-specific clothing. Stuart left them, heading into the men's locker room.

"Stay there." He explained. "I'll be out as soon as I can. Try to look inconspicuous." To Abe he added, "Slouch."

Within minutes he had returned, looking like an entirely different person. Where before he was a small, disturbingly froglike, but otherwise completely forgettable man, now he was... well, now he was a small, remarkably froglike, but unmistakably noticeable star. Norma had to admit she was impressed with the transformation. His shoulders bulked up to three times their normal size with padding, resplendent in a light green doublet and emerald tights, a gold crown perched on his head, and yes, that big gleaming chromed plastic sword, Stuart was without any question the quintessential Frog Prince. The greenish pancake makeup helped, of course, though she was dismayed to realize how little of it he actually needed. But there he was. Every inch a prince. Every inch a frog, too, but nobody's perfect.

Abe's reaction was a bit less complimentary. "You dated this guy?" He whispered incredulously.

"Shut up."

"Come on, come on!" Stuart hissed. "You guys are really lucky I had a spare costume in my locker. We're not supposed to. We're supposed to check them out individually and then check them back in at the end of the day. They keep track. Like library books, bar codes and everything. But I snuck out an extra for just in case. So you're really lucky. I couldn't have brought you down to the costume warehouse as easily as I could here. Not without an ID. Okay. Follow me. We have to be really fast."

The three of them took off at top speed. Well, two of them did. Abe and Norma were off, walking at a near sprint, and had cleared several yards before they realized that Stuart was no longer with them.

"Hey!" the prince half-barked, in as low a voice as he could without attracting attention from the other people still moving through the hallways. "*My* fast as possible, not *your* fast as possible... Frog, remember?"

He lifted a giant rubbery webbed foot and wiggled it at them exasperatingly, his eyes bugged out wide. Then he stomped after them and past them, as fast as his giant fake frog feet would carry him. The two of them followed close behind him, doing everything they could not to explode in laughter.

"Did he take you back to his pad?" Abe asked Norma as they headed through the next set of doors, just out of earshot.

"Shut up."

"Did you listen to hip hop?"

"Shut up."

"Did you touch his tadpole?"

"Oh, shut up."

Before she had time to say anything else, the last set of gates closed behind them and all three of them were in the Park.

51

NORMA WAS RIGHT—THIS WAS the perfect place to hide out. Hundreds of thousands of people coming through every week, dressed in all manner of souvenir clothing, plus all the staff workers in their own elaborate costumes. It didn't matter how conspicuous Abe looked here, not when there were hundreds of people in every direction who looked even more so. There were at least a thousand cars already in the parking lot, and that lot miles away. So even if whoever was following them could trace Norma's car, it would be a long time before that would lead them to her actual location.

Norma looked at Abe, and he looked back at her. Now what? He couldn't imagine asking her to ride the rides, and there was nothing he could think of needing in any of the shops. But they had to go somewhere. "Where should we..." he began.

Norma had clearly been thinking this through. "France," she answered.

Tucked away in a corner of the Park, a miniature version of the great capitals of the world was open for tourists. Abe and Norma settled in to a small café nestled at the base of a fake Eiffel Tower, and ordered more coffees (much fresher this time around) and a basket of croissants. If you had to run for your life, this was definitely the way to do it.

"How long do you think we can stay here?" Norma asked, brushing crumbs from her mouth delicately.

"Here here, or here Paris?" Abe asked back.

"Both, I guess. I can't figure out whether so far you've just been really lucky, or the people after you have been really clueless."

"I wish I knew," Abe said. "You seem to be taking this whole thing in stride."

"Not much choice," Norma responded. "Besides—yesterday I was facing another day in a soulless store, spritzing people with perfume they didn't want, and instead, here I am having café au lait in Paris with Abraham Lincoln." She giggled.

"Can't argue with that," Abe said. He raised his cup. "To la Proclamation Emancipatión," he said in his best French accent, which was pretty terrible.

Norma raised her cup to his with a clink. "Viva la President," she answered back, in her own idea of a French accent, which was worse.

"Is it my imagination," Norma asked quietly, "or are there suddenly a lot of people here who are overdressed for the occasion?"

"Well, we are in Paris, home of *la mode,*" Abe answered jauntily, then noticed what she meant. Heading toward them, though still far enough away that it could be a coincidence, were quite a number of nondescript men in sunglasses and suits. "Au revoir?" he whispered.

"Toot sweet," she whispered back. And they made another run.

THEIR NEXT DESTINATION WAS an inspired one on Norma's part, Abe had to admit. Standing in the Hall of Presidents, looking up at the full-sized replica of himself, surrounded by all the other American Presidents in an ersatz representation of Independence Hall, Abe felt all the old feelings of awe and resentment. But Norma had miscalculated—there didn't seem to be any backstage area in which to hide. Or rather, there was a backstage area, and they were in it. "Don't just stand there," Norma said. "Put your coat back on!"

"I don't have the coat anymore," Abe shot back. "I think I left it in your car somewhere."

"Then take his!" Norma responded, stripping the coat off the animatronic figure a lot more violently than Abe liked to see. He immediately made a mental note that if he were ever lucky enough to find himself in a similar situation with Norma, he would do all his own undressing. It seemed a minor miracle that she managed to remove the coat without snapping off either of the 16th President's arms. "Here," she said, thrusting the coat at Abe. "Put this on. The hat, too," she added as an afterthought.

"No hats," Abe replied weakly, still trying to hold firm on that one last principle, but the look she shot at him allowed no further protests. He put on the hat. Norma, meanwhile, was bodily removing the dummy of the former President and throwing it unmercifully into the wings.

Abe winced. "What are you doing?" he asked, bewildered.

"Just stand where he was—no, like this" She demonstrated, striking a Presidential pose. "We're running out of time!"

Sure enough, through the proscenium curtain Abe could hear the sounds of a crowd gathering in the outside seats. She wasn't really suggesting that he... that he... "What am I supposed to do?" he asked her.

Norma shot him another flabbergasted look, as if the answer should be obvious, to him of all people. "Who cares? Wave your arms a lot. Move your mouth when he speaks."

"But I haven't been here in years—I don't know what he's going to say—my mouth won't match!"

"Abe, you're a robot," Norma hissed. "It's not supposed to match."

"But what are you going to do? There's no place here to hide!" There truly wasn't—even in the semi-darkness, Abe could make out the animatronic Abe Lincoln's feet sticking out from where Norma had stashed him.

"Trust me," Norma said. "I know what I'm doing. Just shut your eyes a sec, okay?"

Abe had been given far weirder commands in the past few days, so it was no difficulty to simply obey. But it suddenly became much more difficult when he heard the unmistakable sounds of a woman undressing. What was she doing? Going into drag as Teddy Roosevelt?

"Okay, you can look," she called out. There was an odd catch in her voice, as if she were simultaneously proud and ashamed. Abe opened his eyes and took her in, from the platinum blonde waves to the flesh-colored sequined dress to the haunted echo of a distant past reflected in her large brown eyes—a look that he knew he shared, and he suddenly understood everything.

"Norma Jeane," he said, awestruck.

"Happy birthday, Mr. President," she replied. And just as the curtain started to rise, revealing them to the next round of theme park visitors, she hurled herself into John F. Kennedy's lap.

52

THE FIRST SHOW SEEMED to go okay. Luckily there was a spotlight that shone on every presidential figure just before he spoke, giving Abe a much needed cue to get ready to flail his arms around and move his lips. He was even familiar with most of the lines he had to mouth—the bulk of them were all taken from well-known speeches. Norma's role was trickier. She basically just froze solid and looked up at the robotic JFK with equally robotic-looking adoring eyes. When the spotlight first hit them, Abe was sure the gig was up. Instead, the crowd roared with approval. Sex appeal had been inserted into inappropriate places to sell tickets for so long, people simply took it for granted to find it here.

Abe wanted to run again as soon as the curtain fell. How long did she think they could keep this up? But together they decided that it was probably the safest place to hide for the time being—they could see everything, there were emergency exits behind them, and it did seem like the least likely place for anyone to look. And it didn't hurt that there was supposed to be an Abraham Lincoln standing right where he was, making it the least likely place in the Park for him to stand out. As for Marilyn—Norma, he corrected himself—she seemed to be making it work for her.

If he was attracted to her before, she dazzled him now. It all made sense. No wonder she looked familiar to him, like coming home. Her—no, Marilyn's—movies had been a regular staple on his mother's television while he was growing up. Abe flushed with guilt at making the exact same mistake he always condemned others for doing, mistaking the living person for the dead famous person. But this was somehow different. He felt certain that he knew her. For the first time in his life he understood why it was so important to everyone to know what was going on inside Abe Finkelstein. This went beyond the simple curiosity about celebrities that pushed tabloid sales into the billions. Looking at Norma, seeing Marilyn Monroe, Abe wanted to get inside her, to see how she ticked, how she felt, what it was like to be her. He also wanted to get inside her in other ways, but this was a family park.

In between shows, Abe did everything he could not to stare at Norma in her new incarnation. She politely kept her own gaze away from his, as if afraid to catch him in the act of false adoration. They didn't talk.

Norma was waiting for the inevitable questions. The evening and morning had gone so well—it might not have been a date, but she had begun to really, really like Abe and loved the Norma she was with him, a Norma whose back story didn't matter in the slightest because it was the same as his own. But once she saw him looking at her in full Marilyn mufti, everything seemed to change. He had the same hungry look that all men got when they found out her secret, and it was disheartening. She wished she hadn't changed into the *Illusions* gown. She could have left, gone a separate way, hidden elsewhere in the Park. But putting on the costume had seemed like the right thing to do—an easy disguise, and something more as well—a way to confess to Abe, to make up for knowing so much about him while revealing so little of herself. But it had clearly backfired. And now it seemed like he couldn't stop giving her that look, couldn't stop staring—not even when she met him with a challenging look back.

"What?" she finally demanded, daring him to say something about Sugar Kane, or Joe DiMaggio, or sleeping in the nude. What he said instead completely threw her for a loop.

"You might want to turn off your necklace."

"My... what?"

"Your necklace—it's blinking. I think you had better turn it off. It might give us away."

Norma reflexively reached toward her neck. What was he talking about? She removed the pendant and looked at it. Sure enough, the red stone, which she had assumed was garnet or cornelian, was actually some sort of bulb, and it was emitting a steady pulsing light. In a flash (literally), Norma realized what it was she held in her hand. Stuart hadn't been lying—she really must have dropped it when she got into her car.

It wasn't an earring, like Stuart thought.

And it wasn't a pendant, either.

It wasn't a piece of jewelry at all.

"It's an EMT," she said aloud.

"You're a paramedic?" Abe asked, confused.

"No—an EMT...an electronic merchandise tracer. With GPS. It must have fallen off the dress. That red gown you hit with your car. The drycleaners must have removed it when they fixed the tear. Lord's puts them on everything worth over a thousand dollars—it's to prevent shoplifting. They must have activated the tracer."

"Wait a second." Abe started out slowly. "Are you telling me... we're currently being chased for shoplifting?"

Norma looked away in apology. "It was a really great dress. And I took it back."

"*Shoplifting?!?*"

"I know, I know." Norma reached around the curtain and tossed the tracer into the empty seats. "We have to get out of here. If those people are from Lord and Taylor's, we'll have a lot more work losing them than if they were just the FBI. You should see what they do over knitwear."

Abe raised an eyebrow but didn't respond. There wasn't time. As he and Norma bolted toward the edge of the stage, they were met by several men in suits, pouring in from what seemed like every direction. There wasn't time to think or to react. There was only time to flail. Grabbing the first weapon to come to hand (and which turned out in retrospect to be the arm of Richard Nixon), Abe flailed away, knocking down two men at once and giving a third one a nasty uppercut with the edge of Nixon's fist. Norma, meanwhile, had incapacitated two of her pursuers by shoving over William Howard Taft, crushing them beneath his vast form. As Abe continued to fend off the two remaining agents (FBI? CIA? Mall security?), Norma headed for the back exit, only to be stopped in her tracks by a giant of a man in a suit, standing in wait with his arms outstretched, as if ready to scoop her up. There was no way around him. She was trapped.

Norma reached down into her purse and pulled out the only weapon she could wield with any sort of accuracy. She aimed straight for his eyes and pushed the trigger. "Would you like to try *Illusions?*" she cooed, pushing him out of the way as the perfume shot into his eyes and nasal passages, making him wince with pain. She'd wanted to do that for years. It felt even better than she had imagined. Yelling for Abe to follow, Norma took off around the corner as fast as Marilyn's stilettos would carry her.

53

ABE AND NORMA RAN down the back alley that separated the hall of Presidents from the rest of the simulated old-American Towne Square, not daring to look behind them to have their worst fears confirmed. Wrapping his fingers around Norma's tiny hand (he was holding her hand!), Abe gave a tug that was a bit stronger than he had intended (he was breaking her arm!) and almost on instinct headed around the corner to a fence marked "Cast Members Only."

They ducked around the fence to find a selection of doors, one clearly heading out to the parking lot, one into a cinder-block building with an anomalous Alpine gabled roof, and the third one just leading... down. Not having a car handy, and not being Swiss, Abe took a mental leap of faith and headed toward the third door. They ran down a flight of steps, and then another, which finally spilled them out into a long corridor, lined by visible concrete blocks and lit by vaguely bluish fluorescent lighting that hummed faintly. The bottom half of the walls were painted a bright blue color, the ceilings were lined with heavy industrial pipes and ductwork. Just before Abe and Norma shut the door behind them with a slow thud, they could hear the sounds of at least two sets of feet echoing off the stair treads overhead at a rapid pace. The corridor stretched out in both directions for longer than they could see, with occasional hallways branching out on either side. The effect was somewhat like being in an undersized, unfinished airport, or possibly a vast anthill whose occupants had almost but not quite mastered the art of masonry. There were no people in sight, but every few hundred feet there were abandoned battery-powered vehicles, golf-carts, bright yellow utility trucks, and herds of two-wheeled Segway scooters.

"Which way?" Norma asked, out of breath. Without a coin to flip or enough time to get past "meenie," Abe took a wild guess at what seemed to be the longer tunnel with the most branches and pointed—making the gesture with Richard Millhouse Nixon's disembodied arm, which Abe still clutched tightly in his hand, gesturing elegantly in its striped grey flannel sleeve. Norma grimaced and headed in the indicated direction. They had run what seemed like the length of a city block, when a distinct echoing sound reached their ears—the noise footsteps make when they travel in groups greater than two. But because of the echo, it was impossible for them to tell from which direction the feet were coming.

"Which way now?" Norma asked again, as Abe tried to figure out which way the steps were headed based on the reverberations.

He looked at her, admitting defeat. "No idea. You pick."

Norma shrugged. Then she reached over and plucked the robotic arm out of Abe's grasp. She looked in both directions, then ahead. There were two more intersecting paths in the near distance, not quite plumb enough to be an intersection. Running to where the four tunnels met the closest, she closed her eyes, pointed the arm out, and spun. Abe wanted to tell her they didn't have time to play games, but the way Norma's dress clung to her with her every movement, all Abe could think was don't stare... *don't stare...*

don't stare... as he stared without hesitation. Fortunately this was one of the rare times when he actually kept his mouth shut.

Norma stopped spinning as abruptly as she started, the arm pointing imprecisely toward one of the paths. "This way," she said assertively. Her reasoning being as good as anything he could have come up with, Abe followed without a second thought. When had Richard Nixon ever steered anyone wrong? Okay, maybe that wasn't the right question. But then again, if her choice worked out, maybe she would do that breathtaking spin again.

The corridor was almost identical to the one they had left, with the same abandoned industrial vibe reminiscent of a Soviet orphanage—visible concrete block walls barely covered with off-white paint in a shade that looked like it was probably dingy even in the can. But the cheerful blue strip lining the walls had at some point switched to a garish dark green. The fluorescent lighting did its best to erase any lingering cheer. The only reminder of where they were came from brightly-tinted images of smiling animals in bizarre combinations of period clothing which occasionally decorated a seemingly randomly placed door or staircase, each character holding a sign labeled with chains of initials which meant nothing to either Abe or Norma. The sounds of footsteps kept coming, still with no indication from which direction, but almost certainly closer than before.

"They're right behind us!" Norma cried, grabbing at Abe's arm.

"Are you sure? I think they might be in front of us."

They were both right. Four men appeared in the distance, running down the hallway from both directions, headed straight for them. They were also in excellent running condition.

There were no golf carts in this section of the tunnels. But there were plenty of Segways. Norma jumped on one.

"What are you doing?" Abe croaked.

Norma rolled her eyes. "What does it look like? Either get your own or grab on!" She pushed a button and the scooter hummed to life. Abe looked at the scooters, then looked at Norma. He grabbed on. Nothing.

"You have to lean forward."

He leaned forward, slightly, trying not to push his body too much against hers. They moved a little.

"Lean forward—harder!" Norma commanded, her own body draped forward across the handlebars as far as she could to counterbalance his upright frame. He rested his weight against her. They shot forward. She smelled incredible.

"Oof! Not so hard!" she gasped, and they chugged forwards at a much slower speed than either had anticipated. The two agents behind them were still behind them, but not by much. The two other agents were straight ahead of them, still running at top speed. There was another hallway branching off a few feet away, but no way to guess who would get there first.

They reached the corridor almost simultaneously, the men reaching arms out to grab at Norma. Abe swung the Nixon arm in response, aiming high. The arm connected with a soft thunk. The man staggered, then grabbed the arm and pulled it towards him, knocking Abe off the scooter. Abe fell and rolled, his horizontal body doing much more damage than his vertical one ever did. Both men lay sprawling on the floor, all three struggling to get upright first. Norma sped back, reaching an arm down and grabbing Abe by the collar.

"Hey!" he yelled, but it was enough leverage to get him up and onto the scooter behind her again. They rolled off just as the other two agents reached their fallen comrades.

They had reached a more populated part of the tunnels. Norma steered past a pair of cowgirls and a six foot tall man in a tiger suit without a head.

"Are you sure this is any faster than just running?" Abe asked, as they rounded another turn at a molasses pace.

"It's faster than us running," Norma said. "I don't know if it's faster than them running."

Apparently the agents didn't know either. Looking back over his shoulder, Abe saw all four of them now on Segways themselves, and beginning to catch up.

"Go faster!" Abe said. "Hit the gas!"

"There is no gas!" Norma yelled back. "I don't think it goes any faster—try and lean forward more, okay?" Abe leaned forward more, his body pressed closer to Norma's. It worked—they were moving a bit faster. A horn beeped, and a giant bear in a flowered hat and a tutu drove past in a golf cart, nearly tipping them over.

"Watch where you're going, assholes!" the bear yelled back at them. Norma and Abe heard a squealing of tires and a burst of more honking as the golf cart reached the group of pursuing agents. They heard a crash and a yell as the bear collided with at least two of the agents. Then the louder crash of several Segways smashing into each other and the concrete walls. Abe looked over his shoulder. Only two pursuers were left.

Abe leaned as far forward as he can, his frame pushing against Norma in a way that seemed barely legal. But it wasn't enough—they might as well be horizontal, it wouldn't add any more momentum.

"Throw that stupid arm away," Norma hissed. "You're poking me."

"I don't have the—oh, right." Abe responded, straightening his body away from hers as much as he could without reducing their velocity. "I um, got rid of it. The arm. Sorry."

She caught the embarrassment in his voice, and decided she really didn't want to know. Not now, anyhow. "You need to lean more—they're gaining again!"

"How'd you learn how to drive this thing, anyway?" Abe asked, doing his best to lean forward more with the upper half of his body while still leaving his lower half aimed backwards.

"Really bad date," Norma answered.

Her tone made it clear he shouldn't ask any more questions. So did the corridor, which was about thirty feet away from a dead end. This was it. They dismounted the Segway without a word. It wasn't that there were no more turnoffs they could take (though there weren't). It wasn't that there was just a lone stairway heading up, leaving them with no other options besides heading straight back toward certain capture (though there was). It wasn't that they only had seconds to make a run for it before the men in suits caught up to them (though they were rapidly closing in). It was the big illustrated character waving at them from the entrance to the stairway. With the unmistakable caricatured face of Abraham Lincoln.

They had no choice. They went up.

The stairs led to another cinderblock hallway, but this time one that looked familiar to Abe. He was not surprised when the two of them ran through the first unmarked doorway to find themselves in a large storage room with a galley kitchen along one wall, a pair of restrooms with male and female mice waving from their doors, and an abandoned souvenir stovepipe hat.

"I know this place," Abe said. "We're at the exhibition."

Norma followed him through the swinging doors into the museum-like hall. It was deserted, the lights out except for the glow of the exit signs, the animatronics stilled. Either history wasn't he draw they had hoped it would be, or the powers that be had decided that the best way to increase attendance was to limit the hours it was open. Stepping into the darkened room, suddenly surrounded by the slanting shadows of at least a dozen robotic versions of himself, Abe shuddered. The darkened stillness of the Hall of Presidents had been fun, but there had been only one Abe. Seeing himself reflected back at himself in so many different ages and poses—including the famous deathbed scene—was like stepping into a funhouse. It gave him the creeps.

But it also gave him an idea. "I think we need to split up. If they're after me, no one will follow you if they see you leaving here alone. And if they're after you, you can take them back to the store and just give them back the dress, right? They won't do anything to you if you can prove it was never stolen, right?"

Norma wasn't so sure. Tampering with the electronic monitoring device was a punishable offense all by itself, even if she hadn't done it on purpose. But Shosha would vouch for her honesty. All those years of not stealing from the company might finally pay off. And if all else failed, she could keep the Marilyn costume on. She felt powerful in it—like she could get away with anything.

"What are you going to do?" she asked.

"Hide out for now," Abe said. "I think I have the anima-tronic thing down, thanks to you." He smiled. "For now I'm just going to go back to the old homestead." He gestured toward the model log cabin. "With all the other Lincolns here to inspect, maybe it won't occur to them. If you get out—*when* you get out—" Abe corrected himself quickly, "I need you to do me a favor."

He took her through his plan, was pleased to find she thought it might work, and said goodbye. Norma wished him luck.

"Be safe," she said.

"You too." And then

ABRAHAM LINCOLN

Finkelstein

AND

Norma Jeane

MARILYN MONROE

Greenberg

GOT IT ON (!!!)

Abe leaned back against the fake cabin, looking up at the stars and stripes painted on the ceiling, triumphant. He could feel his heart pounding through him as though it would burst out of his skin. It was incredible, it was delicious, he was the greatest man in the universe having the most profound life-altering mind rush ever experienced.

Norma had had better.

54

ABE DECIDED TO SPEND the rest of the night in the small mockup of Lincoln's boyhood log cabin. After his similar quarters at the complex, this was less difficult than he otherwise might have found it. The space inside was just large enough for him to stretch out without any parts of him poking out the doorway. There was no furniture—just what turned out to be some trompe l'oeil paintings on the far wall that gave the suggestion of comfortable rustic furnishings. It was a good hiding place for a few hours, Abe thought, but it would be an even better trap. If they didn't know he was here already, he could do with some sleep. If they did, his options were limited anyhow. With no car, no phone, and no money—why hadn't he thought to ask Norma for some money?—all he had was the plan he had laid out for Norma. If she could manage to pull it off...

Abe slept fitfully, shooting awake at every sound. But the pursuing footsteps he dreaded never materialized. As the red dawn light began to filter in through the transom windows of the exhibition hall, Abe stretched and rose. He washed as best he could in the nearest bathroom, pausing with shock at his reflection in the mirror—so much more haggard than he was used to seeing himself, and at the same time (because of that fatigue and the three days' growth of stubble around his face) so much more like Abraham

Lincoln than he had ever seen himself. It felt like looking at yet another old portrait—him but not him, at the same time. Only in this case, the portrait mirrored his movements. It was like seeing a ghost. He stuck his tongue out at the image, only to see President Lincoln razzing him back. Very, very weird. When he got out of here, the first thing he would do would be to dye his hair, or get something pierced, or at least start wearing more leather or Hawaiian shirts. Or all of the above. Anything to keep from having that visceral reaction again.

If he got out of here.

Abe wandered back out and through the exhibit, trying not to stop and actually read all of the display placards he couldn't see the last time he had been here. He wasn't sure how much time he had, but he was reasonably sure it wasn't much longer. He wondered where Norma was right then, what she was doing. Whether she made the phone call he suggested, or whether she went right to bed, then woke up and called the cops on him. He thought they connected. There was that amazing kiss. But Marilyn was always an impressive actress.

Whoa. Abe stopped himself. He couldn't believe the line of thought he was pursuing. If anyone had no right to compare a person to some past ancestor, it was him. Norma had no more inherent artifice than he had inherent integrity. He hated himself for making the assumption, and knew she would never forgive him for it, if she knew. But at the same time, she, more than anyone else he knew, would understand. He wondered for the millionth time in his life what it would be like to have an identity that didn't come with so much baggage. To just be yourself. Life would certainly be easier.

Abe took another tour around the exhibit, looking for something heavy. It wasn't as easy as he thought it would be. Most of the larger solid props were made of fiberglass or even cleverly painted cardboard. But there in the "Boyhood" diorama was a long-handled coal shovel (complete with basic arithmetic homework scrawled on the back) that looked as though it would do the trick. He hefted the shovel and headed toward the center of the hall.

So little real time had passed since the last time he had stood before this case, looking at President Lincoln's rough draft of the Emancipation Proclamation. But he barely recognized the person he was then. The scenes—even his outfit—were almost identical. Yet so much had changed in the interim. He remembered looking at the document with a feeling of connection, and of desire. He had wanted to smash the glass and take it up in his hands, and run away with it. Well, here was his chance. Funny how it wasn't what he wanted any more.

He put the shovel down and ran his fingers over the glass vitrine. If there was any way to do this without breaking anything, so much the better. He didn't see a lock anywhere— could they really have been so trusting, or so uncaring, as to not protect the Proclamation's safety? He tried lifting the top, or sliding the sides of the case—no luck. There was no lock because it had been fashioned to be solid. It was probably hermetically sealed to keep any particulates in the air from damaging the antique paper. Well, so much for that. Abe lifted up the shovel and closed his eyes. Wincing, he carefully brought the shovel down upon the glass.

Too carefully. The blade glanced off the top of the case and rebounded, striking Abe above the eye. An alarm began to sound from speakers all around the ceiling. The thing was protected, all right. He took a deep breath and struck the case with the shovel with all his strength. The glass barely cracked, but it was a start. Over and over, Abe pummeled the top of the case with the shovel, until he was finally able to break a sizable enough hole to reach a hand in. The cacophony of the alarm system was joined by the wailing of approaching sirens as Abe emancipated the Proclamation from the case.

Still grasping the now-battered shovel, Abe slowly made his way to the far end of the room, climbed past the mock proscenium wrapped in red white and blue bunting and up over the twin American flags into the balcony of the Presidential Box of Ford's Theater. Abe felt something soft brush against his hand and bounce down into the box as he flung himself over the flag-draped railing and into the nearest seat. He leaned down to retrieve it: Lincoln's stovepipe hat.

What the hell, Abe thought. He placed it carefully on his head.

55

A BE HID IN THE shadows behind the curtains of the box, looking down at the exhibition hall below. There was no way out from here except back the way he came. There was a door in the rear of the box, in the exact location of the famous door through which the actor John Wilkes Booth appeared to shoot the 16th president during the fateful performance of *Our American Cousin*, the policeman guarding the door having gone out for a drink. But in this mocked-up version the door led nowhere, only for show. Not that Abe was going anywhere. But it was a comfort to know he couldn't be ambushed from behind.

The alarms were shrieking at a level that made thinking impossible, and the faraway sirens grew louder and nearer. Abe felt his heart start to beat at an erratic pace. Did sirens mean ordinary cops, or would they come accompanied by whatever government goons had been after him in the first place? Were all those well-dressed men after them yesterday—there must have a dozen of them, all told—really just after them because of some stolen dress? Was that possible? How much actual danger was he in?

And if he was in real danger of losing his life, if the stakes were that high, then even if Norma did follow through, would his plan even work? He felt something crush within his hand and looked down at the now crumpled, priceless document he had wrested out of its case. Without realizing it, without thinking at all, he had practically crushed the papers into a ball. It was bad enough he had really done this, taken Lincoln's rough draft. But to not even have the reverence to treat it as carefully as he did a library book? It was like realizing he had just taken a leak in Duchamp's urinal. Blushing with embarrassment so pure it felt like pain, Abe sat down in Lincoln's chair and began smoothing out the creases on the page against his knees. At such an immediate close range it caused actual goose bumps to rise on his skin. He was holding the same piece of paper first held by Abraham Lincoln.

He traced the words with his fingers, pausing with his eyes closed as his fingertips delineated the words "I Abraham Lincoln, do hereby proclaim." Words leaped off the page to his attention: "An act to suppress insurrection," the word "abolition" crossed out and altered to "abolishment." He caressed the words the way he would a woman's skin. Such a beautiful piece of writing, both in how it looked and in what it stood for, the words coming straight from Lincoln's heart and emended by his brains with the purpose of ending real suffering. These were the words about which Lincoln later said, *"I never, in my life, felt more certain that I was doing right, than I do in signing this paper."* This was real; this was a real, genuine piece of history. And unless things somehow changed for the better for him, and soon, Abe was going to destroy it.

The sirens ceased and the lights in the exhibit came up to full power at the same time. He heard doors slamming, feet running. Not too many of them, maybe a couple dozen. Then a combination of police uniforms and dark security guard suits rushed in from all doors, many with guns already out and ready. No one saw him at first, sitting peacefully in his eyrie looking over the entire space. Their ordered ranks dissolved into chaotic searching as they spread out through the labyrinthine displays. In their quest to find him they paid little regard to the exhibits, pushing down explanatory dividing walls to get a clearer line of vision, and knocking over the animatronic figure of an eight-year-old Abraham who then gesticulated wildly on the floor. Abe sat quietly, waiting. He practiced the stillness he had learned from the Hall of Presidents. Maybe they take him for a mannequin and assume he'd left the building. Maybe he could still get away.

"Hi, Abe." Abe heard the familiar voice before he saw the familiar figure. Ed stepped out from behind a mock theater curtain. "Nice hat."

"Thanks," Abe said. Something seemed different about Ed in the morning light. He seemed smaller, somehow. Diminished. It took Abe a minute to figure out what was missing: Nita. Ed wasn't alone. The two burly bodyguards from the complex had accompanied him, bulging with extra lumps in all the places you didn't want to see lumps. But without Nita's quietly targeted menace at his side, Ed just seemed like a nerdy professorial guy in an expensive suit. This man had caused him two days of trepidation? Abe looked over his shoulder at the sealed door behind him, half expecting to see Nita's cocked eyebrow leading the charge from behind, but she didn't appear.

"These other agents, they're all here because of the alarms. Someone here must have tried to steal something. Something valuable, judging from the numbers. Know anything about that?"

"Maybe," Abe said. "Maybe not."

"Well, they'll arrest you if you do. Or you could just come with me."

"And get my brain sliced up? I think I'd rather take my chances with them."

"There he is!" a man shouted and a trio of cops rushed over to where Ed was standing. They stopped, seeing Abe in his full Lincoln regalia. They hadn't expected to be facing an escapee from the Hall of Presidents. Was he even human, or just a particularly good robot? One gave a low whistle. Three guns rose, pointing at Abe's chest.

"Come on down, now," one of them said. "Put your hands up."

"Don't come any closer!" Abe said. He held up the wrinkled document, trying to make it look both incredibly precious and incredibly fragile. "I've got the Emancipation Proclamation. The original. If any of you take one more step closer, I'll destroy it!"

No one moved.

"No you won't, Abe," Ed said. "I know how much those pieces of paper probably mean to you. I know you know how much they mean to America. You couldn't do it if you tried."

"I can, and I will. I'll tear it up! I'll tear it into shreds and then I'll... I'll eat them!"

"Fine," Ed said. "Do it. Go for it." He slowly, deliberately took a step closer, the two armed bodyguards following immediately behind.

"Don't make me do this!" Abe yelled, desperately hoping they wouldn't continue to call his bluff. He thought he could do it. He had been steeling himself to the possibility that he might have to do it, that had been his plan from the time he and Norma first opened the door and found themselves within the exhibition hall. But if push looked likely to come to shove, did he honestly have it in himself to rip up such a fundamental piece of history?

The guards took another step forward, toward the box. They were only a few steps away from being able to climb right up next to him. Time was running out. Ed lifted his hands like he was holding an imaginary knife and fork and began making eating gestures, daring him to do it.

"This isn't just some copy!" Abe yelled down. "I'm not faking it! This is the real thing!"

"We know, Abe. To be honest, we're willing to lose it. We'd rather not. We'd rather end this amicably and put those papers back safely. But honestly, Abe? Let's say you do destroy it. So what?"

"So... what?" Abe couldn't believe his ears.

"So what?" Ed repeated. "You don't think we can recreate that in just a few hours? No one would ever know we'd done it. Archival paper, original inks... Lincoln himself wouldn't know the difference. This day and age, we could probably just Photoshop the fucker onto manila paper from Staples and brown it over the toaster a little and most people wouldn't even notice. What's the big deal? It's just paper."

"It's not just paper. It's history! It's priceless! Surely you don't..."

Ed gave a sharp little laugh. "What makes you so sure that's the real thing?"

"I... it's... it isn't?"

"It might be," Ed responded. "Or it could just be a perfect replica made specially for this tour, for insurance purposes. You do know the dinosaur bones you see in museums aren't the real thing? They'd be too heavy to stand. Nineteenth century paper and ink can't stand up to so much light and movement—you really think they'd put something that valuable here?" Ed gestured around, his arm sweep taking in both the museum-quality relics and the theme-park kitsch.

Abe stared at the document. It was real, he knew it was. It had to be. And yet, if it were a copy... He didn't know what to think. "You're bluffing," he called down. "It's real and you know it is. Otherwise you'd have come up here and grabbed me by now." He pinched the top of the pages tightly between his fingers and thumb, daring himself to start shredding. A tiny rip appeared at the margin, its jagged outline cutting into Abe sharper than any papercut.

"We told you, Abe," Ed said, "We'd rather not do anything to damage that document. But if the only thing stopping us from getting you down is you eating that piece of paper, go for it. Bon appétit. It doesn't matter."

"The Emancipation Proclamation doesn't matter!"

Ed sighed. "Of course it matters. But your tearing up and swallowing that draft doesn't stop Lincoln from having written it, doesn't stop it from having been rewritten and proclaimed and passed into law and actually emancipating a few slaves. Hell, the real copy went up in flames in Chicago in 1871. Everything about that document that *matters*," he took his time on the word, looking Abe right in the eye, "is already done and gone. You're just holding a souvenir. And souvenirs," Ed took another step forward, "can always be replaced."

Abe felt his grip loosening on the papers, felt them slipping from his grasp. He still had the beaten up coal shovel, but they all had guns. What would be the point?

"Come on down, Abe," Ed said. "We just want to talk with you a little more."

Abe took his time climbing down. Three agents immediately ran to retrieve the papers he had left behind. They had been bluffing. Of course.

"You're under arrest," one of the nearest cops began. "You have the right to…" A crash of doors opening from all sides and suddenly the room was filled with people pouring in, tall men in dark suits and string ties and stovepipe hats, and curvy women with platinum blonde locks and all manner of seductive evening wear. From wall to wall, everywhere you looked were Abraham Lincolns and Marilyn Monroes. Norma had come through.

Before anyone could see what was happening, Abe was surrounded and escorted away from his captors in an undulating wave of Lincolns. The cops pointed their weapons in all directions, bewildered. Abe could hear crashing and thumping as the gathering quickly descended to a melee.

56

FINKELSTEIN—OVER HERE!" IT WAS Harold. The last time Abe saw him he had hoped to never run into him again. Heck, the first time he had run into him he felt the same way. But now he could have hugged him. Abe ducked around a pair of Lincolns and followed Harold's lead into the kitchens.

"Fancy meeting you here."

"Norma called you?" Abe asked.

"Well, I didn't just decide to show up because I heard there was an Abe Lincoln flash mob," Harold riposted. "She's something else."

"Is she here?" Abe asked, holding his breath. He hadn't seen her, but then again, with that rushing wave of Marilyns washing over the room, he also didn't *not* see her.

"Out front. In the parking lot. You'd better skedaddle. I brought you something." Harold thrust something into Abe's hands.

Abe looked at it. "A Yankees cap?"

"Best I could do. You'll blend in better than you will wearing that thing."

Abe sheepishly removed the stovepipe hat.

"Looks good on you," Harold said.

"So I gathered." Abe handed the hat to Harold and put on the cap. He felt ridiculous, but looking at the sea of stovepipe hats through the kitchen porthole windows he figured Harold had a point.

"Probably want to lose the tie, too," Harold said.

"With pleasure." Abe removed it, feeling as if a noose was being lifted. "Thanks."

"Get out of here," Harold answered. "You make it out, you can buy me lunch. If not, maybe we'll get adjoining cells." Abe made a move to the back door, but Harold shook his head no. "I just came in that way. Couple guys are watching that one. Front way's better." Abe looked at him, panicking again. He had to go back through the crowd of armed searchers? "Don't worry. I'll create a distraction."

Harold put the stovepipe hat on his head and loosely draped the tie around his neck, heading out into the exhibition hall, yelling the words of the Gettysburg Address at top volume. He didn't look anything like Abraham Lincoln, but maybe that was the point. Abe adjusted the baseball cap to what he hoped was a flattering angle, and headed out after him. Harold was right. In the crush of top hats and bleached blonde finger waves, not to mention navy police and FBI caps, Abe felt as if he had suddenly changed teams. No one even glanced at him as he made his way out through the fighting mob.

Abe crossed the room as quickly as he could, passing an Abraham Lincoln attempting to swat an FBI agent with his collapsing top hat, and a Marilyn, cornered by a pair of cops, brandishing a fairly deadly-looking stiletto in self defense. In the corner, Harold was still running zigzags though the hall while yelling "A HOUSE DIVIDED AGAINST ITSELF CAN NOT STAND! SIC SEMPER TYRANNIS! I CHOPPED DOWN THE CHERRY TREE!" with several officers in close pursuit. In another corner he saw a particularly sultry Marilyn leaning coyly against the wall, chatting up a man in a suit who was clearly hanging on her every word. He found himself drawing nearer, fascinated by the glistening lips and the vivacious sparkle in her eyes, before shaking off the vision and heading for the glowing exit lights.

Abe was within sight of the open front doors when a figure stepped out of them, blocking his escape. He recognized the woman with a feeling like a sucker punch to the gut. Nita. He pulled the brim of his cap farther down over his eyes. Maybe she wouldn't recognize him.

She locked eyes with him, with an almost audible click.

"I um," he said. "I was just..."

"Relax, Abe," she said. "I'm not here for you."

"Um." He struggled with the idea. "You're not?"

"Nah, you're off the hook. One of the Marilyns is wanted for check kiting. Been after her for years. Figured this was as good a place as any to try and grab her."

"Which one?" Abe asked. He hoped it wasn't the one he had in mind.

"I don't know, they all look alike to me." Nita responded. "Ed'll flush her out, if she's here."

"So I can... go?" Abe wasn't sure what to do. Was this a trap?

"Well, the cops want you, but that's not my department. I'm sure Ed still wants you. He always actually cared about the historical stuff. But after the stunts you pulled yesterday no one who counts will release any more funds in your direction. You lucked out."

"Because of the fire?"

"The what? No, that wasn't such a smart move. Don't be too surprised to find your taxes audited for the next few years."

"So—why?"

"Do I really need to spell it out for you?" Nita said, looking distressed. "Look. What you want to do with your social life is your business. Let's keep it that way."

"I don't..."

"Abe. When we thought you were having some sort of past-life regression, you were interesting. Lots to study, never happened before. What made you tick? Well, we found out, and we're officially no longer interested."

"You found out...?"

"What triggered the flashbacks? Some dude named Joshua Speed. What made your MRI results light up like the fourth of July? The name Joshua Speed. What name did you call out when you jumped the intern? Speed again. I Googled him. Personally, I don't think he was all that hot. But hey, whatever you're into. Just not on our watch."

"You think I'm gay?"

"I don't care what you are. More importantly, the U.S. Government doesn't care what you are. You can yank your stovepipe to Joshua Speed, or Marilyn Monroe or Mickey Mouse for all we care. The American people will fund a lot of things," Nita concluded, "but one thing they won't spend money on is research showing that President Abraham Lincoln was gay. You touched the third rail. Not gonna go there."

"Right." Abe suppressed a grin. If this was what got him off the hook, he'd take it. "So you don't need to cut into my brain?" he asked, just to make sure.

"Can't promise you that. But we can always cover that when you're dead."

Abe was sorry he asked. He should have quit asking questions while he was ahead. "Guess I'll get going. Lots of attractive men in the sea," he said.

"Good luck, Abe," Nita said.

"Thanks. I like you better as Good Cop," he said.

"People always do." The glint in her eye was steely. For the first time, Abe appreciated just how lucky he was that she was letting him escape. Abe held out a hand for her to shake.

Nita looked at it like it was some new species of cockroach. She shook her head, briefly. "I didn't see you. In fact, we never met. You got that?"

"Got it."

"Get out of here."

She didn't have to tell him twice.

Out in the parking lot, Norma was waiting, resplendent in sequins and platinum waves.

"Ms. Monroe," he greeted her, gallantly touching the brim of his cap.

"Mr. DiMaggio," she responded.

She took the hat off and placed it on top of her head. "Get in," she cooed. "We've got about 30 minutes before this dress has to be back at Lord's, or we're in big trouble."

She gunned the engine, and they were off.

About the Author

M. E. Roufa has ridden an ostrich, appeared on *Jeopardy,* and can crochet a mean banana. In her spare time, she works as an award-winning advertising writer and creative director whose work has appeared everywhere from the Super Bowl to the sides of shampoo bottles. *The Norma Gene* is her first novel.

Acknowledgments

Thank you first of all to my editor, Jay Nadeau, for your continuing support and guidance. To my first readers: Josh Kilmer-Purcell, Hope Provost, Mike Gerber, and Meir Lakein. Thank you to the incomparable Melanie Forster for your good advice and stunning cover design. I am indebted to the staff at the Abraham Lincoln Presidential Library and Museum for taking the time to answer my questions, and for actually building Abe's cabin. Thank you to Sheilah Parsons, Nile Jones, and Maria Torres for helping me grab the freedom to write. Finally, thanks to Levi, Aderet, Pinchas, Batya, Noam and especially my personal hero, Eliyahu Teitz. Hey, you're mentioned in a book!